Avenger

Other Books by Heather Burch

Halflings

Guardian

A HALFLINGS NOVEL

Avenger

BOOK THREE

Heather Burch

ZONDERVAN®

ZONDERVAN.com/
AUTHORTRACKER
follow your favorite authors

ZONDERVAN

Avenger
Copyright © 2013 by Heather Burch

This title is also available as a Zondervan ebook.
Visit www.zondervan.com/ebooks.

Requests for information should be addressed to:

Zondervan, *Grand Rapids, Michigan* 49530

ISBN 978-0-310-72824-5

Cover design: Cindy Davis
Cover photography: Dan Davis Photography
Interior design and composition: Greg Johnson/Textbook Perfect

Printed in the United States of America

13 14 15 16 17 18 19 /DCI/ 20 19 18 17 16 15 14 13 12 11 10 9 8 7 6 5 4 3 2 1

Chapter
1

The blur lasted only a second before Nikki Youngblood's face exploded in blinding pain. *And I thought karate tournaments were ruthless.* Even the gentlest blow of this Halfling put her past competitors to shame; half human, half angels were lethal. Her lips throbbed with the beating of her heart, and for a few horrible seconds she wanted to call time out and collapse onto the ground.

But she wasn't a quitter, and the pain rumbling through her was only more incentive to pummel the Frenchman into the ground.

Even if it wasn't the smartest choice she'd ever made.

Nikki advanced, ignoring the cheers and gasps around her. A smattering of Halflings now dotted the courtyard surrounding the Cinderella-style castle, similar to the one where Nikki had been living like royalty since she and the others arrived. Though to her knowledge, Cinderella never kicked any butt, so any fairy-tale similarities between her and the blonde princess ended there.

Her lips were numb, a thankful reprieve from the pain of them smashing against her teeth as the Frenchman, Deux, made contact with a powerful fist. She didn't taste blood yet, but she could feel her mouth swelling. For all she knew, there was blood seeping from her lips — she was simply too adrenaline-driven to care.

If she was in a competition, officials would call the fight at the first sign of a cut. But this was no tournament. There were no senseis, judges, or black belts hoping to showcase their abilities as masters and students. And no called fouls when things got rough.

Nikki stood in a cat stance, trying to form some type of strategy, and used her newfound powers to take in her surroundings. It struck her that the French countryside was quite picturesque, and would be like a storybook — Beauty and the Beast, maybe, since Cinderella didn't fit — if not for the guy beating her to a pulp.

Pulp. That's what her mouth felt like.

She saw the fist coming and caught it in midair. When Deux tried to pull away, she held firm, stopping him and letting this new power — this new strength she'd begun to tap into — course though her, but carefully. Nikki knew what she was capable of. A night of stalking her demented godfather, Damon Vessler, had taught her that.

Her fingers squeezed until she heard Deux's bones begin to pop. His clear blue eyes clouded with a mix of surprise and dread.

"Oooooh" and "ewwwww" echoed from the crowd of spectators. *No disapproving groans. Mace must still be in the house; otherwise he'd be breaking things up.* One thing her boyfriend couldn't abide was Nikki fighting for no reason. Boyfriend —

that sounded strange to her ears, but accurate. She and Mace were a couple. Mostly.

She released her grip marginally. After all, she didn't want to break Deux's hand, just disprove his theory that female Halflings were the weaker part of the species.

Nikki shoved his fist back, knocking him off balance.

Off to the right, someone said in a thick French accent, "I think you have misjudged her power, my friend. Or perhaps you have misjudged your own."

Snickers from the onlookers on both sides of the earlier argument. She tossed a glance behind her to the tall glass doors.

No Mace. She could continue the fight.

Deux was shaking his hand, massaging it, trying to encourage fresh blood flow. "You are waiting for Mace to return and rescue you, no?"

Nikki set her jaw and punched Deux in the face. His head jolted back, causing his carefully layered hair to whip.

"That hurt." A red welt materialized on his cheek and jaw, but a smile sliced through the darkened flesh. He wiggled his brows. "I think I am in love."

Maybe it was the fact that love had gotten her into more trouble than any person — human or Halfling — deserved, or maybe it was the cocky, condescending way he looked at her, but his words unleashed her fury. And her fury always meant real pain. Nikki sailed into a combination of kicks and punches that a fifth-degree black belt would envy. Each made contact, but not with the intended target. Over and over Deux cupped his hands and caught every punch. Kicks were absorbed by arm blocks. Even the low kick to his knee was halted by a shin block.

"You are good, Cherie. In a few years, you might even be a real opponent." He yawned.

A few chuckles from the crowd, along with some calls cheering her on and some telling Deux his skills were still amazing.

Even when outmatched, there's always a way to win. Find the hole in the machine. Then throw a wrench in it.

So Deux was a better fighter. It didn't matter. One thing this journey, this new life, had taught her was that things could change in an instant. Her whole world had. One second she was a semi-normal teenage girl, the next she was a Halfling. But her transformation of sorts gave her one serious advantage: the awareness brute strength — even Halfling strength — wasn't the only way to win a fight.

Nikki smiled and blinked a few times, ignoring the pain now flooding her lips. She lowered her hands and loosened her body posture. When she dropped a shoulder and cocked her hip flirtatiously — a move she'd learned by watching Glimmer — Deux's hands fell to his sides.

His gaze drifted down over her while she pretended not to notice. And to add to her attractive assault, Nikki pulled the two pencils out of her hair — her makeshift hair clasps — and tossed them to the ground. Her long hair cascaded around her shoulders, and when the wind grabbed it she shook her head, letting the breeze have its way. Deux was helplessly pinned — a boy attracted to a girl, one who suddenly seemed interested.

"I could learn a lot from you." Nikki's voice dropped to a purr. "Like those blocks. Could you teach me?" *Being this bad shouldn't come so easy.* But she didn't want to linger on that truth.

"I would enjoy teaching you many things, Cherie." He took a few steps toward her, one brow arched seductively.

Except it wasn't seductive at all. It made her want to snicker. She bit her cheeks to keep from laughing, because he was playing right into her plan. He mistook her reaction for more flirtation and winked.

For a while, she listened as he instructed her on the blocking technique. She took it all in and waited for the right moment to strike. When Deux rocked back on his heels and crossed his arms over his chest, the opportunity arrived. He was no more ready for an attack than a duckling in a pond was ready for the alligator lurking just below the surface.

Snapping with her signature jumping front kick, she planted her foot against Deux's stomach. Rock-hard abs softened and his body flew back as if yanked by a string. He landed on his behind with a roar of laughter rising around him.

From his seated position, feet straight out in front of him, he shook his head. "I can no longer consider dating you, Nikki. I'm sorry, but trust is paramount in a relationship."

She giggled — just couldn't stop herself — and reached out a hand to help him up. "You can trust me."

"It is not you I'm concerned about. I cannot possibly trust myself with such a wild animal. You are driving me crazy." Before she could pull away, he tightened his grip on her hand. His foot slid against hers. After a powerful tug, she landed on top of him.

She tried to roll off, but Deux's arms were suddenly everywhere. As she tumbled, so did he. She squirmed, but he wouldn't let go. With each passing second, she struggled harder to break the hold. No luck. The crowd was chanting, for her, for him, for both of them.

When she had the upper hand and was almost free, they cheered for Deux. But when he clamped his powerful arms on her, they cheered for Nikki, shouting ideas on how to break his hold. *Fickle crowd.*

11

Grunting and now face-to-face on the fresh grass, Nikki reached behind her back, curled her fingers around his thumb, and pulled.

Deux arched his back and let out a yell so loud that Nikki felt terrible. But she was free at least. She sprang to her feet, turned, and hit a brick wall.

Mace.

He glowered at her from eyes filled with a curious blend of concern, anger, and maybe a tinge of disappointment. Her wrist was in a stranglehold. *Drat, trapped again.* This time in Mace's iron grip as he dragged her from the courtyard and into the house.

"Can I not leave you alone for two seconds without you getting into trouble?" Mace tried to slow his racing heart, but when he stepped outside and saw Nikki and Deux fighting, rolling on the ground, his pulse had gone into overdrive and wasn't likely to slow down anytime soon.

"He was helping me."

Fresh fire coursed down his body. "He was helping himself to you."

Her eyes — now darkened to melted gold — narrowed on him. "You said yourself that Deux is one of the best fighters there is."

"So?" *Brilliant argument there.* He just kept imagining Nikki and Deux rolling on the ground, and something, some horrible monster inside him, wanted to grab Deux by the throat and ...

Oh. That's what this is about.

He watched Nikki blink, those feather-soft lashes hooding her eyes for a few seconds. She pulled in a deep breath and let it out slowly. Her cheek was smudged with a bit of dirt, and the corner of her mouth had a drop of dried blood on it. It too was caked with dirt.

He lifted his hand to her cheek. Fingertips touched the soft skin and she pressed into him. "Did he hurt you?" Mace whispered, praying Deux hadn't, because he'd hate to accept the Frenchman's hospitality then kill him in his own courtyard.

"Only my pride," Nikki said, nuzzling into the press of Mace's hand.

His thumb drifted over her bottom lip. "You're bleeding."

"A sucker punch. I shouldn't have fallen for it." Her eyes snapped open. "What should I have done differently?"

"Stayed out of the fight."

She leveled him with a look.

"Okay, okay." He stared at the ornate ceiling and worked the muscle in his jaw. He hated to see Nikki fight, but fighting was a certainty in her life. She was a Halfling. And even though she'd only just learned the truth about her angelic power, she was already enmeshed in the epic battle against darkness.

Since discovering what Nikki truly was, Mace had learned Halfling females tap into their power later than the males, around age eighteen or nineteen; at seventeen, Nikki was a bit of an early bloomer—like Vine, his "brother," who'd earned the Over-Achiever award for tapping in at fifteen. Mace was still amazed Nikki had adjusted so quickly—before her angelic side had begun to emerge, even their fully angel guardian, Will, had thought she was human. "Everything changes when we tap in."

"For me more than anyone."

That much was true. Nikki's life had been orchestrated by her godfather, Damon Vessler, who'd planned on turning her into a dark Halfling once she tapped into her power, and then using her to create an army at his command.

Since Mace first met her, in a field where she was being chased by hell hounds, he'd tried to protect her from ... well, from all of it. But that wasn't fair, and in doing so, he'd almost lost her. He'd have to help her take on the evils herself, no matter how hard that was for him. "When I came out you were already on the ground. How'd you get there?"

"He pulled me down when I reached to help him up."

Mace chuckled. "And you said *his* move was a sucker punch? Seriously, Nikki, you fell for that?"

Her mouth cocked in a sheepish grin. "I should have known."

"Yeah." Mace ran a hand through his hair. He'd rather be running his fingers through hers, smoothing the messed-up strands, but that would only distract him. Though he itched to remove the blade of grass stuck in her hairline. "As soon as you felt him pull, you should have dove, caught him off guard. He wouldn't expect it, and it may have given you a few seconds to get away. At the least it would have—"

"Given me the upper hand," she said. Her brows dipped.

Thinking. Ah, he loved her when she was thinking. Beyond the glass door, another fight ensued. Deux and Vine this time. From what Mace could tell, the two looked pretty evenly matched. *Go, Vine.*

"Watch how Vine fights, always thinking ahead—always." He laced his arm around her waist and pulled her close while she studied the two combatants.

She smiled. "Thanks for helping me. I think your judgment may finally be clearing."

What was that supposed to mean?

"Don't be offended, Mace. It's just that your opinions haven't been the most sound where I'm concerned."

"You mean trying to leap into an airplane filled with titanium, and then letting Vessler get away?"

"You were with me when the airplane landed. You couldn't have known Vessler would make it out."

The whole scene entered his mind like it did every night when he fell asleep. He could hear gunshots, knew Nikki was in the plane, but the titanium zapped his strength, making him unable to leap inside. The kryptonite-like metal had caused his wings to feel like giant anchors; the closer he got, the worse it was. Finally, he'd moved to the other side of the plane and spotted the open cargo door. He got Nikki to safety while Raven — his rival and brother-in-arms — followed the plane. Will had contacted the other Halflings, who'd met the plane when it landed outside of St. Louis. *Sorry, Vessler, no titanium wingcuffs for you.*

Nikki's voice drew him out of the memory. "I really didn't think I'd make it out alive. Vessler actually told me to leap to safety at one point. Like I have wings."

"You'll have wings, Nikki. You've tapped into your angelic power, so it's just a matter of time now."

He could see she didn't believe it. "At least the titanium was intercepted. And thanks to you, Vessler was so wounded he'll be out of commission for a while."

When her body posture changed, he knew she'd gone back there in her mind as well. Tiny frowns appeared and disappeared on her face, each attached to a fact she'd not yet been able to accept. She'd shot Damon Vessler. Twice.

"You could have died, Nikki."

"I don't know what I was thinking, going after Vessler alone." Ever since getting her back, Mace had watched closely, trying unsuccessfully to understand her actions. Her darker side had been shocking, and the confusion over what she'd briefly become was taking a toll on Nikki as well.

He tilted back to look at her. "I know I asked you this before, but do you think Vessler may have been putting something in your drinks?"

She stiffened. "Mace, I know you want to believe that. And I do too — more than you can imagine. But I'd been away from Vessler and his influence — potentially spiked beverages included — when I decided to go after him."

"But Nikki —" Her fingers rose and rested against his lips.

She leaned in and placed her head against his heart. "I remember wondering if there might be something wrong with the water. He'd always fill my bottles for me. And once when I was finishing a cup of coffee, there was this little bubble of something in the bottom. I figured it had been dirty, but when I handed it to the housekeeper, she got really nervous."

Against his chest, he felt Nikki squeeze her eyes shut. "I don't know what he was doing to me. What I do know is, I have to be responsible for my actions. And I almost murdered Damon without a second thought."

"It wasn't you, Nikki. It had to be a product of whatever he was giving you. Your mood would change almost instantly. Remember when I found you at the beach house?"

She nodded, but he felt an unsettling distance between them, an invisible wall she raised whenever this subject came up. But that wouldn't stop him this time.

"It was like a veil came over you. Like you weren't in control anymore. And I think that's why you went after Vessler."

"And *I* think that's what you need to believe." She laced her fingers together at his back and held on to him, but he pushed from her.

"What are you saying?"

The gold in her eyes lost its shimmer. "Exactly what I said. You need to believe I was just a robot under someone else's control. If you don't, you have to consider the possibility that I have become the monster Vessler worked so hard to create."

"Nikki, that's crazy. You're not a monster."

"Aren't I? I shot him — twice — and I wanted to do a lot more." She shook her head. "I'm sorry. I'm not who I used to be. And I'll never be that carefree, innocent girl again."

Mace chose to hold her close rather than argue, despite the cold feeling that swept through him. Fact was, Nikki had changed. They'd all changed. And he wasn't sure how to navigate that new mountain before them.

He looked over her head to the door facing the courtyard. "Based on how Vine's fight is going, I don't know if we'll be welcome here much longer. We can only beat up our host so many times." Nikki gave a small laugh. "Come on, let's get the others and head back to Viennesse." Their ancestral home in Germany and across the Rhine Valley from Deux's compound. These days, Viennesse felt like the only safe place. And even that surety was slipping.

It was a short trip from the ruins to Viennesse, but Raven couldn't get there fast enough. Nikki was in more danger than he'd ever imagined, and if he hadn't questioned the heavenly angel who'd appeared as he'd petitioned the Throne, maybe it would already be too late to save her.

After Nikki's standoff with Vessler, and after she'd left with Mace, he'd prayed for some assurance that she would be okay. Instead, he discovered the exact opposite. The cold reality of what awaited her now fueled his speed. Night had fallen, but he could see perfectly as he sailed through a puff of low clouds and descended on the Viennesse castle. Built on a mountaintop, it has been chosen as a formidable foe for all human invaders, though what was coming after Nikki was neither human nor demon. And it had come for one reason: to destroy Nikki, the woman Raven loved and would never have.

But one thing he could do was protect her. Right? Why else would the angel have warned him about what was coming after Nikki? He'd find her, then he'd make a plan. Until he had visual confirmation she was still alive, his only focus would be getting to her side. True, he knew next to nothing about the evil being sent to destroy Nikki, and he honestly had no clue how to defeat it. But he did know that if Nikki could be saved, he was the one to do it.

Raven began running the moment he touched down and headed for the front door, shoving both doors open and rushing inside as his wings — sore from the long flight — tucked behind him.

Winter and Nikki sat in the library just off the main hall. He should have known where to find her. Nikki had a weakness for quiet spots.

They both stood when he barged inside. Normally, he was confident and self-possessed, almost cool in his demeanor. Doing the hair toss thing and planting his thumbs in his pockets as if to impart information only he possessed. But not this time.

Both females noticed.

"What's going on? Where have you been?" Winter took a cautious step toward him.

"Where are the others?" He shot a glance out the side door that led to a private patio.

Nikki is safe. For the moment.

Winter shook her head, a blanket of silky, dark hair falling from her shoulders. "Scattered throughout the castle. Raven, what's happening?"

He stopped only long enough to meet her gaze. "A seeker's been released from the pit."

Winter dropped into a nearby chair, the blood in her face draining, leaving her even paler than usual.

Nikki split her glances between the two of them. "Wha — what's a seeker?" He tried to hide the fear, and pain, from his eyes as he watched her. He soon had no choice but to look away.

Winter's eyes slowly drifted up to meet Raven's. "Sent here?"

There was no denying the terror in her voice. If Raven had thought meeting up with the other Halflings would somehow reassure him, he'd been dead wrong.

"Why? And how do you know?" Winter said.

"He's hunting Nikki."

Mace came in, sailing around the doorjamb, his narrowed gaze landing on Raven. "I thought I saw you." As soon as the words left his mouth, he dropped to silence, sparing a moment to take in the looks on everyone's faces. "What's going on?"

Raven nodded toward the door. "We have to get Nikki out of here. A seeker's coming."

"What?" Mace crossed the room and pulled Nikki to his side. "What are you talking about, Raven? Will hasn't sensed anything — "

"Will doesn't know everything. The thing's on the way. And he's after Nikki."

And, while you have her in your arms, I'm the only one who can protect her.

Mace's grip tightened, and though Nikki had no idea what a seeker could be, it was something terrible enough to strike fear in Winter, Mace, and even Raven. Four hours ago, she was sparring with a Frenchman in a mock fight. Was she really about to have to run for her life … again? Nausea wove through her and Nikki placed a hand on her stomach as if mere touch could keep the contents settled. She was supposed to be safe here. Vessler and his horrible plan for her were a half a world away. Like that mattered: Mace had once told her the enemy, the *real* enemy, wanted her.

Mace shook his head. "If a seeker had been released, Will would know."

"Well, you can go on telling yourself that, but you might be wasting the last minutes we have to get Nikki out of danger. I got my information directly from the source."

Mace fisted his hands and took a step toward Raven, leaving Nikki behind. "If a seeker is coming, there isn't anywhere safe to go."

Raven threw his hands in the air. "So go find him. Ask All-Mighty Will what we need to do."

Mace reached back and grasped her hand. "Come on, Nikki."

Her palm was sweaty; she hadn't realized until he gripped it. "I don't feel well."

Winter stood and dragged her chair a few feet to where Nikki stood, and along with Mace lowered her into the seat. "I'll stay here with her. Go find Will."

Mace dropped a kiss on her forehead. "I'll be right back. Don't worry, because everything will be fine."

Fine? She wanted to scream, but her mind couldn't get the sound to travel to her mouth.

Raven dropped onto his haunches at her feet, the midnight blue of his eyes so intense it jolted sanity back into her system. "Listen to me, Nikki." He closed his warm hands over hers, so softly she felt her breath catch. "We have to go. We have to run. It's the only way."

Thoughts, jumbled thoughts, bounced around in her head. "Safe, here," she managed.

"I know it's hard to understand, but a seeker's like a tsunami. He'll rush through this castle and destroy everything. And he'll take you when he's done, even if I and every Halfling here tries to stop him. As long as you're here, no one is safe."

Her eyes trailed up to Winter.

"I don't know, Nikki. Seeker's are ..." But her words dropped and she looked at Raven. "Maybe you're right."

Raven squeezed Nikki's hands just enough to pull her from the chair. "We can be a thousand miles away from here in two hours. But we can't waste any more time."

Winter dropped a hand on Raven's shoulder. "You may be right, but perhaps she *should* stay. Will is here, and at least ten Halflings. What can you do on your own that we cannot do here?"

Raven traced the lines of Nikki's face as if she held the answer. His only concern seemed to be keeping her safe, and his promise to protect her was imprinted in every inch of his being. She thought he might concede, decide it was best to be here at Viennesse. *How many times have the Halflings bragged about how fortified the castle is?* Raven opened his mouth. He was going to agree.

That's when they heard the scream.

Chapter
2

Glimmer and Vegan ran through the front door, scream-ing Will's name. Raven rushed forward and caught them in the hall, barreling into Glimmer and stopping her forward momentum. Instead of pushing him off, she clung to him like a small child; even from the library Nikki saw the visible quake that started in her arms and worked its way down until her whole body shook. She'd never seen Glimmer so ... helpless before.

In the rush of words, Nikki heard, "Deux, Paix, and Tronc. All dead. We found them in the courtyard at their home."

Nikki's mind went numb. The Frenchman she'd fought ear-lier in the day? Dead?

"Something ... something *shredded* them," Glimmer said.

"Where is it now?" Raven yelled.

Vegan now leaned on the wall for support. Her golden brown hair scattered over her arms, her usually peaceful face streaked with worry. "We didn't see it. It was gone when we got there." Tears rolled down her face. "We only went back to France to get my jacket. I left it there earlier today."

Keeping Glimmer tucked beneath his arm, he stepped toward Vegan. "Can you think of any reason why it would have gone there instead of coming here?"

Vegan's eyes were terror stricken. "Why would it come *anywhere*? What do you know, Raven? What did that? No human or demon could do what we saw."

"A seeker."

Her knees gave out and she slid to the floor. "I don't even think they had a chance to fight."

"It's after Nikki," Raven said gravely.

All eyes fell on her. Glimmer's voice cracked. "How do you know?"

Raven stood tall and looked Glimmer directly in the eye. "Trust me, I know."

She buried her face in her palms, and Nikki wondered if she too was trying to block the horrible sight she'd witnessed at Deux's house. Glimmer's hands dropped suddenly. "Will it come to Viennesse?"

"Not if I can get her out of here."

They're really dead, Nikki realized, the thought fully saturating her mind. The French Halflings were dead because ... because a beast was after her.

Fingers clamped around her arms. It took her a moment to process they were Raven's, and they were shuffling her toward the door. "Let's go." *Everything is happening too fast.*

"Wait!" Will's booming voice reverberated down the hall, bringing a measure of calm to Nikki's chaos. "If a seeker is on the way, we prepare to fight."

Fight? Like the French Halflings fought? Nikki pivoted to

look at him, but her movements were stiff. Will's words seemed confident, and of anyone he would know what to do. Not to mention there was safety in numbers — especially with Will at her side. But how many would die because of her? She shuddered. *How many more?* These were her friends. Her family. She tried to clear her thoughts. "Where's Mace?"

Will nodded down the hallway. "He's rounding up the other Halflings. We will all protect you, Nikki."

"Can you promise me no one will die?" Her voice was solid, strong. And hearing it brought more conviction. No one else was going to die because of her.

Those giant silvery-blue eyes dropped to the floor. "You know I can't."

Nikki slid an arm around Raven and drew strength from him. She knew what they had to do. "Then I have to go."

Winter stepped toward her and placed both hands on Nikki's arms. "I'll go with you."

Raven shook his head. "Not yet, Winter. We'll go first, in hopes of keeping it away from here. Two of us should be able to escape easily. If we don't get airborne in time to reroute the seeker, though, Will is going to need everyone here to fight. As soon as I can find somewhere safe to tuck in for the night, I'll get word to Zero and you can catch up to us."

Winter's eyes narrowed on him. "You have a plan, right?"

Raven tried to hide his reaction, but Nikki felt him bristle. "Of course. But if you've got some ideas, I'm open."

Winter let out a long breath. "Circle the sky, Raven. Fan Nikki's scent in as many directions as possible. It's your only hope to confuse the seeker. Then find someplace very populated to hide — somewhere belowground. Try the tunnels under Paris. The mixture of smells will interrupt her scent, and you should be safe there at least for tonight. Contact us as soon as possible."

Raven answered her with a nod. He turned to Nikki. "You ready?"

Nikki tightened her arms around Raven's neck, throwing a last look to the Halflings and Will.

A moment later, they were leaping up into the night.

For the last hour Raven had been circling, just as Winter suggested. Usually, Nikki loved sailing above the earth, seeing the world below with nothing but wind and whispers surrounding her. But this night, she felt like live bait, as if each exhale drew a beast closer and closer. She hoped that was the case. If not, it could mean the seeker was at Viennesse. They'd covered ground over Switzerland, Germany, Austria, and were now entering France.

Her arms ached from the stranglehold she'd kept on Raven. "Can we check on them?"

She felt the muscle in his neck roll against her forearm. "Not tonight. We still have to find a way into the tunnels. I've only been there a few times, and it was years ago. Besides, Winter told me to check in tomorrow."

"Since when do you follow instructions? Especially from a girl."

"Since your life is on the line. Winter has lived a very long time. I trust her instincts on this one. There's too much at stake to not get her thoughts."

"What about Will? He's lived longer than anyone. He may have known what to do."

"The only thing Will would have done was try to talk us into staying, wasting what time we had." Raven narrowed his gaze on Nikki. The look spoke more than words. *Discussion's over.* He projected every ounce of intensity he possessed into those midnight blue spheres. Fierce protection and temptation mingled, a realization that cut through every fiber holding her together. She was stripped bare. It was a hideous, wonderful feeling. Especially as he seemed so focused on his mission that, for maybe the first time ever, he didn't realize what he was doing to her by just being himself.

"We're here." Raven nodded. "Take a look."

The world below was a velvet-dark surface dotted with a million golden lights. Some spiked high into the sky as if reaching out for her, while others remained, alive, on the ground, snaking through the jungle of illumination in long steady lines. It stole her breath.

Raven paused, airborne, his wings stretched out to hover above the crawling lights below. "Never gets old," he said. The hint of pleasure lasted only a moment before he was back in action, descending on the streets of Paris.

He touched down in an alleyway and took a few seconds to get his bearings. "Okay, there's a way in from a museum at the end of this street. Not sure how easy it will be to get inside though."

Her muscles creaked and groaned in protest. "Are you considering breaking into a museum? Raven, we'll end up in jail."

He slid a hand through his wind-ruffled hair. "I'd send you there and lock the cell door myself if I thought it would keep you safe."

Nikki cocked her head and planted a fist on her hip.

Raven looked her up and down. "You learn that from Glimmer?"

She dropped her fist.

He grabbed it and placed it back on her hip, then readjusted her head with both hands on the side of her face. "It looks great on you. Makes it look like you mean business. You should do that more often."

From far down the street, music drifted toward them. "You bring out the worst in me, Raven."

He took a step, bringing them closer. "I bring out the best in you, Nikki. Always have. Get used to it."

No thanks. But the words caught in her throat. "Come on, let's go vandalize the museum."

Raven followed close behind as she left the alley. They stepped out onto the street, and no one seemed curious why the two teenagers had just come from an alley leading nowhere. When they paused to wait for the street light, Raven slid his hand into hers. The light changed and he prodded her, but she stayed unmoving, staring at their interlocked fingers.

"Don't flatter yourself," Raven said, but there was a hint of playfulness in his tone. "I just want to keep you close."

For a moment, she felt foolish. Given their history, the foolishness melted quickly and was followed by a cold dose of reality. Raven had taken advantage of every opportunity to woo her. "Sorry. I didn't realize you just wanted to keep me close. I thought the hand holding was a pitiful last attempt to romance me."

Raven stopped cold and turned into her. "No." His face was so close, she could feel every brush of his breath as he exhaled. "If I wanted to romance you, I'd have done this." He took her by both arms and spun her around. His fingers trailed along her neckline and drew the long strands of her hair over her shoulder. Hot breath, then a kiss against the back of her neck.

Then he spun her back around to face him, looking at her with the same serious look as before.

Nikki's lungs shrank and wouldn't accept the oxygen she willed into her being.

"Try not to confuse the two. It's humiliating. For you."

She nodded.

"If you're done messing around, we need to get moving." He placed his hand around hers once more, and after a tug to prod her the two ran until they reached the giant doorway leading into the museum. After judging the distance, Raven grabbed her, snapped his wings open, and leapt, shooting straight up. It happened so quickly, she wondered if the people sitting at the dimly lit café across the street even noticed. Or if they did, they likely thought their minds were playing tricks after seeing teenagers, loitering in a doorway, then a flash of white, then nothing.

Even she still had trouble processing it.

They landed on the museum near a rooftop window. Raven tried to open it but it was welded shut.

"Can't you leap inside? The building is big enough, right?"

"Yeah, but I don't know what kind of security system they have. If it's movement, we could set off an alarm." He pointed to a metal door in one corner of the rooftop. "Stairwell. My guess would be the alarm systems are set up to trigger on the individual floors. I think if we stick to the stairs we'll be okay."

"Then why did you try the window?"

Raven paused when he reached the door. "Are you going to ask this many questions all night? It's getting on my nerves."

Nikki looked down at the padlock and chain securing the door. She heaved a breath. "What now?"

Raven considered the handle for a few seconds then grasped

the thing and ripped it from the door. The chain and padlock fell to the ground. Nikki's jaw dropped with them.

"You just ripped a metal door open," she squealed. Her hands fell onto his shoulders and she shook him. "Raven! Did you see what you did? *You ripped apart metal.*"

His head bobbed as she shook him. There was no mistaking the smile spreading across his face. Maybe Raven had surprised himself too.

The levity didn't last long. He reached through the hole in the door and swung it open. "Get inside," he ordered.

The stairwell was dark, but as she'd learned from being in Zero's tunnels what now felt like a lifetime ago, she could see in the dark. Nothing for a Halfling.

"The entrance is in the basement, so I'm hoping this stairwell will take us that far. If not, we'll have to cross one of the floors to get to the front stairs. That's where I've gone in before."

"Do you think they're all okay, Raven?"

He stopped mid-step and turned to her. "You really need to put your energy into staying alive, Nikki. The other Halflings can take care of themselves." When she continued to stare at him, he softened, but only slightly. "Look, they know what they're up against now."

She searched his eyes for the lie, but couldn't find it. "You really think this worked, don't you? You think they're all right."

"Yeah. I wouldn't have left with you if I didn't."

She forced a smile. "I hope you're right."

He winked. "Count on it, baby. I'm always right."

Nikki rolled her eyes and grabbed his hand to tug him down another flight of stairs. *Finally, the Raven I know how to deal with.*

"When we get to the bottom, the stairway narrows. And it's

kind of creepy. Don't go too fast, and stay close. I won't let any rabid Parisian rats nest in your hair or anything."

"I hope it doesn't narrow too much," Nikki said.

"Why? Scared of enclosed spaces?"

She blinked innocently. "No, I'm just afraid your ego might not fit."

The tunnel into the Paris underground was indeed tight, indeed creepy, and indeed a place Nikki was glad to be out of. The instant they stepped into a larger space she began the ritual of combing imaginary spiders from her hair. The combing was especially vigorous since there was a good chance they weren't all imaginary. She'd rested her hand against the tunnel wall at one spot, and when it quivered beneath her touch, she screamed. Raven clamped a hand over her mouth to quell the sound. "It's just a spider."

Just a spider. As if that somehow made it better.

"I thought you were tough," he scoffed.

"I don't like spiders."

He pointed to her foot. "How do you feel about centipedes?"

She practically sucked in all the air from the room, but before she could shriek Raven's hand was over her mouth, once again muffling the sound.

"You're really good with the whole inconspicuous thing."

The centipede continued his trek toward the tunnel wall. "Inconspicuous?" She motioned around her. "Who's gonna hear?"

"I would." The small voice came from behind them and Nikki jumped. "Sorry," the shadow said.

Nikki thought maybe the narrow tunnel they'd left wasn't so bad after all. She could see, but the voice came from a space she couldn't penetrate, and a stranger was certainly worse than some bug. Even if he was polite. Looking closer, she realized the shadow was a rock wall and the voice came from behind it. A small hand slid out from the rock and waved. "Hi. I'm Dane."

Raven's brows rode high on his head. He shrugged at Nikki then addressed the hand that now clung to the edge of the rock. "Hi, Dane. Is there a body attached to that hand?"

From about four feet off the ground, a small head appeared slowly from behind the stone. Brown hair, then large brown eyes framed by glasses, then a small nose. He stayed positioned like that, staring at them as if deciding whether to engage in a conversation or run to find authorities. He couldn't be more than ten years old, and the strong French accent seemed odd coming from such a small boy. Finally, a bow-shaped mouth appeared, teeth chewing one side in apparent nervousness. "So, how'd you find my hideout?"

"Your hideout?" Raven repeated slowly.

"Yeah." Dane's eyes filled with confidence. "This is my hide-out. This room here. I discovered it a year ago and it's all mine. No one else comes down here, and no strangers are allowed. There's nothing to see. Just my toys and stuff. So just go back out the way you came in."

Raven crossed his arms. "Look, kid, I don't have time for this. I'm looking for someone. Greta. Does she still use the tunnels?"

Greta? Nikki cut a look to Raven.

Dane, still mostly hidden behind his rock, laughed. "I don't know what you mean. This is just one room, one way in and out, so however you got down here, you need to leave the same way."

"If you're going to be the self-proclaimed tunnel guard, you probably shouldn't tell people there's one way in and out, then tell them to leave however they got in."

Dane's eyes grew troubled. Black-rimmed frames slid down his nose a bit. "Greta's been gone awhile. Oh, my brother will know how to help you. He knows everything."

The boy materialized, all four feet of him. He ran to Raven and grabbed his hand. "Come on. I'll take you to him. He knows everybody. He knows everything about the tunnels."

"Idolize much?" Raven mumbled, then threw a pleading look to Nikki. He tried to pull away from the kid, but Dane would have none of it. By the looks of his small hand navigating Raven's larger one, he was used to leading unwilling people.

The boy walked them through a series of spaces that could be considered rooms, each containing walls of some unknown material. It could be concrete, or maybe very smooth rock, or even dirt rubbed slick from years of wear. Nikki fought the urge to reach out and touch. Whatever the rooms were made of, they were a spider's heaven, no doubt. She ran her hands over her hair again ... just to make sure.

"Do people actually live down here?" she whispered to Raven, hoping his new appendage wouldn't hear.

"Some," Raven said.

Nikki shuddered and couldn't imagine calling this home. She needed sunlight, fresh air, trees. Then they crossed a larger space littered with people, and a woman reached to lift a child into her arms. Pain pierced Nikki's heart. Home was where your family dwelt. Underground or otherwise. At least Dane had a home; she couldn't say the same anymore. "They don't have a choice, do they?"

Raven stopped to look at her, the bespectacled boy dangling

at the end of his arm. "Most of them don't," he said in a whisper. "A few are fugitives, others are homeless. None of them want to be found. It's kind of a separate city down here. Believe it or not, they all watch out for each other."

Nikki's eyes found Dane, and for the briefest of moments she saw him homeless on the streets of Paris. A bubble of emotion rose to her throat. She dropped to her haunches and reached out to grab the boy and hug him. "Thank you so much for your help, Dane."

Statue still, he stared straight ahead. One side of Dane's face slowly broke into a lopsided smile when Nikki released him and stood up.

Finally free of the boy, Raven sank his hands deep into his pockets.

Dane blinked a few times, gauged Nikki with an unsure look, and reached to drag Raven's hand from the safety of his jeans.

Raven swatted at him with his other hand, but Dane wouldn't be deterred. He grasped Raven's wrist with all his fingers and tugged until the cloaked fist was free and back in his grip.

"We're almost there. My brother hangs out at the Cave."

The Cave, Nikki learned, was a dimly lit room that appeared to serve as a gathering place for anyone over sixteen. Several people mingled at a handful of tables, and some stood among a few pieces of inspired artwork — mostly chunks of shining metal twisted into abstract designs. She searched the space for a friendly face but found none. One table of girls stopped talking to turn around and glare at them. A man traversed the room walking so close that when he passed she was almost knocked down even though she stepped aside. None of it fazed Dane.

But Nikki felt like she'd just stepped into a private party where she not only wasn't invited, she certainly wasn't welcome.

Old movie posters dotted the walls, and music — a style she'd never heard before — filled the air, giving the place its own alternative vibe.

"I'm liking the tunes," Raven said to her as Dane dragged them toward a table of tough-looking guys in the corner.

"It's different. If Lenny Kravitz married Alanis Morissette, this is what their offspring would sound like."

Raven laughed.

A guy with short hair and big muscles — highlighted by the tight white tank top he wore — stood from the table and stepped out. "Yo, Great Dane. What're you doing here?" His voice was gruff, and Nikki began to think following Dane was a mistake.

Dane released Raven, ran toward the guy, and jumped. He landed in his arms.

"Whoa," the guy said, ruffling Dane's hair. "You are getting way too big for that, lil' bro."

Nikki sighed with relief. Beside her, she swore Raven did the same. "You weren't scared of him, were you?" She felt wicked for saying it, but she couldn't resist.

Raven cut her with a look. "No. And even if I *had* been, we need their help."

Dane beamed, and as the older guy carried him over, Nikki saw the resemblance in their faces. Same bow-shaped mouths, same brown eyes. Same accent.

"This is Frank. He's my brother. He knows everything."

Frank had yet to crack a smile in their direction, and Nikki's heart increased with the ticking seconds. "I don't know who you two are or what you said to get this far, but strangers aren't welcome down here."

He threw a glance behind him, signaling the other boys at the table to stand. The half dozen guys made a half circle around Raven and Nikki.

Dane pushed back from his brother. "Frank, they're my friends. He's looking for Greta."

Frank scrutinized Raven, and Nikki could only wonder what the intense examination was about. Who was this Greta, and why was she so important? And how did Raven know her? One more quick motion of Frank's head and the pack of guys slithered back to the table.

"Greta's not here. Why are you looking for her?"

Raven took a step toward him. "What does it matter if she's not here?"

"Everything matters in the tunnels, my friend. If you want help, you should work on your attitude."

Raven relaxed. "Yeah, I keep hearing that. Greta brought me down here a few years ago."

Frank answered by raising his brows.

"Anyway, she brought me down here because I was ... injured ... in a fight."

Frank loosened his grip on Dane and the boy slid to the floor. "Makes sense," Frank said. "Greta always was one to bring in strays."

"Was?"

"She's dead."

If Nikki hadn't been looking at Raven, she might have missed the way he practically doubled over with the words. He stared at the floor for a long time. "What happened to her?" The muscle in his jaw twitched.

"She was trying to help a mutt like you."

Chapter
3

Dane hugged his brother's legs "I miss Greta. She always brought me candy."

Nikki wanted to cry. For Raven, for Dane. For Frank, who obviously cared for Greta too — more than his steely shell could hide.

"I'm sorry," Raven said. He slid his hand into Nikki's and started to turn. "We'll find somewhere else to stay. We just needed a place for the night."

Before they could get to the door, the stone walls carried Frank's voice to them. "We'll help you, Halfling."

Raven stopped in his tracks. Nikki risked a peek over her shoulder and stared at the muscled giant.

"What's after you?"

Raven turned slowly.

Nikki followed, and her confusion must have been glowing on her face, because Frank directed the next statement to her. "I'm a Xian and a Seer."

Okay, maybe he could help. After all, Xians already understood the spiritual realm surrounding them, and if he was also a Seer, like her, he might actually be able to tell them where to head next. Of course, her Seer abilities hadn't helped at all during this whole nightmare. She didn't even know what a seeker looked like, and until Raven appeared at Viennesse she'd hadn't realized she was in danger.

Frank almost smirked at them. "Even if I wasn't a Xian, you both fit the profile."

"Profile?" Nikki echoed, still a little freaked. No one had ever blatantly called her out as *other* before.

Frank gestured to Raven. "Light hair, blue eyes on the guys, and dark hair, golden eyes on the girls. Sorry, but you sort of stick out like a cannibal in a vegan restaurant."

"Okaaaay," Nikki said, wincing at the metaphor.

"And since I'm a Seer, I know something's hunting you."

Nikki ran forward and gripped Frank by the arms. "Please tell me everything you know. Can you see it? Can you see where it is now? I haven't been able to sense a thing." *Let it be far from Viennesse.* Or, if the seeker was after them, she prayed they'd succeeded in rerouting it. Though if it had picked up her scent … Had she put everyone in the tunnels in danger?

Raven pulled her off Frank. She forced herself to focus on his thumb gently rubbing the underside of her wrist instead of the thoughts swirling through her mind.

"What's after you, Halfling?"

Raven opened his mouth to speak, but stopped and looked down at Dane.

The motion wasn't lost on Frank. "Go get me something to drink," he told his little brother.

Dane sighed and moped off in the direction of a doorway.

With a glance back to make sure they boy was out of ear-shot, Raven said, "A seeker."

Frank's mink-brown eyes narrowed. "Don't know that one. I've met with hell hounds, watched Halflings fight demons, but a seeker? Wimpy name. How bad could it be?"

"Worse than anything you've seen. It's like a million razor-sharp knifes slicing at once, leaving you in ribbons. And it never stops hunting until it finds the target."

Frank pointed to Nikki. "You, right?"

Nikki dropped her head.

Dane returned, and when his brother wouldn't take the can of soda he offered, he sat it on the ground at their feet.

So far, no explosion about drawing the seeker into the tunnels. That had to be a good sign. Though why *wasn't* he yelling at them? Did the guy have no sense of self-preservation? Nikki felt the questions rise in her throat and the fear accompanying them. Especially for Dane, who had already lost someone he cared about — Greta — because she had stuck her neck out for someone like Raven. *Someone like me.* "Look, I don't want to stay down here. Raven brought us here because we didn't know what else to do. Just point us to the nearest exit and we'll go."

Frank rocked back on his heels. "Just like that?"

"We can't just let them *go!*" Dane pleaded, his small hand patting the sure-to-be rock-hard stomach beneath Frank's tank.

Nikki marveled at her ability to mess everything up. If she survived this latest nightmare, maybe she'd write a book. *Ten Thousand Ways to Ruin Someone's Day.* "Yes, we will leave just like that. It's not your concern and we've put you in danger."

As Frank stared at her, Nikki realized his features were chiseled enough to belong to a Halfling. But he was sporting a five o'clock shadow and springy arm hair, as well as eyes that were far from blue — not to mention he didn't possess the Halflings' smooth manner and breathtaking beauty. Instead he looked beat up by life, but stronger for it. There was wisdom and fearlessness in his gaze.

"Well, you're wrong about a couple of things." Frank reached to the ground and snagged the soda. "First, you're here. And that makes it our business. Second, you didn't put us in any more danger than what we live in day by day, baby. So stop with the pity party."

Nikki closed her mouth abruptly.

"I may not know anything about seekers, but that doesn't mean we aren't afraid to fight whatever tries to infiltrate our domain."

Raven reached a hand to Frank's shoulder in a brother-in-arms sort of way. She'd learned warriors had their own language, one Raven and probably Frank spoke fluently. "I appreciate that, but this creature just destroyed three of our friends. Halflings named Deux, Paix, and Tronc."

Frank slowly sat the soda can back on the floor. When he rose, Nikki could tell he was struggling to maintain his composure. "They were our friends too. You sure? Deux is an amazing fighter ..."

"We're sure."

Nikki chanced a glance at the corner table. The guys seated there reacted to tragedy the same way — all dropped their heads a degree, while one rubbed a hand over his face and another leaned back, sniffed, stared at the ceiling.

More pain and sorrow to leave in her wake.

Frank moved a millimeter closer to Nikki and trapped her in his stone-cold gaze. Beside her, Raven bristled. Frank's entire composure had shifted once more — now something was boiling in the depths of Frank's eyes. His teeth were clenched so tightly, she wondered if his jaw might shatter. As he took a predatory step toward her, Raven countered with a defensive stride between them.

Tension rose until Frank reached out and grabbed her by the shirt. "Stop it, Nikki!"

Now what did I do? She tried to ready for a punch, an attack of some kind, but instead he pulled her to his face. Nikki wanted to search for Raven, but couldn't drag her eyes from Frank. "W-what?"

He drew her even closer and growled, "Stop it *now*."

Where is my sworn protector while I'm being manhandled by this Xian bully? Beside her, she actually felt Raven relax.

"I — I don't understand."

"It's not about *you*, little Halfling. This is the battle we've chosen. Stop feeling sorry for us. Stop feeling sorry for yourself. It reeks like yesterday's trash. You want to help? Be a fighter. Be a soldier. Stop being a baby." Frank released her with a shove. "You were called into this war. Start acting like you're worthy of it."

Well.

Raven clapped a couple of times. "Thank you. I've been wanting to give her a wake-up call for a while now."

Nikki's cheeks were fire hot and she couldn't utter a single word. Not that she wanted too. Crawling into the nearest crack in the unidentifiable wall seemed a much better solution. Who was she kidding? Frank was right. She spent half her energy feeling bad for, well, everyone, even though they didn't feel bad for themselves. She needed to get over herself.

The boys continued to talk, but she caught only bits and pieces of the conversation. Something about seekers, victims, knowledge. How much energy had she spent worrying about the circumstances rather than taking action? Too much. She purposed to do what Frank challenged her to do. Be a warrior. Be worthy of the battle.

She tuned back into the discussion just as Raven explained what had occurred when the seeker arrived at the castle in France. As she listened, all the pieces of the puzzle settled into one giant question. "Why would the seeker go to Deux's home rather than Viennesse?"

The boys stopped chattering and stared at her.

Warmth — the first she'd felt internally since entering the subterranean world — surged through her like hot soup on a cold winter's day. It was the heat of knowledge, the realization that she'd stumbled onto something that could help them. "Don't you see? That's the clue. My scent is all over Viennesse, and in a much heavier concentration than it ever was in France. If it was tracking me, why would it start anywhere else?"

Frank rubbed his chin and stared at the ground. "Maybe it was following the freshest scent?"

Nikki raised her hand. "The freshest would have been coming from France to Viennesse."

"She's right. So, what does that mean?" Raven glanced between the two of them.

Frank shrugged. "Don't know. We need help. Wisdom."

Dane jumped up and down. "The Owl! We need to ask the Owl. He knows everything."

Raven pointed. "I thought your brother knew everything."

Dane's eyes expanded behind his bubble glasses. "He knows even more of everything than Frank. The Owl has been alive for forever."

"Who's the Owl?" Nikki blinked.

Frank winked. "He's an old dude. Kind of quirky and strange."

"Great," she muttered. "Just the sort we tend to attract."

"Where's he at, Dane? Seems like he left awhile ago."

He did." All the blood seemed to drain from the small boy's rosy cheeks. "He's in the dungeon."

Raven flashed a plastic smile. "Dungeon? Perfect. Let's go to the dungeon to talk to the Owl."

Frank turned to the group of five guys who'd been huddled around the table, and with a slight nod one of them disappeared for a moment, only to jog over with a thick, heavy raincoat that looked like it had been designed for a seven-foot-tall giant.

"Well, what are you waiting for, miss worrywart? Put out your arms."

Nikki could only stare at Frank as he enrobed her in yards of rubberized fabric that happened to have sleeves. "There's only one way in and one way out of the dungeon, and this might be the best chance we have of holding your scent in once we reach the surface."

Her lips begged to ask how that level of protection was possible, but the looks from everyone else convinced her it was best not to argue with the bruiser in the white tank.

As Frank and the corner table crew, Raven and Nikki, and Dane made their way out of the tunnels, the coat dusted the ground with every step Nikki took. *At least I know every inch of me is covered.* They traversed a long corridor, opened a creaky door, and started up an impossible amount of stairs leading to the surface. "Why not *garden* or *palace* or even *courtyard*?" Nikki mumbled.

Frank stopped, backing up the traffic behind him. "Huh?"

Nikki shrugged and a thousand pounds of yellow rubber slicker bobbed with her shoulders. "Cave, dungeon. Those

43

names are depressing. And why not bring a few plants down here to brighten things up a little?"

Shock twisted Frank's features. He pointed at Nikki but directed the words to Raven. "Is she kidding?"

Raven nudged her with his shoulder. "What's up with you and the Suzy-Homemaker thing? It's not like you, Nik. It's freaking me out."

What was *up with her*? She shrugged beneath the yellow blob again. *Nervous energy, I guess.* Since she'd been instructed not to feel sorry for herself, her mind had to stay busy doing something. Apparently mentally redecorating the underground tunnel systems of Paris was the answer. She snaked her hands from under her too-big cuffs and saw her palms were sweaty. She lightly blew on them as Frank turned to continue up the stairs.

"The dungeon got its name when a section of tunnel collapsed, closing it off from the rest of the underground," Frank said to Raven. "That's where we'll find Solomon."

"Solomon?"

"The Owl."

Already Nikki felt the whoosh of fresh air swirling around her ankles. She opened the raincoat slightly to let some of that fresh breeze in, but clamped it closed right after. She hoped no one had seen her brief mistake.

The last doorway opened onto a Paris street, but she barely got a glimpse. Frank turned to her and wrapped the raincoat tighter, then tugged the hood up and over her head. It felt like she'd been submerged in some sweaty fog. "Stay close and, uh, don't breathe."

She held her breath for a few seconds until she heard him chuckle. Nikki sank a fist into his arm from behind.

"Solid punch," he said. "For a girl."

That comment awarded him another hit.

The nine of them walked single file, Nikki hovering near the middle of the pack, able to actually smell the boys' taut attention. Their alertness crackled through the air. She wondered why guys she didn't know — who weren't even Halflings — would put their lives on the line like this, so ready to face a creature beyond their worst nightmares. Her appreciation grew.

She felt a small hand reach up into the sleeve of her raincoat and entwine his fingers with hers.

Dane was whispering about the entrance to the dungeon. "See the row of trees behind the edge of that building?"

"Yes," she whispered back, adjusting her hood slightly.

"That's the entrance to the university. That's where the Owl — I mean, Solomon — likes to hang out. He used to be a professor there, but when he went cuckoo — "

"Cuckoo?" She tried to look down at him, but her vision was again blocked by yellow. She pushed the material back.

"Yeah, like a clock. You know." His head tipped from side to side and his voice rose to a chirp. "Cuckoo, cuckoo."

"Stop it, Dane," Frank hissed.

Nikki's attention returned to the entrance ahead.

Dane squeezed Nikki's hand, and when she looked back down at him he did the cuckoo clock impersonation again, this time silently. By the end he had to press his hand to his mouth to keep from giggling.

She was glad for his moments of levity when they made it into the next tunnel system. Nikki now understood the name *dungeon*. No other handle would fit this dark, stale place.

"We're almost there," Frank said when they reached the end of yet another long staircase leading into the depths of the dungeon. "If we have any … uh … interruptions before we find Solomon, just stay close and keep quiet." His gaze burned a laser hole through Nikki. She widened her eyes at him as if to say, "What?"

He didn't answer. And five minutes later, she found out what "interruptions" were.

A group of guys stopped them as they entered what Frank had said would be the last room before the entrance to Solomon's place.

Nikki lowered her hood and tried to do a quick head count — not that it was necessary. They were outnumbered. Frank stepped forward after the initial pause, and Nikki marveled that Raven was letting someone else lead. She was suddenly aware of his proximity to her. Close. Always close, always there, and always ready. It was like having a personal pit bull.

The leader of the other group stepped out as well, and Nikki watched the anger build as he stared down Frank.

"We're just here to see Solomon." Frank held his hands up in a *back off, we don't want trouble* kind of way.

The guy opposing him had dirty jeans, long hair, and enough tattoos that a kid with a Matchbox car could drive forever along the green paths on his muscled body. A scar marred his face from cheek to jaw, and when he turned his head to spit on the ground, she saw the scar ran the length of his neck too, hiding beneath the collar of a soiled T-shirt. *Guess they grow them tough down here.*

"Look, Skully, I don't need any problems right now. This is important."

Skully stiffened. "Important? Like you told my sister she was important?"

Uh-oh. This could get ugly.

46

Raven moved and slid Nikki behind him.

Frank shot a glance back to his guys and winked, which led to a few snickers.

Nikki rolled her eyes. *Ugh. Could guys ever resist being ... guys?*

"Tell her I said hi."

"You can tell her after I'm done with you." Skully rolled his shoulders, hiked his jeans a little, and readied to fight.

And so did the rest of the guys. Both sides.

Raven stepped forward, between Skully and Frank. "Look, I can appreciate this little fight over your sister's honor, but we don't have time. Someone needs to tell me where to find Solomon. Right now."

Yep, that's more like Raven.

Skully dropped his hands and scoffed. "Who's the newbie?" He nodded in Nikki's direction. "And what's up with the banana costume?"

Nikki kept her head down, not making eye contact. She probably did look like a giant piece of fruit. But at least she didn't look as if she'd been stamped like a package of USDA beef.

"My name's Raven, and you're wasting my time. Where's the Owl?"

Skully stepped until he was inches from Raven's toes. "I guess you're confused about how things work down here. First of all, no one orders me around. And second, you're probably just scared to fight because you know we'll slaughter you."

Raven fisted his hands around Skully's shirt and lifted him off the ground. "And apparently *you're* confused about what *I* said. But since I'm still in a relatively good mood, I'll make myself clear. Tell me where Solomon is, or I'll use your head to carve a new tunnel."

Nikki swallowed, watching as her dark Halfling dangled a huge, muscled man six inches off the ground without breaking a sweat.

Frank stepped in, placing a hand over Raven's in a silent plea to put Skully down. Raven flashed Frank a look then slowly lowered his prisoner, who practically collapsed when his feet touched the floor ...

After a few tense moments and stares from the other dungeon guards, Frank broke the silence. "Just let us pass, Skully. I'll be more than happy to pick up our dispute later."

Skully crossed his arms over his chest, but not before taking a step back. "Can't do it."

Frank swept a hand toward his guys. "You know you don't want to fight us."

"And what would it do to my reputation if I just let you through? I owe you, Franky."

Frank huffed a breath. "You do." He pointed a finger at Skully, then a thumb at himself. "You and me then. If I win, we pass. If you win, we leave."

Raven's hand slapped against Frank's chest. "I'm not going anywhere. And I'm not trusting our fate to a guy I've never seen fight."

Frank started to argue, but Skully cut in. "You choose a fighter from our side to represent us, then. We'll choose one from yours."

Raven shook his head.

Skully shrugged. "Fine. Try to work your way through us, but you're only burning hours. I'm merely giving you a way to save time. If your man wins, we let you pass. If ours wins, I'll listen to your reason for seeing Solomon."

Power games. Gah! Why can't guys find a better way to settle disputes?

Skully walked back to his group and Frank walked toward his, then motioned Raven to his side. Raven put his arm behind Nikki so she would follow. *Always keeping me close.*

"I know these guys," Frank said, in a hoarse whisper. "Skully will pick you to fight. You're the new guy and you insulted him."

"I also lifted him off the ground."

Frank nodded. "Yeah, even more reason for him to choose you. He's a cage fighter, so he knows his close combat. You can't grapple with him down here; he'll be all over you. The guy's like a monkey with a thousand arms and legs once he's on the ground. If he gets you in a sleeper hold, it's lights out. I hope you've got plenty of stamina, Halfling. You're gonna need it."

Nikki's heart was racing. Raven was a great fighter, but this guy sounded like a pretty tough opponent — even if he was a human. She looked down and saw Dane was still clutching her hand under the yellow slicker. She'd forgotten until he squeezed.

Frank leaned in, clearly as oblivious to his brother's presence as she'd been. "Look, I know you're a Halfling, but I'm telling you, strike fast, strike hard. He won't go down easy."

"Got it," Raven said. "Let's just get this over with as quickly as we can."

Skully's sharp voice prevented any further strategy. "You ready to choose, Frank?"

"Yeah." He stepped forward until he was a few feet away from Raven and Nikki. Then he looked at Raven, then frowned, then focused his attention on a thin, sickly guy hovering near the back of Skully's crew. Nikki wasn't sure whether his pensive expression was good or bad.

Raven must have noticed too, because his eyes shot to Frank. "Don't do it!"

Raven lunged forward and placed a hand on Frank's shoulder to spin him around, but Frank's voice already filled the room. "We'll take the guy in the back."

Nikki felt intense anger fly off Raven in waves. She just couldn't sense why he was so irate. Skinny-boy didn't look nearly as tough. Maybe Raven figured Skully would still attack Raven as retribution.

Then the skinny guy made his way to the front of the pack and paused by Skully. Once closer, Nikki could see the vines of knife wound scars layered on his arms.

"No weapons," Frank said, face draining of color. Nikki worked to keep herself steady as well. She knew from her karate training that undersized opponents often find creative ways to compensate for their size. And what better way than to master something no body can withstand?

Skully held his hand out while a variety of knives were handed to him. The thin guy's eyes were cold and calculating, not a hint of fear in his posture. He leaned over and whispered something to Skully and they both smiled at Raven.

Skully nodded toward Raven. "We'll take the new guy."

Raven stepped out.

"Not you. The one in the raincoat."

Chapter
4

This is stupid. Completely stupid. Here we are running for our lives, trying to hide from a creature so evil and so destructive it could rip all of us apart, and this group of guys just wants to puff out their man chests. And they think they're so clever, picking the poor kid in the raincoat.

"No." Raven said, turning toward her.

But it was too late. Nikki stripped off the coat and threw it to the floor. She felt her hair fall in a cascade down her shoulders and heard the gasps from the onlookers. *Huh. Gasps from guys. Go figure.*

She stomped out from the side wall where she'd been gathering her frustration. She felt like her body was engulfed in empowering flames, and her eyes must have turned to molten lava, because Skinny's brows rose slowly as he stared.

She could hear laughing from the back of Skully's group.

Typical immaturity. Always having to fight to prove who's tougher. Always quick to pound someone into the ground.

Nikki's adrenaline rose, coursing through her veins, filling her with righteous anger. *They need to be taught a lesson in a language they understand.* Not that she wasn't quaking a little on the inside at the prospect. Skinny Boy undoubtedly knew how to fight. But so did she. And the longer they stood sizing each other up, the closer the seeker came. Which made this whole show of caveman strength even more utterly ridiculous. Nikki growled in frustration.

Skinny rocked back on his heels, making her even angrier. So much so she fisted her hands and yelled at him, "Come on!"

More laughter. Ugh, when this was over, she was going to kill them all. One by one. Then she'd dress them in evening gowns and hang them from the Eiffel tower. *Where'd that come from?*

"A girl?" Skinny said with a thick French accent as he lumbered nonchalantly toward the center. "Please, Skully. You insult me."

Nikki surged forward, catching him by surprise, and landed a power-packed back fist to his face. All that anger, all that frustration released in a single blow.

Skinny staggered, one step back then another. His head bobbed once, eyes going glassy, before he dropped like a leaf from a tree, his limbs wavering and folding as he went down.

Silence.

Then a roar of laughter. It came from all sides and filled the room, scattering the tension. Nikki turned to face a smiling Raven. "Will taught me that."

Raven winked at her, his eyes animated and sparkling in the dim cavern light. "It's definitely effective."

She rubbed her palm over her fist as she walked back to him.

Raven took her hand in his. "You okay?" His tone dropped to that purr he reserved for only her, and his fingertips trailed over her skin, causing goose bumps to materialize on her arms.

"I'm fine. Bleeding a little," she said, trying to ignore how his touch made her feel. "Must have caught one of his teeth on my knuckle."

Around them, people were trying to help the wobbly, skinny knife fighter to his feet.

"Don't move!" someone yelled from farther in the corridor. The crowd cut a path for the voice until Nikki could see an older man rushing toward her. Dane had interlocked his fingers with the man's, but the man was trying to get away. Dane did that slick-as-an-eel thing he did and clasped tighter.

"No, no!" the man yelled down at him, and Dane let go.

"Solomon?" Raven leaned over and asked Nikki.

"Guess so," she answered. As the man approached, all she could think was *cuckoo, cuckoo, cuckoo* — especially when he snatched a do-rag off one of the boy's heads as he passed by. Two fully functioning hands — now free of Dane — tied the bandana into a loose knot. Solomon grabbed Nikki's hand, mumbling about blood, and wrapped the fabric around her fist.

All this for a tiny cut?

He squeezed hard, pinching her fingers. "It's the blood," he said, pulling her close to his plump face. His breath wasn't all that fresh and his eyes weren't all that clear. *Cuckoo, cuckoo.*

Nikki leaned back.

He leaned forward. "The seeker tracks your blood."

Instinctively, Nikki slammed her free hand over the wound. Her heart kicked up, this time beating out of more fear than anger.

"Did your blood touch the ground?"

"No," she said.

He grabbed her arms and squeezed. "Don't let your blood touch the ground. The blood cries out. That's the easiest way for the seeker to find you."

Over Solomon's shoulder, she watched Skinny wipe his mouth as if removing the Nikki-blood plague, then step farther and farther away until his back bumped the wall and there was nowhere else to go. He continued staring at her like she was the reaper come to collect his soul.

No one laughed now. Raven eyed Dane, then Solomon. "How'd you know?"

Solomon ruffled Dane's hair. "He came and found me."

Raven's gaze narrowed. "Dane didn't know it was a seeker. How'd you figure out a seeker was involved?"

"It wasn't that difficult. Dane said you were being hunted. Something worse than demons and hounds. That narrowed the options. When he told me you came with a question about why a creature would track you to a place you'd barely been rather than finding you at your customary dwelling, the answer had to be spilled blood. A seeker."

Customary dwelling. He must mean Viennesse.

Raven's shoulders dropped a degree, and Nikki was reminded Raven didn't trust anyone. *Well, he's still alive, so you can't argue with success.*

"You know about seekers? Do you know how to defeat one?" Raven said with enough encouragement in his voice to lift Nikki's spirits.

"Oh, no." The man shook his head.

Hopes dashed.

"I don't even know how to fight a seeker, and I'm not sure anyone ever has successfully."

Okay, that removed all hope.

"I can tell you what I know about how they track, what they do to their victims." Gray eyes found Nikki. Wrinkle lines framed Solomon's watery gaze as he tried to force a smile. "But it's best not to dwell on that if you're trying to stay ahead of one."

"Stay ahead?" Raven spat. "What, for eternity? We have to figure out a way to stop this thing, not keep running from it."

The old man grabbed Raven by the shoulders and yelled, "I can't tell you what I don't know, half-man."

Dane grabbed Nikki's unbandaged hand and mouthed "cuckoo."

Solomon let go. "I'm sorry."

"Right." Raven's eyes slowly went from saucer size to normal. "We'd appreciate all the help you can offer."

"Come with me," Solomon motioned them into the darkest part of the tunnel.

One hour later, after numerous glasses of lukewarm tea at the Owl's kitchen table in his underground apartment, they knew little more than when they'd arrived.

The only helpful tidbit was that seekers knew but one thing: find and neutralize the target. "So, basically, they never rest and they never stop hunting?" Raven asked, circling back to what the Owl had told them.

Solomon rifled through the mix of journals and books he'd scattered across the table. "Here it is. I wrote this a few years back when the seeker caught my attention. I'd spent a year in the Middle East researching biblical monsters—"

"Biblical monsters?" Nikki interrupted. "Like demons?"

Solomon reached around his tea mug and pulled a black leather-bound book to him. "Much worse than demons. Vile things that aren't allowed access to the earthly realm. It's all in

Scripture — if you've a mind to look closely enough. Leviathan, the behemoth, the angel of death, they're all there. This creature seeks whom he can devour. The word *devour* actually translates to *shred*. Seekers shred their victims."

Nikki's heart plummeted to her stomach.

Raven pushed his tea away. "I am so going to regret asking this, but why does it shred its victims?"

The Owl swallowed, his gray eyes darkening. "It's trying to remove the soul. It digs into the victim in hopes of capturing it."

"Yeah, I didn't think I wanted to know."

"The issue is souls can't be removed. Once a physical person is dead, the soul sails on its own." Solomon sipped his tea.

Nikki's brow puckered. Mr. Cuckoo wasn't making any sense.

She chewed on her lip. "I remember reading in my Bible that to be absent from the body is to be present with the Lord. So, everyone who dies goes to God?"

Solomon patted the leather book again, and Nikki realized it must be a Bible. "To be absent from the body is to be present with *your* lord. Whoever that is. If you serve the Throne, then the Giver of Life is your Lord. If you reject him, the hater of men's souls is your lord. Either way, your soul is gone from the physical body instantly."

"Unless you're a Halfling," Raven mumbled.

"But the seeker tries to dig through you to find it after you're dead?" Nikki tried to stop the nausea the mental picture raised.

"That's what I understand, at least. Seekers aren't my specialty. I have a friend who has spent more time than me studying them. I think you should talk to him."

Raven stood. "No time like the present."

"He won't be reachable this late at night. He's in the Bernese mountains."

56

"Swiss Alps. One of my favorite ski areas." Raven began to gather the tea kettle and cups "Can you give us directions?"

"Of course," Solomon said. "But don't you think you should sleep here tonight?"

Nikki yawned. "I'm exhausted. But I don't want to put anyone at risk."

Solomon reached to pat her hand across the table. "For those of us in the underground, we specialize in risk."

Choices, choices. Raven glanced down at Nikki. She looked spent. Dark circles under her eyes, worry tilting the edges of her mouth into a frown. Even now she was gorgeous.

And exhausted. Yeah, they needed to rest a few hours. Winter had suggested the tunnels to him as a safe place for the night, but he'd managed to keep them one step ahead of the seeker, and maintaining that advantage was paramount. Plus, there was something really delicious about being her guardian, the only one protecting her. For the first time ever, he had Nikki to himself, and she truly trusted him. But no matter how much he enjoyed their current arrangement, his feelings had to take second place to her safety.

"Solomon," Nikki said, leaning forward. "We need to get a message to a friend in Germany. Do you have a computer with an internet connection?"

Raven stood. "No time, Nikki." He dragged her out of her chair and she rested against him. "If we want to stay ahead of the seeker, we have to move. Tonight. Now." He briefly stared at his hand, wrapped around Nikki's wrist, realizing the decision he'd made the moment he pulled Nikki to her feet. He couldn't allow them to connect with the others, as that meant sharing her — and it seemed like sharing her meant more risk. Too much risk. For all of them.

Her long exhale assaulted him, and he tried — unsuccessfully — to avoid drawing Nikki into his lungs. Her breath was sweet where it blew against his skin. Ignoring the Owl, he cupped her face in his hands. "You can rest while we fly," he whispered. "We've been here too long already."

She nodded, the motion causing strands of her hair to dance over his fingertips. Man, it felt good to have Nikki alone. And he simply wasn't ready to give that up.

Chapter
5

Raven pumped his wings, taking in the snow-dusted mountains below him. His arm was numb with a thousand prickly spots begging for fresh blood flow, but he wouldn't readjust. Nikki had fallen asleep, her skin against his, her breathing heavy with exhaustion. She'd groaned once, and he'd drawn her closer, rewarded by her nuzzling into him and whispering his name. There, in his arms while he hovered above the mountains, everything was perfect.

Except for the fact they were being hunted.

He spotted a cabin and a thin sliver of road leading to it. Smoke rose from a chimney and the ground around the building glowed warm yellow with the illumination of lights from inside. Solomon had said they would have to wait until morning to talk to his friend, but Raven had never been one to listen to other people's opinions about what he should and shouldn't do. He dropped altitude and landed silently at the edge of woods beside the house.

On the ground, he could give his full attention to Nikki. Her long hair fell in windswept waves around her shoulders and spilled over him. Her eyes were closed, and those impossibly long lashes rested against her skin. When a breeze worked its way around the mountainside and collided against them, Nikki burrowed deeper into Raven's arms.

He closed his wings around her, sheltering her from the cold. *What are you doing?* a small voice whispered inside his soul. Nikki had said she wanted to be with Mace, that he was her match. But Raven knew she was wrong. At least, he *believed* she was wrong.

And it wasn't just her. No one thought Raven and Nikki were right for each other. The words Winter spoke to him when they were on the yacht echoed back. "What will happen when you're not the shiny new penny anymore?"

Raven pushed all the negative words aside. He wanted Nikki, and knew they had a connection no one else could fathom. And that made it right.

He roused her by gently kissing her cheek. His lips lingered against her skin. She smelled different this close. With his powerful senses, his mind clicked off the fragrances as they entered his nose: coconut shampoo, baby powder, lotion. He lifted one of her hands to his face. Yep, hand lotion, vanilla. And there was that aroma that was simply *her*. The smell of wind and life. It was Nikki, and it was freedom. The one thing he never thought he'd have.

He wasn't just in love with her. She was his salvation.

Her eyes fluttered open. Taking in her position in his arms and the surroundings of his gray wings, a slow smile spread on Nikki's face. "Are we safe?" she whispered.

"You're always safe with me, Nikki."

"I'm starting to think you're right." She yawned, stretched like a cat, but he wouldn't let her slip that easily. His hand pressed to the small of her back.

"Then why don't you stop fighting me?" His lips brushed against hers, and for a moment she melted into him. But just as quickly her mouth hardened and she leaned back.

"I'm not going to do this, Raven."

He studied her eyes, still inches from his face, yet suddenly miles away.

"If this is your plan, take me back to Viennesse."

The muscles in his body twitched, and he hoped she hadn't noticed her words caused him to loosen his hold. Since when did Nikki react to him like this, and with such conviction? Since when was he no longer irresistible?

"Take you back? That's a stupid idea."

She cocked a brow. "Maybe, but I didn't come with you so you could try to change my mind."

"If your mind couldn't be changed, you wouldn't be so worried about it." Though his grip had loosened, his hand pressed into the small of her back. He knew what that did to her.

She lifted a hand and pushed firmly against his chest. "I'm serious."

Maybe I am in trouble.

"I don't want to put them in danger, but I've hurt Mace over and over by being drawn in by you. He saw us kissing when we fed the dolphins, and at my house the night my parents died, and I . . . I left Viennesse with you." She gathered fistfuls of hair in both hands. "I can't believe I did that. How's he going to feel?"

"The same way I do, like we need to do whatever it takes to keep you alive," Raven spat.

Her eyes cooled. "I won't hurt Mace again. If you're going to play the "get her alone and make her forget her boyfriend" card, you can forget it. Because I'm not playing that game with you anymore."

He'd gotten plowed by an ATV once, before he'd tapped in; this felt about the same.

"We have to concentrate on staying alive, staying ahead of the seeker. All our energy needs to go there. If you're not committed to that, take me back."

She was right, even though it killed a part of him to admit it. Raven released her and opened his wings. "Okay, okay. What's our next move?"

The wind caused her to shutter while she scrutinized him, no doubt judging his motives. "You're still willing to help me?" There was a new strength in her voice, her posture.

"Of course."

"And you won't be trying to ..." She pointed between them and made small circles with her finger.

Frustration increased but he fought it. "No."

Nikki's chin dropped and she eyed him. "Not at all?"

He released an angry breath. "Not at all, Nikki."

A mix of triumph and relief were visible in her crooked smile. "Good. Thanks." She turned and tromped toward the cabin's front door.

"As I said, what's our next move, oh dear person I see only in a platonic manner?"

"Our next move is to go wake up Solomon's friend. And if you keep up that tone of voice, I'll dig my fingers into your eye sockets."

Huh, so this is what it feels like when the shine wears off.

Introductions had gone as well as one could expect. Christopher, Solomon's friend, invited them in with barely a word. Raven had entered slowly, trying not to gawk at the weirdness of it all. *Hello, we're here to pick your brain. Why? Oh, we're being chased by a seeker. Got any coffee?*

Once they were inside, he was only slightly shocked to see the entirety of the cabin's walls were covered in shelves and shelves of books. Books to the ceiling. No paintings, no photographs, just books and the occasional window. Every direction held evidence of either an untidy housekeeper or a very one-track mind. Stacks of folded clothes had taken over one corner, while piles of dirty ones comprised another.

The tall, thin man had been kind enough, though he'd taken one look at Nikki, one glance at Raven, and demanded there would be no discussions until they'd all rested. "It will take all of your strength. All of your cunning to stay ahead. Tonight, you need your rest," Christopher had said, like some Dad trying to make sure his kids got enough sleep before the big algebra test. Moments later he'd shooed Nikki into a small bedroom and shut the door behind her, leaving Raven alone with him in the living room.

Why were the men who helped them always such weird dudes?

After several minutes in the Twilight Zone that was Christopher's cabin, Raven slipped back outside, trying to wrap his mind around the situation.

He wouldn't sleep, of course, so he sat on the front porch beneath a patio heater that actually kept the temperature comfortable. The quiet and stillness of the Swiss Alps closed around him like a protective armor. He lingered there, thinking about all the things he should leave tucked into that other protected place, his heart.

Nikki's words had stung. But he'd give her what she'd asked for. Shoot, he'd slice open his side and give her a kidney if that's what she needed. Maybe by backing off, she'd actually see the truth. That's what she'd wanted him to do on the boat, and in the end she'd raced off to his favorite place, choosing his motorcycle, just because she had an urge to be near him again. She just had to see he wasn't a back off kind of guy. Regrettably, that was part of the path he'd chosen. A choice that hadn't quite gone as planned.

But her ability to pull away this time was something different. Nikki was different. Maybe she'd been battered and knocked around so much, she finally settled into who and what she was. Even Mace wouldn't be able to deny determination and strength came off her now in undeniable ripples.

She'd become a survivor. That, he could use.

And that, that quality he'd helped her hone, might be the thing that drove her away from him.

The door creaked open.

Nikki peeked out onto the porch, pulling the colorful afghan she'd found tighter around her shoulders. "I thought you were going to sleep." She'd almost panicked when she'd left her cozy bed and found he was no longer in the living room. But a pale light from the front porch slipped beneath the door, and she'd breathed relief before coming out to him. Raven was still there. Guarding her.

"I guess I'm just not tired," he said, and turned back toward the endless sea of blue-white mountains.

She stepped onto the porch and a shiver entered her feet and climbed up her body. "It's cold out here." She considered the mountains, the smoky gray moon hovering above. "Is sitting out here really necessary?" *What is he looking at?*

Raven pointed. "See that peak over there? It reminds me of my favorite place to ski."

Nikki settled onto the porch swing beside him. "You're exhausted, Raven. Why are you out here thinking about skiing?"

"Keeping watch. I don't like being surprised." There was a hint of bitterness in his voice.

"If you're talking about what I said earlier — "

"I'm not."

Off to the right, the wind moved a tree enough to collapse the small peaks of snow on the branches. Sparkling flakes fluttered to the ground.

"You only said what you've said all along."

Ugh. That bitterness again, barely hidden under his resolve, but poking through each word like weeds in a sidewalk crack. Though he put on a good front, when she turned to study him, she saw it — the wound. She'd damaged something in him, and for that she was sorry.

An animal howled in the distance, drawing her attention from the Halfling she seemed destined to hurt. The long, moaning wail bounced off the mountains and played against the hardened snow around them.

Fear clawed across her shoulders. She pulled the blanket around her and looked at Raven.

"Relax. It's just a wolf."

"You sure?" Nikki scooted a little closer.

"Yeah, probably miles from here."

"Raven?" She glanced over to view his profile. His hair

fanned across his forehead as if the breeze had its way with the strands. His eyes were rimmed with red, but it only added intensity to his features.

"Yeah?" The slightest move of his head angled him toward her.

"What if there's no way to beat the seeker?"

Raven's eyes slid closed. Defeat, or something like it, radiated from him. "Then we'll just keep running forever."

Nikki closed her eyes too, and didn't realize the amount of breath leaving her lungs until she heard the hiss from her own lips.

He slowly slid an arm around her and pulled her into him. "It won't beat us, Nikki. I won't let it."

Oh, she wanted to believe that. Believe *him*. Because he'd never let her down yet. Even when it seemed he'd abandoned her, he hadn't. Like when he left a train accident to chase after some guys in a van. She'd later discovered they were the bombers who'd blown up the tracks, hoping to kill every last passenger. By going after them, Raven intended to destroy the threat. For good.

But he'd come back for her in the end, as if he'd known exactly when she needed him. And he came back to Viennesse as soon as the seeker was released.

She pushed back from him for a second. "How did you know about the seeker?" Why hadn't she thought to ask sooner?

"An angel showed up at my ruins and told me."

Told him? Not Will, the Halflings' guardian. Not Mace, who'd practically made keeping her from any harm his fulltime job. An angel told Raven.

Nikki's gaze drifted from Raven's face to the snow-rumpled road leading away from the house. "Why would an angel tell *you*?" Each word was cautious, carefully chosen, but inevitable.

As was his answer. "Maybe the angel knows something about *us* that we don't know."

He met her gaze straight on by tilting her chin until she surrendered. There was no seduction in his midnight eyes. They simply sparkled as if a thousand diamonds danced beneath their glasslike surface. There was no hint of flirtation. Just a solid, convincing look he forced her to take in. To get the message he'd been proclaiming since they met. That he was her destined match …

Thanks a lot for confusing the one area I thought I was clear on. Nikki swallowed. "You need to sleep. Go on in and I'll watch for a while." But when the faraway wolf howled again, Nikki scooted closer to him.

Raven cleared his throat, stifling a chuckle.

"I'm not scared to stay out here and keep watch." She hated how unconvincing she sounded. After fighting a few hell hounds, she was still wary of any large, lumbering canines, and wolves fit into that category.

He shrugged away her suggestion and focused on the mountains again. The previous moment, with talks of angels and messages, was officially gone. "No. Go back inside. You'll need to be rested for tomorrow."

"I'm wide awake, Raven. I slept on the way here, then for another three hours inside. It's your turn. I need you to be fresh tomorrow. After all, my life's at stake." Even she knew it was pitiful attempt at humor.

His eyes were almost cold. "Don't joke about it, Nikki." His gaze shot from her eyes to her mouth to her hair like he was taking it all in and snapping little pictures of her as he went.

She tried to swallow again, but her throat was swollen and

her tongue had become thick with apprehension. Little pictures. Little memories … in case …

Maybe they shouldn't have left Viennesse. It seemed like such a smart and brave idea at the time. *No, I did the right thing. The others are safe. That's what matters.* At least she kept telling herself they were safe. Mace would understand that's why she left, wouldn't he? It seemed no matter the choice she made, someone was always destined to be nicked in the fallout.

Beside her, Raven's eyes closed far too long to be a blink. Ah, her chance. "I'll stay out here with you a bit," she said, glancing over. "Here, lean your head on my shoulder."

It seemed to take great effort for him to open his eyes. "I know what you're trying to do." But already his words were heavy with sleep.

"Come on, I'll tell you a story." She reached over and placed her hand to the side of his face, leading him to rest on her blanket-covered shoulder.

With a sigh, he stopped resisting. "I won't sleep."

"Umm-hmm," she purred. The tension in his muscles relaxed and his breathing slowed.

"Once upon a time …" Her voice was barely a whisper, soft enough she didn't interrupt his journey to the land of sleep, but loud enough he couldn't possibly accuse her of foul play.

His shoulder twitched once.

She held her breath then ventured on. "Once upon a time, there was a girl named Nikki. And she was soooo much trouble, it was determined that one handsome prince wouldn't be nearly enough. So the great Throne sent three …"

Chapter
6

Winter and Glimmer watched the sun rising over the Viennesse courtyard. Golden streaks of light spiked into the sky.

Glimmer rubbed her face with her hands. "Feels safer now with dawn approaching."

Winter nodded, tried to smile, but it died on her face. It wasn't safer. The seeker could hunt as well in the day as the night, but Glimmer was still young and didn't need that knowledge weighing upon her. Winter often wished *she* didn't have to know. But that was the penalty of living a long life.

Not that Glimmer had been completely spared the truth behind the seeker. She and Vegan had found the dead French Halflings. Winter knew what seeing that level of carnage was like. It'd taken her decades to erase the memories.

She placed an arm around Glimmer, who shuddered at the cold touch.

"Sorry," Winter said. "Sometime I forget that popsicles aren't very comforting."

"You're the most elegant popsicle I've ever met. Actually, you're the only living, breathing, Halfling popsicle I've ever met."

Winter cast a glance heavenward. "What can I say? I'm special."

No one really talked about Winter's ice-cold skin. She was a freak, like they all were, so a peculiarity like hers didn't seem to matter — except when trying to comfort a friend.

"Do you think it's still on the way?"

"No," Winter said. "It would have reached us by now."

Glimmer hugged her own shoulders, as if trying to hold in her body heat. "You think it went straight for Nikki and Raven, don't you?"

"I should have insisted on going with them." The sun continued its trek, rising higher and higher and chasing away shadows along the courtyard. "It all happened so fast."

"I've never seen Mace so mad." Glimmer's golden, red-rimmed eyes widened.

"He's probably still fuming, but what could we do?"

"Any word from Raven?"

Winter shook her head, causing hair to spill over her arms. She dragged a hand down its length and pulled it over one shoulder. "No. Though I know he won't let any moss grow under his feet."

"What?"

"Sorry." Another thing Winter often forgot was the need to use modern phrases. The other Halflings were a lot younger than her. Even though none of them looked over twenty — herself included. "Raven won't stay put for long. He'll be on the move, and hopefully he'll outsmart the seeker."

A visibly worried Glimmer chewed on her fingernail. "I've been praying for him to have wisdom."

"You still have a crush on Raven?"

Glimmer smiled behind her hand. "More than ever. The way he grabbed me when I came in last night after Vegan and I found—"

A noise at the door drew their attention. Vine entered the room with a cup of coffee. "This is for you, Glim. It's got chocolate syrup and extra sugar—just the way you like it."

Winter held back a smile. *Speaking of crushes . . .*

Vine placed the mug into Glimmer's hands like it was a Faberge egg being handed to a princess. "Do you want some cookies to go with it?"

Glimmer accepted the mug, wrapped her hands around it, and smiled at Vine. "No thanks."

Winter watched red pop out across his cheeks—a stark contrast against his luminescent skin and that robe of white-blond hair.

When Vine didn't leave, Glimmer questioned him with a look.

He continued to watch her from an uncomfortably close range until Winter cleared her throat.

"Oh. I'll just go. But, I was wondering if . . . you know, if you're . . . okay."

Glimmer dropped her gaze.

Vine backed toward the door. "You know what? Never mind. I'll check on you later. Okay, so, um, if you want more, just yell. I'm in the kitchen. I mean, I'll be in the kitchen."

When he left, Winter pointed to the door and scrunched her nose. "How cute is he?"

Glimmer did a one-sided shrug and rolled her eyes. She started to take a drink, but Zero came flying through the hall before she could safely tip back the mug. "Got a hit on the seeker," he said as he passed their door, pausing only long enough to make a moment's eye contact with Winter.

Zero was shaken, but trying to hide it. Mace was right behind him, not hiding a thing. Winter and Glimmer rushed to the door and fell in line with the group following Zero into the kitchen.

By the time they were gathered, Mace looked about ready to explode. "What's happening, Zero?"

Winter's heart went out to him. He'd spent the night pacing the floor and wondering if Nikki was still alive. Several times, she'd seen him trying to leave in hopes of finding them, but his duty to the other Halflings kept him. If the seeker arrived at Viennesse, he claimed he'd be abandoning them, and Winter partly agreed. Besides, all he'd known was Raven might take her to the underground tunnels of Paris, like she'd suggested, and even if he'd followed that advice, there were miles of tunnels. There'd be no way to find them.

After much argument, Winter had convinced him to wait until Raven made contact. As Mace met her eyes across the kitchen, she hoped Raven made that contact soon.

Vegan moved to Zero's side as he spoke. "The seeker killed a guy on a university campus in Paris."

Winter's eyes went back to Mace. He looked like he'd been struck by a brick. "Is it — ?"

"I don't know who it is, but the report said the guy's flesh — what was left of it — was marred by scars. They thought it might be someone who's been in his share of knife fights."

The room released a collective sigh. It wasn't Raven.

When everyone continued to stare at Zero, he lifted his hands. "That's all I got."

Mace spun from the group and headed toward the door. Winter followed closely. "What are you doing?"

He turned to face her, the challenge evident and powerful. "I'm not waiting any longer. She's out there, Winter. I have to find her."

"Raven said he'd send us information as soon as he could."

Anger bubbled beneath the blue of his eyes, causing them to look like glass under pressure. They might shatter at any moment. "I'm not trusting Nikki's fate to Raven. You can sit here as long as you want, but I'm going to Paris. There has to be answers there."

Vine stepped out from the group. "I'm with you, bro."

"Me too," Glimmer said.

Winter weighed the options. "Okay, I'll go as well. Zero, will you keep searching for information on the seeker?"

He nodded. "I've got some programs running back history—if there's any written record of seeker attacks, I should find them, but it might take awhile. Vegan can help me."

Vegan opened her mouth to protest, but Winter stopped her. "He's right, Vegan. You should help Zero. You know more about his computer system than the rest of us, and the two of you work together well. You'll do us the most good by staying here."

Vegan's mouth twitched with aggravation, but she conceded with a sigh. Winter, Vegan, and Glimmer were a team. In fact, she couldn't recall the last time they had been apart. But everything had changed when they'd been sent to help the males. Unfortunately, it took all of them to keep Nikki Youngblood alive.

Nikki stared over the table at Christopher, who had cluttered the space with books and notepads. Unlike Solomon, he was tall and thin and lost in a sea of loose papers. "I've been intending on getting this stuff organized," he said.

Her frustration grew. She'd rested. So had Raven — sort of. But now it was daylight and she felt like a beacon-lit target from staying in the same place for so long. And Christopher didn't seem in much of a hurry.

Raven entered the kitchen and spun a chair backward, straddling the seat and crossing his forearms over the back.

"Make yourself at home," Nikki mumbled.

"Thanks."

He'd been chilly to her since the night before. But that was for the best, even though his cool demeanor and impassionate looks leached any warmth from her body. She'd sat on the porch swing while he dozed — and for that moment of time, she'd relished the feel of him against her, his defenses down, simply and wonderfully Raven. But awake, he was a different person, thanks to her ultimatum. Every practiced defense he possessed was on full display, just because she'd dared challenge him.

And Nikki didn't like being bullied. She'd made her decision, and it was Mace. Now that Nikki was a Halfling, she couldn't keep the two guys in a constant fight for her affections. It had been wrong enough when she thought she was a human, but now . . . Now it was detestable. Mace was her match. She knew he was, even though it made little sense; Mace was constantly pushing her to be a better person, even when it was painful, while Raven loved her the way she was. She was better suited for Raven — the two of them both dangling over that dangerous cliff called darkness. But her heart belonged to Mace. He was her true love.

Except . . .

Nikki couldn't erase the words Raven spoke the night before. *Maybe he knows something about* us *that we don't know.*

Christopher stood and offered Raven some coffee, and when he shook his head, the man sat back down. "Why don't you tell me what you've discovered and I'll try to fill in the blanks."

"We know the seeker tracks blood."

"Yes," Christopher agreed, reaching for a yellow pad. "Since Cain killed Abel, the blood cries out from the ground."

"Cain and Abel, as in the first murder?" Raven asked.

"Yes. He tracks your blood. Wherever it spills, wherever you leave a drop on the earth, it's like a homing device. You see, a spirit of anger grew within Cain, causing him to kill his brother. That spirit became the first seeker. Tracking blood that's hit the ground is a seeker's strongest ability. They are only released only at the most intense moments of betrayal. Once out, he will track your scent, your energy, your fear. But your spilled blood screams to him. Spilled blood screams in the spiritual realm ... for those who have ears to hear it."

Nikki's heart dropped. "I know what you're talking about." She turned to Raven. "When I was in the Hummer in Vessler's garage, I found some blood on the seat. When I touched it, I saw a flash of my dad's face."

Raven reached over and took her hand when her voice cracked. "You knew it was your dad's blood? Just by touching it?"

She nodded, drawing strength from his hand against hers. "Yes."

"So, your ability as a Seer is growing." Raven squeezed, and for an instant all that icy coldness melted. "The guy in the Hummer killed your parents?"

She nodded again.

Christopher flipped some pages. "Do you know about water?"

They turned to him.

"We really are starting from scratch here, aren't we?" He placed the pad on the table. "Seekers are from the pit. They were not meant to ever reach this realm, but occasionally one is sent."

"It's after me," Nikki said.

"Lucky you." Christopher tapped his pad. "Things of this realm confuse them."

Raven leaned forward a little. "Things like water?"

"There's no water in hell so they have trouble with it, can't navigate well through it." He snapped his fingers as if trying to dumb down the explanation. "Water's dimensional property is confusing to them."

"That's great to know if you're a fish, but we can't exactly hide underwater."

"Not just underwater, behind water. Say you're looking through a giant aquarium. You can see the seeker clearly. But it has trouble seeing you."

"That doesn't make sense, because scent would travel around the aquarium," Raven offered.

"Of course, it would smell you — uh, her — but it couldn't easily find her. Many things of this realm create difficulties for the seeker. Water is the biggest."

"What else?" Raven tossed his head.

"Temperature changes. Extremes. If you're trying to stay ahead of it, going from cold climates to warm are difficult for the creature. It doesn't adapt well. But you can't stay anywhere too long, because eventually it will adapt."

"What about the midplane? Is she safe there?"

"No. The midplane is the doorway to both the heavenly and earthly realms, so the seeker has to pass through it to reach this realm. If he can go in once, he can go in again. Traveling the mid-plane can get you places quickly, but don't linger there too long."

"It's hopeless." Nikki didn't mean to say it out loud, but facts were facts.

Raven gave her his full attention. "It's not hopeless. Stop saying that."

"He's right," Christopher agreed. "The seeker also relies on your emotion to draw him closer. Your fear, discouragement, all those things are like smoke signals to the creature. When he gets close, he'll rely on your emotion to draw him in. In fact, it's rumored that once he gets in close proximity, he can no longer get a fix on your scent and has to rely on your emotions to bring him to you."

"If he can smell me from far away, he can smell me up close. What you're saying doesn't make sense."

"In close proximity, he frenzies. It's not like he can't smell you, it's more like you're all he smells. All around him. So he can't find you. At that point, he has to rely on your fear or something like that to draw him to you."

"So, the aquarium isn't any good if you're hiding and ter-rified? He can't see you, he smells you everywhere, and your fear will lead him right in." She gave a quick nod. "That's what you're saying."

Christopher's face fell. "Unfortunately, that sums it up. The water wouldn't do much good in that case. Once you leave here, stay full of faith that you will overcome. You *will* find a way to beat the seeker or to send it back to the pit."

"How do you know all this?" Raven didn't seem like he was questioning Christopher's information, just how he gathered it.

"I have a friend who came up against a seeker years ago. It became my life's study after ... after ..." He gathered some papers to his chest. "Anyway, as I said, you'll find a way to beat it or send it back to the pit. I have faith you will."

Nikki spoke up. "I have faith." She thought back to the faith ball Will taught her to hold on the yacht.

Raven cut her a hard look. She had no idea why. He was the one who'd helped her tap into the well of faith within herself. Mace had tried, but mostly ended up frustrated with her, and she with him, while Raven had gently guided her fingers over his until she felt the sphere of faith vibrating in her hands. That's when she was able to hold it for herself.

When she looked over to give Raven an appreciative smile, he dropped his gaze and almost looked ... guilty of something. *What was that about?* It didn't matter. He'd taught her how to use her faith. Which may help save her from the seeker. Right now, she'd forgive him anything.

She could keep up a positive attitude if it would help her stay alive. After all, without it, she was doomed.

"I think you should talk to someone else," Christopher said, after a few moments consideration. "Her name is Kaylyn Quick, she's a ..."

"A Xian. I know her." Raven shrugged. "If it's the same Kaylyn."

Nikki leaned toward him. "Do you mean the singer?"

Raven ignored her. "What does Kaylyn have to do with this?"

"Her uncle fought a seeker once."

"What happened to him?" Nikki asked.

Christopher answered her with silence. He rose and filled his coffee cup. "Kaylyn may know some things that can help you. I've not talked to her in a while, but I have contact information here somewhere."

He rummaged through a drawer then handed a card to Raven. Nikki was about to ask Christopher if he'd let them send an email to Zero when she noticed the change in Raven. His foot tapped noisily, and he acted like a few hundred ants were trekking down his spine. "What's wrong?"

He stared at the window for a second. "Nothing."

She wasn't convinced. Her shoulders began to tingle in that way they'd done when hell hounds were close. "Raven . . ."

He held out his hand to silence her. "Something's happening." He rose from the chair and went to the window.

Nikki stared at the books and notepads. That's when she sensed it. "Hounds."

"I forgot to mention that if a seeker doesn't find you quickly, hell hounds will be released to help in the search. Since they drop in and out of the midplane after you've used it, they can sometimes get to you more quickly."

"Time to go," Raven said, pulling Nikki to her feet. All positive thoughts were gone.

They threw the front door open, but it was too late. The hounds were making their way across the snowy meadow, their hideous black forms and fur-matted paws beating against the ground. Seven hounds in all, the most Nikki'd ever seen at one time. Her lungs sucked the cold outside air and it chilled all the way down, causing her T-shirt to feel way too light. Christopher had offered them warmer clothes the night before, but there was no time to get them now. "What do we do?"

Behind the hounds, a smattering of wings materialized, dropping from the sky at such a rate it forced another breath into Nikki's already full lungs. In the mix she spotted Mace.

Three Halflings flanked him. From the distance, she couldn't make out faces, but she didn't need to. She knew Vine by his hair. Glimmer's bow and quiver of arrows were held ready as she ran toward the cabin, aiming at the hell hounds closing the distance to Nikki. Winter, her dark hair streaking behind her as she ran, pointed to the lead hound, and Glimmer let her arrow fly.

It cut through the air and found its mark. With a yelp, the hell hound skidded to a halt and turned to face Glimmer. Blood ran from its side in a red-black river.

"Get her out of here," Mace screamed to Raven. "We'll follow you when we can."

Chapter
7

Raven lifted Nikki in his arms and leapt into the sky. She squirmed against him as she looked down and saw the fight. Hounds moving toward the Halflings, Glimmer sinking another arrow, and Vine leaping onto one hound's back. "Raven, we have to go back. We have to help them."

"No. If the hounds found us, the seeker might be close behind. And if you get so much as a scratch ... Our best chance is to get you away from here."

Nikki couldn't help the convulsions that started in her stomach and wrenched outward, finding voice in a desperate wail. She clung to Raven.

"Don't cry, Nikki," he whispered, and pulled her into more of an embrace than a hold. His wings flapped against the mountain air, causing the two of them to rocket toward the midplane.

She couldn't stop shaking, and realized part of it was relief. She'd seen Mace. That meant he was alive.

"Mace and the others will find us when they've killed the hounds."

"How?" She couldn't think clearly — the image of Mace landing, his powerful legs propelling him toward her, and his authoritative voice booming the words, "Get her out of here" kept rolling over and over in her mind.

"Christopher will tell them where we've gone." His voice was almost soft.

"What if the seeker gets there before they can kill them all?"

Raven stopped in midair — like hitting the brakes after careening down a roller coaster's deepest hill — and considered her for a moment, then rocketed west so quickly it jolted Nikki's head straight back.

He dropped onto a mountaintop. Raven set her on her feet, and when she wobbled he grabbed her shoulders to steady her. "We're about a hundred miles from the cabin, so this should be good enough."

"What are you talking about?"

He picked up an ice-covered stick and examined the meaty part of her upper arm. Before she could protest, or even react, he raked the stick across her skin. Searing pain filled her senses. "Raven what are you — " But as bright red blood appeared on her arm, she knew.

Raven dredged the tip of the stick in the blood and dropped it onto the ground.

A second later, they were airborne again.

"Sorry about that," Raven said, nodding down to the scrape. "Your blood's on the ground, and apparently that's irresistible to the seeker. It should draw him here. Hopefully, Christopher is right and it's spilled blood, not blood on you, that is easiest for him to track."

Her gaze followed his below her shoulder. A jagged line marred her skin. "You did the right thing." But even she wasn't convinced by those words. He traveled farther west then shot straight up.

Before long, they entered the midplane.

There was no question they were in another realm. The midplane — the zone between heaven and earth — resembled the world she's always known — with trees, hills, rivers and forests — but all of it was bathed in a warm golden glow as if the sun had burst and scattered its particles into the air. It was beautiful, serene, and only safe for a short while, since they were being tracked.

Raven touched down at a stream and released Nikki slowly. "Doing okay?" He studied her. Her shell-shocked eyes and bewildered look proved she was unsettled from seeing Mace and Glimmer, and it made him wonder if he was doing the right thing. *She is alive. That's all that matters.*

She squeezed her upper arm. "My arm stings a little."

He took her by the hand and led her to the water. "Let's wash out the cut. That wasn't exactly a sterile hunk of wood."

She nodded and he reached a hand into the water. He drew his cupped palm toward her, but paused. Raven's gaze left the wound and considered her face. *What if . . .*

Nikki peered down at the wound and nodded. "I agree. Don't rinse it." He felt her pull back slightly. "It'll leave my blood in the stream."

He let the liquid drain through his fingers then wiped his hand across his jeans.

Of course, there were *other* ways of helping heal a wound. Not that he should try. But as she squeezed her forearm and frowned down at the cut, he knew *should* didn't matter.

Before she could protest, Raven licked his lips and pressed them to the cut.

She flinched, a hiss escaping her lips. "Raven, ouch." She pulled from him, horror filling her golden eyes. "Why did you do that? My blood is on you now. That makes you a target, genius."

Her lips were a hard straight line, but as she clutched her arm with her free hand, her eyes ablaze, all he could think was, *Man, she's hot.* Hot mad, but also hot sexy. He allowed himself a half smile. "Did you know your cheek dimples when you get angry?"

She smacked his arm. "This isn't funny, Raven. That burned! And was ... incredibly stupid!"

She dropped her attention to the wound. It had healed, like he knew it would. Nikki blinked a few times, then ran her hand over the tiny, silvery scar.

Raven sniffed. He knew Mace had done the same angelic healing thing when she'd burned her hands.

"You healed my arm with your spit."

"Wow, it sounds really gross when you say it like that."

"It burned, Raven. Why did it burn? Mace kissed my hands after the lab fire and it was far from painful." She grabbed his chin with her finger and thumb and peered into his mouth like the answer was there, resting on his tongue.

He pulled away from her, though part of him wanted her to continue her scrutiny. "Yeah, well, Mace is a little purer than I am." Raven shrugged and sat down on a rock. "Bitter blood in me."

"But your eyes have lightened, so you're not close to falling into darkness anymore, right?" It was both a question and a plea. Nikki dropped to her knees on the ground to look him eye to eye. Maybe to make sure she understood the whole iris-darkening thing. Either way, he liked her like this, all interested in him and full of questions. Especially when she leaned in a little closer. "Vessler fought me on the lawn of my house, and you and Mace knew I was a Halfling because you watched my eyes darken."

"I was there, Nikki. You don't have to tell me what happened." *But keep talking.* She'd dropped her hands to his knees; heat from her fingers radiated through his jeans and vibrated into his gut.

"Your eyes were slowly darkening until ..."

"Until I met you."

She withdrew her hands quickly. "But they're light now."

"Things can change in a heartbeat, baby."

She grabbed his upper arms. "Raven, don't joke about that, okay?"

Yes, his eyes had lightened. When Raven began the journey to keep Nikki alive, his eyes were nearly black, a sign he was shifting to the darker side of his nature. A side she made him no longer crave. "Everyone is one breath away from choosing evil, Nikki. For me, it's just a shorter trip."

She didn't like hearing him talk like that, he could tell. Well, too bad. It was a fact. If Nikki really had chosen Mace, what did he have to live for, anyway? To fight for?

Tears welled in her eyes, and she tilted her chin back to hide them.

Raven forced out a long breath. If she only knew what that

combination of fearlessness and fragility did to him. "The lock was rusty."

Her tears ceased. "What?"

"On the metal door at the museum. The door was rusted around the lock. That's how I could rip it open."

"So, you didn't tear metal?"

"No. We're strong enough to bend metal, but rip it open? Not likely."

Her eyes narrowed, but a smile was teasing at the corner of her mouth. "Why'd you tell me?"

He shrugged and stood. "Seemed like the right thing to do."

Nikki tugged on his pant leg until he reached down to help her from the ground. "See, Raven? You're not nearly as close to the abyss as you think you are."

He wished that was true. "Come on, let's go to a concert."

The pounding thud of both bass guitar and drum took turns vibrating Nikki's lungs. "Really loud," she said, cupping her hands over her ears.

Raven was leading her around a hallway that ran the length of the stage. "You're a Halfling. The more you tap in, the stronger your senses are."

Tapping in — the full realization of her power and ability — would be nice, especially if that ushered the arrival of wings. Nikki shrugged her shoulders up and down a few times. No. Nothing felt different.

Raven skid to a stop and looked down at her from his six-foot-plus stance. "Don't worry, you'll get them soon enough."

Embarrassment warmed her cheeks.

"I love this song," he said.

Nikki listened a moment. Yeah, she'd always liked it too, but a few decibels quieter. Something about the look in his eyes made her happy inside. His eyes. Those round lakes of fervency and fire that could turn velvet soft in an instant. So many emotions could traipse across their diameter, it seemed wrong not to give them a few moments attention.

The light in the hallway was dim, only adding to his persistence. Yes, that was the other thing about his eyes. Whether they were studying the terrain for escape, sorting details necessary for conquest, or stopping her heartbeat with their softness, those eyes held more persistence than some armies. Suddenly, she felt bad for the way she'd treated him earlier. Raven was Raven, and part of what made him that was his determination — even in pursuing her. She'd warned him to stop or she'd leave, and he stopped. Very contrary to his nature. But, he'd done it. For her.

Always for her.

He didn't come any closer, but somehow the moment felt more intimate than it had seconds ago. His eyes closed, shutting off that well of optic emotion. He breathed deep. When he spoke, his words were soft as silk and far away. "The first time I heard it on the radio, I'd been out snow skiing in the Swiss Alps. I returned to the ski lodge, and it had been ..." His eyes snapped open and looked not so much at her, but through her, like he was reliving a beautiful memory through her irises. "I don't know, it had been, like, a perfect day."

He exhaled and her mouth went dry, because she realized as he talked he'd had very few of those kinds of days.

"The sun was just coming up, and it washed everything in

gold; the lodge, the mountains, even the snow. I'd found some untouched powder on a mountain I'd never noticed, and—"

"And you claimed it as your own."

He blinked himself fully from that moment and fully into the present.

"Yes." That was all he said. And it was enough.

"I've never snow skied."

"I'll take you."

Nikki felt something smooth run over the back of her hand and glanced down. Somehow, their fingers had interlocked. "Kiddie slope, please."

He moved toward her, but only marginally. The kind of move that could be a press of gentle wind, or the twitch of a muscle ... or the motion of a man trying to keep his distance.

"You have eternity, now, Nikki. You're a Halfling."

Yeah, eternity if someone didn't murder her. Unfortunately, she seemed to attract the murderous types. But it wasn't that part of his words that snagged her attention. *You're a Halfling*. Eternity she would spend with her match. Mace. Or Raven. She'd been so sure, so certain, but now ...

Well, now, Raven was doing the one thing she didn't need him to do, and it was the one thing she'd asked him to do. Step back. Give her space. Stop pushing.

In his normal state, he was way too cocky, way too cute, and way too irresistible.

But this was worse.

He'd stripped all that, and she was getting a glimpse at the man beneath the ultra-cool exterior. And she liked what she saw.

"It's about us, you know."

Nikki frowned, hoping *he* hadn't caught a glimpse into *her* mind.

He nodded above. "The song. Spreading your wings, you reach the horizon. My heart feels like it's gonna die. You disappear into the morning and once again I cry. As you fly."

"It's about Halflings?"

Raven winked. "Well, she claims it's about me, but I'm not the only Halfling Kaylyn has ever known."

Arrogant Raven was back in full form and sort of shattering the moment. Nikki threw out a breath. She turned and headed deeper down the hall. "This song is *not* about you," she grumbled.

After a series of twists and turns, they reached a backstage door guarded by a guy dressed in a black T-shirt with the words Event Crew written in tall yellow letters. It may as well have said Stop.

Raven didn't seem to care. "I'm here to see Kaylyn."

The guy's eyes widened for an instant, then he laughed. "Yeah, you and about six thousand other fans."

"I'm not a fan, I'm a friend." Raven pointed to the black walkie talkie on the guy's waist. "Call back and find out."

Off to the right, a wall hid the stage. That didn't stop gorilla man from motioning toward it. "Kaylyn is still onstage, so why don't you go on out and watch the show."

He was very persistent. Very persuasive. And wasn't about to budge. He did that typical cross-the-arms-over-the-chest-and-spread-the-stance-a-little thing guys always used as a way of saying, "I'm not moving." Was that supposed to deter Raven?

"Get Kevin Finley on your radio before I use it to …"

Nikki's hand against Raven's arm stopped the words. *Thank goodness.* "Raven, we can just wait. Maybe when she's off stage, he won't mind calling back to clear us."

The guy laughed again, sending a streak of anger down her back. "Yeah, I'm sure I'm gonna do that."

Maybe it was the fact that the big guy made fun of her, maybe it was that Raven just didn't want to wait anymore, but he struck forward and back-fisted gorilla man in the face. She watched in silence as his knees gave way and he folded. Raven caught him on the way down.

Chapter
8

"Will's move works well."

Nikki closed her mouth. "Was that really necessary?"

"Nikki, you're running from a creature that has already killed others to try to get to you. I'm not worried about steroid boy's bloody nose. Occupational hazard."

She rolled her eyes as he took her hand to help her step over the clump of muscle mass in the doorway.

Once inside, no one seemed to care that they were there. They passed a crew of three guys carrying wound black cords. Nikki waited for one of the guys to yell at them, but no one spoke.

Raven stopped after they passed by and turned to flag them down. "Hey, you know where I can find Kevin Finley?"

"Green room, down the hall" one said, and they walked on.

Nikki placed a hand on her chest. "You almost gave me a heart attack. We aren't supposed to be back here, Raven. Don't draw attention to us. Or if you're going to, warn me first."

"Warn you when I'm gonna speak?"

She sank a fist into his shoulder. When two girls passed by, Nikki dropped her head.

"Stop acting like a thief. Nobody cares that we're back here. Just act normal."

Nikki broke from Raven and stood with her hands propped on her waist. *Normal. Riiiight.*

"Just act like you belong here, okay?"

She let out a huff as he grabbed her hand and dragged her into a room that was, surprisingly, green.

"Raven!" A thirty-something guy jumped off the white leather couch and came at them. Nikki shrunk back a little, tugging on Raven's arm.

Two seconds later, the two guys were in one of those slap-on-the-back bro hugs. "How are you? What are you doing here? Is Kaylyn in danger?"

Raven shook his head. "No, nothing like that. We just need to see her."

The guy Nikki assumed had to be Kevin flashed a frown. "You have any trouble getting back here?"

"I sort of had to knock out the guy at the west door. He'll wake up soon, might need his nose reset. So the door's been unguarded for a couple of minutes."

Kevin nodded and yelled over his shoulder, "Mike, go relieve Ben." He looked back over to Raven. "It's an obscure door anyway. Ben's a new guy."

"Some initiation," Raven said, and introduced Nikki to Kevin, who turned out to be Kaylyn's manager.

"You guys look hungry." He led them deeper into the room, which had cleared out when Kevin made a show of waving his arms. A table ran the length of one wall and offered trays of sandwiches, veggies and dip, fruit impaled by little decorated toothpicks, a warming dish filled with meatballs that smelled like heaven, and an array of bottled drinks — everything from Perrier water to IBC root beer. "Help yourselves. I'll get Kaylyn as soon as she's off stage."

"Cool, thanks."

Raven started to reach for a plate, but turned to Nikki instead. "Go sit. I'll make you something to eat."

I guess that will work. She shuffled back toward the door and sank onto the couch. A huge mistake, as it must have been covered in sleeping powder — the cushion all but folded her up in overstuffed luxury. She watched Raven turn his attention to the food, but the moment she let out a long, surrendering sigh, he was beside her.

Bending at the waist, he slipped off her shoes and swept her feet onto the soft white leather. A throw blanket decorated the oversized chair in the corner, and Nikki watched through half-lidded eyes as he shook it a couple of times before draping it over her body. An instant later, everything was dark, and safe, and warm. But a song about wings and the horizon played in her head.

She woke to voices. Kevin and Raven stood over her. She was pretty sure they'd been whispering for a while, but had grown comfortable once they realized she was asleep, their voices rising with their conversation. She peered through her lashes.

Raven looked good. Fed. Awake. But lying there, Nikki felt uncomfortable. Should she continue to pretend she's asleep? Or just hop up and say, "Hey, sorry I happened to wake up and am now interrupting your private conversation"? But then the smell of meatballs hit her nose and she decided waking was better than starving.

She stretched and yawned — just to give them a little fore-warning — then blinked her eyes to chase out the remaining sleep.

"Good morning," they both said.

She hugged the blanket and sat up.

The two guys chuckled, and Raven stepped over to smooth her hair. She reached up, felt the tangle, and decided to die of embarrassment right there. "You guys weren't supposed to let a family of gerbils nest on my head."

Kevin grinned. "It doesn't look like a family —"

Raven cut him off. "No, just a couple rodents." His cheek quirked in a one-sided smile and he winked.

How charming.

"I'll take that plate now," Nikki said to Raven.

Kevin stumbled back. "Oh, sleeping beauty has a bite."

"No," she corrected. "Sleeping beauty has an appetite."

Raven waved a pair of tongs from the cheese tray at Kevin. "She's also got a killer right hook, so watch your mouth."

Kevin offered her a hand up from the couch. "Well, if she's hanging around with you, she needs to know how to defend herself."

Nikki folded the throw. "Sorry I turned your green room into my personal nap area." She tried to run her fingers through her hair but they snagged instantly.

"No problem. Kaylyn had to do an interview right after the concert, and it's taking a little longer than we expected."

Nikki shot a worried glance to Raven, who was just turning from the table with a full plate. "Don't worry. Stopping on that mountaintop in the Alps bought us a little time."

Nikki's hand went to the cut on her arm Raven had healed with his painful kiss.

He handed her the plate and she began eating like it was the last food she would see for months. Her mouth was full when the person they'd been waiting for entered the room.

"Raven!" Kaylyn squealed, and took two leaps, landing in his arms. An incredibly long and gorgeous waterfall of wavy blonde hair trailed her and sort of entombed Raven when their bodies met.

Nikki swallowed, choked a little on a half-chewed chunk of cauliflower, and tried to melt into the couch.

Blue eyes glanced around the room and found Nikki. But Kaylyn fired her questions at Raven. "Are any of the others with you? Can you stay awhile?"

Raven's nodded to Nikki. "Just the two of us, and no, we can't be here long."

Kaylyn traversed the room toward Nikki. "Raven hasn't been around in *forever*." She threw an accusatory glance at him with those giant, bright eyes. Then she was back to him, clasping his hands. "Did you get here in time to hear your song?"

So she really wrote that song for him? Guess he wasn't full of … himself.

"You sounded great." Raven lit up when he said it. Actually lit up. Eyes, face, all brighter and … happier.

Nikki realized she didn't like his reaction at all.

Perspective. She needed perspective. Kaylyn seemed like a genuinely sweet person; after all, she'd welcomed them, didn't even get mad at Raven for beating up her bodyguard. Didn't get mad at Nikki for eating her food.

She was also beautiful. Of course, Nikki had seen her on TV and on the covers Kaylyn's numerous CDs, but in person it was intensified. She wore studded jeans and a flowing dark blue top that set off her eyes and made them look like they were alive behind her eyelids. Her face was perfect, her teeth were perfect. Her posture was perfect.

Nikki stood up a little straighter.

Kaylyn motioned for Kevin to close the door, the *green* door. "I know you guys aren't here on a social visit, so what's up?"

Raven sighed as if he really didn't want the "getting reacquainted" party to end. "We need information about seekers."

Her pearly skin went chalk white. She wavered, like someone had struck her with a syringe full of something lethal. Raven reached out to steady her. Not a difficult task since he was already standing so close.

Long seconds ticked past before Kaylyn lifted her chin and sort of chased away the moment by slamming it with determination — jaw set, eyes fierce, mouth firm. "I'll help however I can. What do you need to know?"

Nikki admired her bravery — the mention of a seeker had practically knocked the girl off her feet, but she was still ready to help. Nikki cleared her throat. "I'm being hunted."

Kaylyn nodded. "Okay," she said on a long breath. "Let's talk about it."

Fifteen minutes later, they had no new information and Raven was pacing the floor like a caged tiger. Nikki wondered if he might be sensing hounds, but she hadn't picked up on anything. Of course, last time she picked up on the hounds when it was almost too late.

Nikki turned to Raven, hoping her worries didn't set him off. "Do we need to go?"

Kaylyn answered instead. "I need more time. It's been a lifetime since I thought about seekers and I'm scared I'm leaving something out."

Raven returned her plea with a stare, and Nikki was left

wondering what conversation was passing between his and Kaylyn's eyes.

"Okay, let me just run through everything again." Words flew from her mouth so quickly, it was hard to keep up. Now and then she'd tilt her head and stare at the ceiling a few seconds before continuing. One by one, she rattled off things she'd already told them.

"You already know about blood. What about fear?" Kaylyn didn't give them time to answer. "It feeds off your fear when it gets close. And trust me, there will be plenty of terror for it to use."

She paced in a tight line. "You need to stay as fresh as you can. Rest, eat, keep your spirit up, and mostly, pray. Actually, you're going to need to call on some pros for this."

"Pros?" Raven said.

"Yeah, intercessors." Kaylyn tapped her foot, the sequined shoe glistening from the overhead light. "In fact, I've got a friend who leads a church in Philadelphia. You need to go there. And I can let him know you're coming."

"Okay. Why?" *What can a pastor do that Raven can't?*

"Two reasons. You'll be safe there for the night, and right now they're having an all-night prayer vigil — one orchestrated by the Throne. They can intercede for you — for when you do have to face the seeker. You *will* have to face it."

"Am I safe in any church?"

"Only one bathed in prayer. And only for a day at the most. Intercessors can keep the seeker at bay through prayer for a number of hours, but they're human. Eventually, they will tire and the seeker will overwhelm them."

Nikki shook her head. "There's no way I'd go to a church and draw a seeker there to kill all those people."

Kaylyn pointed at her but again directed her inquiry to Raven. "She doesn't know anything about spiritual matters, does she?"

Raven shrugged. Nikki felt the urge to slap him.

"Nikki, the intercessors are warriors. They go head-to-head with the being from hell on a daily basis. It's what they were created for."

"Head-to-head?" Nikki echoed.

"Not physically. More like battling in the realm of the spirit."

"So, the fight with the seeker is a spiritual battle as well as a physical one," Raven said.

Kaylyn nodded. "Very much so. Almost more a spiritual battle than anything else. You need weapons. Faith, peace. As I said, you will have to face the seeker. You can't run forever."

Nikki agreed. "I'm tired of running already. I'd rather just get it over with."

Kaylyn reached over and touched Nikki's arm. "Not until you're ready. Trust me on this one. But Pastor Layton can help prepare you."

Nikki imagined herself being encouraged onto an armored horse at a jousting tournament.

Kaylyn smiled. "Layton will help you prepare spiritually. Right now, your spirit is probably just about dry."

Nikki'd never given much thought to her spirit — practically her entire life had been spent learning to protect her body. But if preparing her inner defenses would help end this nightmare, she was game. She thought back to the faith ball, and the breakthrough she'd had. "I do have faith."

"You *don't* have faith, Nikki!" Raven's outburst shocked her.

"It wasn't your faith, okay?" he almost whispered. His face looked like a small child's.

A thousand icicles sliced through her stomach. "But I felt the faith ball. I held it in my hands. I did what you told me to do and I succeeded."

He looked everywhere but at her. "It was a trick. I used my own faith to make you think you'd found yours."

A short puff of air forced all the oxygen from her lungs. *A trick?* "Are — are you kidding? Why would you — " Then she knew. He'd wanted to do something Mace couldn't. Raven had let her think she possessed something she didn't have — that she needed to have — just to make Mace look like a fool.

Her head was hot, her ears were ringing, and if she didn't get away she was going to scream or faint. The tiny black spots in front of her eyes suggested the latter. *He tricked me.* Boiling anger chased the spots until they all but disappeared in the periphery of her vision. All that time, she'd been frustrated with Mace's slow instruction. Now she understood he was the only one actually trying to help her. And just that quickly, she made a decision. "I'm going back to Viennesse."

Raven grabbed her. "Nikki, you can't. They're on their way here. I was trying to help you back on the boat. I wanted — "

She pulled away from him. "To trick me into thinking I have a weapon I don't? That's not help, Raven. My life is on the line."

He grabbed her again, this time harder, so she couldn't even thrash. "You think I don't know that? Look, I wouldn't have done it if I'd had any idea this was going to happen."

"Oh, right, because it's so unlikely I'd be hunted and chased by people and things wanting to kill me!"

"I figured if you held the faith ball and believed in it enough, it would become a part of you."

"You *figured*? Well, thanks for gambling with my life."

Kaylyn stepped between them, and Raven let go. "This isn't

99

helping the situation. The fact is, Nikki, whether you have faith or not right now, you better find a way to tap into that well inside you. Layton can help you do that."

Nikki swallowed, and Raven's betrayal slid down her throat with all the other emotions that were bubbling to the surface. She was just so tired of being a victim, being hunted. First by hell hounds, then by evil men and demons, now by a monster from hell. It wasn't fair to release all her anxiety on Raven, she knew, but at the same time what he did was almost unforgivable.

Kaylyn's bright blue eyes were now pleading. "Let Raven take you to Philadelphia."

After a long time, Nikki gave a reluctant nod. What choice did she have? She couldn't fly, and she clearly couldn't protect herself on her own. *Why is it even a rebel like Raven has more spiritual power than me?*

"Before you leave, I'm going to need some of your blood." Both Raven and Nikki gave Kaylyn a quizzical look, but she was too busy inspecting items along the table to notice. "You're headed to Philadelphia, we're headed out West. Miles and miles of desert."

Nikki and Raven exchanged shrugs, as if it was the only form of communication they could now share.

"Ah, this should work." Kaylyn brought an empty Perrier bottle to Raven then held out the dented cap. "Bend it back?"

Raven took the lid and smoothed out the crease.

Kaylyn slid the cap back onto the bottle and gave it a couple of shakes; apparently, it needed to fit snugly. She smiled sweetly, turning to face Nikki. "About that blood …"

Chapter
9

I don't think it's a good idea, Kay."
Nikki noticed the nickname and Raven's tone of voice as he said it. It raked against her spine.

"Raven, it might buy you more time. We're leaving within the hour, and I can drop the bottle out in the desert. The seeker likely won't pick up the scent until the blood touches the ground." Kaylyn placed her slender hand on Raven's arm. "Nikki *needs* time."

That seemed to be enough motivation for him. His eyes caught Nikki's as she began to say no.

"Nikki, I'm not going to argue about it." Raven's voice rose a little.

"I'm not giving her blood. No way. Too dangerous."

Kaylyn and Raven shared a sort of conspiratorial look, then the blonde singer was back at the table.

Nikki started to move away, but Raven's arms surrounded

her. When Kaylyn swung around with a cheese knife in her hand, Nikki screamed and tried to wriggle free.

Cold first, then a burning sting as the blade sliced her arm. It didn't hurt that bad, but emotion welled in her. Maybe because these two were putting their lives on the line while she tried to stop them — just like a bratty kid would stop her mom from pouring peroxide on a wound to clean out the infection. Tears stung her eyes and her nose tingled. Ugh. She hated that. She looked away, off to the left, as if courage was hiding in the corner and she only had to make eye contact to possess it. But no courage came, so she bit her bottom lip while Kaylyn held the bottle to the edge of the cut, where a fine line of blood flowed.

Kaylyn's voice was annoyingly soothing. "I'm sorry we held you down, Nikki. But if you're anything like the girls Raven usually goes for, it was the only way."

Just when I figured I couldn't possibly feel any worse ...

Kaylyn pressed her shimmery lips into a straight line. "I appreciate that you're worried about my safety. But believe me, I can handle myself, and I won't take any stupid risks."

Not trusting her voice, Nikki gave a quick nod and uttered a thank you.

"Okay, you guys need to go."

Raven bent and kissed Kaylyn on the cheek. The whole exchange made Nikki's world tilt. Kaylyn was trying to help, but again, Nikki'd been bullied into doing what she didn't want to do. Was she ever again going to have control over her life?

Yes. One day she would. Deep in her soul a promise bloomed, and she knew with absolute certainty that one day she'd choose her own destiny. Awareness filled her. She didn't deserve the people she'd been given, and yet here they were.

She didn't deserve the unmerited favor that surrounded her on every turn. And yet, it sought her like flowers seek the sun.

The sensation overwhelmed her. Something deep within her was changing. Her gaze trailed to Raven first, then to Kaylyn. It gurgled in her stomach and rose to settle in her chest.

A bit confused by it, she stood statue still as waves seemed to flow both outward and inward at the same time, washing over her flesh and splashing through her system.

The green room looked a little brighter. Had someone turned up the light?

"What is it?" Raven's voice reached her through the veil.

She whispered, "Faith."

Kaylyn clapped her hands. "Raven, she's tapping in."

By the time they made it to the church in Philadelphia, Kaylyn had contacted her friend Pastor Layton. The forty-something man ushered them in and closed a massive door behind them. Nikki recognized his face, especially the dark hair and green eyes, from TV, although she hadn't known his name. He was probably on some church show she'd flicked past a thousand times on Sunday mornings.

A gargantuan sanctuary swallowed them, lit only by some dim overhead lights, and she took it in as they walked. At the edge of the chair-filled room a door was propped open, spilling bright light into the space.

Nikki chewed on the inside of her cheek. *Guess they didn't have such a great turnout for the prayer meeting.* But as they moved to the door, a low rumble of voices grew louder. Pastor Layton turned and addressed Nikki with a smile. "I'd like you to meet your intercessors."

"*My* intercessors?"

Pastor Layton grinned. "Yes, they've been praying for you for months. But yesterday I felt an unction from the Throne to call them together. I also called Kaylyn. Can't say why, just felt like I needed to talk to her. I mentioned we'd be having the prayer meeting."

"Kaylyn knew we would come here?"

He shook his head. "Nope. Sometimes with the Throne, we're on a need-to-know basis. You just pray and listen and do what you see yourself doing. Often, you don't know the details. I had no way of knowing Raven would take you to her. But the prayer warriors here have been keeping you covered with prayer for some time."

She frowned. Had they just entered some weird alternate reality? "How — How would they know me?"

"They didn't know you in the flesh, but the Throne placed you on several of their hearts. It will be nice for them to have a face to put with the name."

"My name?" she asked, which felt like the stupidest thing she'd ever uttered. But really, spiritual stalkers?

"Yes. Nikki Youngblood. They also sometimes refer to you as Freedom."

Nikki's gaze shot to Raven. "Did you put him up to this?"

Pastor Layton placed a hand on her shoulder. "Freedom is your Halfling name."

It was also the nickname Raven had given her. She hated it, now more than ever before. Because of all the things she felt right now, free wasn't one of them. She opened her mouth to speak, expecting words to form as she did, but none materialized.

"I'm sorry, Nikki. Perhaps I shouldn't have revealed that to you."

Raven tossed his hair from his face. "Oh, I wouldn't worry about it. She's so stubborn, she probably won't believe you until she's heard it about a dozen times."

Pastor Layton threw his hands in the air. "In that case, no harm done." He turned and led them into a room where about fifty men and women were praying. Warriors, Kaylyn had called them. Hearing the fervency of their prayers, Nikki agreed.

For the first time since the angel arrived and announced that a seeker had been sent for Nikki, Raven was able to rest. Nikki was safe here. Even if the seeker came, it couldn't gain entrance to the church as long as the intercessors were praying. Raven leaned back on the dark leather couch in Pastor Layton's office and was almost asleep before the next breath left his lungs. His eyes burned from too many hours awake and watching, refusing to wonder what would happen if he let his guard slip.

A gentle rapping at the door pulled his attention from the drowsy haze. "Come in," he said, but the words were thick with sleep.

It was Nikki. She pushed the door open and slipped inside, then stood there for a moment, leaning her back against the door frame and giving him a smile that would fill his dreams. A blanket was hanging over her arm. "I need to apologize."

Ahhh. That was nice. He closed his eyes, imprinting her image. "Then do it so I can get some sleep."

"Raven, you're not being very gracious. I'm trying to say I'm sorry."

He tilted his head and peered at her through one open eye. "Trying. Not succeeding."

She tossed the blanket at him hard. It landed in a heap on his gut and an unexpected *oomph* followed the thud. "Wow, you really need more practice at this apologizing thing."

She crossed the room and he scooted just enough for her to sit on the edge of the couch. "I know you would never do anything to hurt me."

Why hearing her say that caused the icy-hot sensation through his body, he didn't know. He opened his eyes fully, because, seriously, with her so close, filling his nose with her scent, it wasn't like he'd be able to sleep now. His hand reached to the soft skin on her face, fingertips memorizing every curve, every smooth line. He paused at the edge of her mouth. Soft lips, waiting to be touched. But he didn't run his hand over their smoothness. Instead, he reached to either side and squeezed gently. His voice came out in sync with the motions of his hand, ventriloquist style. "I'm sorry, Raven. You are *always* right and I am *always* wrong."

This elicited a true smile on the mouth he held, encouraging him to say more. "Raven, you're awesome and amazing and the bravest guy I've ever met. And did I mention hot?"

Nikki giggled and grabbed his hand in hers. "Okay, that's enough. Seriously, I'd hate to vomit on you after such an elaborate apology."

Raven's face slowly dropped the smile he'd worn as her fingers twined with his. And for a while the two of them stayed there, staring into each other's eyes. They really didn't need words. She had this kind of closeness with Mace too, of course, one they'd both built with her while facing the threat of death over and over, experiencing the effects together. But with Raven, it felt more like a mutual connection. He needed her as much as she needed him. Mace needed no one. By nature,

Mace was the quintessential leader — the kind people followed, the kind that never wavered. Hadn't she seen that so clearly at the train crash? The day she fell in love with him all over again. His very personality bred loyalty. Mace was whole. And Raven was damaged. Like a broken flower pot, still working to hold the flowers, trying to keep up, hoping to hold it together — at least until roots worked their way through the clay and caused it to crumble.

And weren't people always drawn to help what's broken? Nikki was. She'd proved it when they'd first connected in the art gallery, shown it through the painting she'd created. She needed Raven. He needed her.

Chapter 10

They were readying to leave when the first bits of apprehension trickled over her shoulders. Raven was unfazed, so Nikki cast her unease aside. "You look rested."

He smiled. "Yeah, I had sweet dreams. You?"

She didn't try to hide the smile. "Yes. Pastor Layton's wife let me sleep in an ultra-comfy recliner in her office after they gave me some instruction about faith and how to fight the seeker."

"Great, you can fill me in on all the details after we go." He gave her his full attention. "What's the main thing you learned?"

"To pray for peace. Peace is a major key in defeating the seeker."

"Pray for peace, got it."

"I wasn't finished. Pray for peace. But prepare for war."

Raven nodded. "Sometimes war is the only way to peace."

Didn't she know it? Rough roads often had the best scenery. And what she'd learned on this difficult journey was fast becoming the framework of who she was becoming. That girl who liked drawing and karate felt so far away from her, except, on some deep level, that girl was still there. Not dead, just … transformed. It was as if she'd been reborn, and because of that everything looked different, like the world was spinning in a new way. Pastor Layton and his wife helped to make sense of the craziness and in listening to them, she'd found a new kind of clarity. And maybe a new kind of determination. Faith was no longer the foolish thing she'd imagined it to be earlier — now it was like air.

Relationships with boys, however, was another matter. Raven was busy folding the blanket he'd used. It smelled like him, a scent she loved. She couldn't deny that. Last night, sitting at his side, holding his hand … it all felt so right. But Mace felt right too. Always. How could this be so hard to figure out? Maybe she never would. Maybe there'd never be a clear picture, and the only answer would be choosing neither.

Pastor Layton met Raven and Nikki at the door to his office. Bags rested beneath his red eyes and he looked like he hadn't slept all night. Oh yeah, prayer meeting. He probably hadn't.

"Time is of the essence," he said, rushing them toward the door that led to the large parking lot they'd entered through the night before. "The intercessors are sensing …" He paused in the hallway, swallowed, and gave a weary shrug. "Well, I don't know what they're sensing exactly, but — "

Raven pulled the door open and they stepped outside. A bright morning sun greeted them, offering the promise of a beautiful day. Which — considering their current dilemma — was a pretty unlikely possibility.

Nikki heard the sound immediately. A deep, guttural howling noise that cut through her flesh and straight into her heart. For a moment, all three looked at one another as if waiting for one to ask the question none of them wanted to answer. Raven led Nikki to the edge of the portico where he could leap. But it was too late.

Something dropped near them from the sky. The massive black creature landed close, grunting and screeching. But there wasn't just one creature; other beings soon intertwined with the monster. Here and there, its form was interrupted by slashes of color and wings.

Nikki started screaming and couldn't stop. In the mess, she recognized Mace, Vine, Winter, and Glimmer, all woven with and fighting the creature and its multitude of long, slithering arms. There was a commotion behind Nikki, and hands closed around her. First just one, then others. The intercessors had undoubtedly rushed to the door and were now dragging her back toward the church. She fought to get free.

"Get her inside," Raven yelled and ran straight for the seeker and the mass of Halflings fighting it.

Nikki yanked against her captives. "I can help them," she said, stretching toward the fight, but she couldn't move. The intercessors were lead shackles holding her steadfast.

Tentacle-like appendages stretched from the horrid black creature. He used two of them to lift his body to a standing position, and once it was planted against the asphalt Nikki noticed the razor-sharp blades on the end of each arm. The Halflings rose in response, Glimmer backing away slightly then drawing an arrow from her quiver and readying her bow.

But the seeker caught her movement and lashed out with one long swipe, slicing her cheek. She reeled back, falling on the ground, while the same razor claw hovered over Glimmer's body, aimed at her chest.

Nikki screamed and finally broke free. She ran toward Glimmer. "Get back," she yelled at the usually fearless girl who'd become frozen on the ground, clutching her cheek.

Nikki stopped in her tracks when the seeker turned its full attention to her. She instantly felt vulnerable. *There has to be something I can use as a weapon.* Her eyes shot to the ground and rested on Glimmer's bow, lying forgotten beside her friend. Nikki grabbed the weapon, but rather than try to shoot it, she tilted the bayonet-like sharpened end at the seeker. When Mace drew the monster's attention by jumping onto its back, Nikki ran forward and planted the bow in the seeker's chest with all the strength she had.

The creature reeled back, staggering a few steps while a thick, black liquid oozed from the wound. Its eyes settled on Nikki like a homing beacon, and before she could move, a long, serrated arm slashed at her. She felt the burn of tearing flesh as it sliced across her throat.

She fell backward as she watched the seeker disappear beneath a frenzied mound of Halflings.

Nikki gasped for air. The wound across her throat felt endless, and each breath she took caused the excruciating sensations to seep deeper into her system. Suddenly Pastor Layton was above her, his hands clamped around her shoulders. She was vaguely aware of being dragged toward the door of the church, and watched in shock as Glimmer rose and retrieved her bow. From a safe distance away, Glimmer shot three arrows into the seeker's chest while Nikki continued to struggle for air.

"Raven," Mace said, when the seeker staggered again, this time from Glimmer's attack. "Take Nikki and leave. Get away from here."

Raven paused only long enough to consider the consequences of the words he was about to speak. "I'll stay here and fight. You go."

Mace stopped moving, but only for the briefest moment. "You've kept her alive this long. Go. Find somewhere safe. We can hold the seeker here until you're far enough from its range."

Pastor Layton ran to the boys, who were now a few steps away from the battle. He directed his words to Raven. "You have to come with me immediately. Plan to stay away for several hours, give your friends time to reroute the seeker. Then bring Nikki back here. We'll pray for that wound when you return."

Layton led Raven back to the portico. He followed, reluctantly, half ready to flee with Nikki and half wanting to battle the seeker with Mace and Vine at his side. "Is she going to be okay?"

Pastor Layton's eyes dropped, and he studied a spot in the concrete sidewalk. "I don't know. Despair has been released into her system by the seeker. It will take over if you don't keep it at bay."

"How do I do that?" Raven said.

"I'm not sure, son, but we'll pray for you to have wisdom." Some of the intercessors carried Nikki out to Raven while the Halflings continued to fight.

Raven took Nikki in his arms and leapt. With her this close, he could see the fresh wound, a smooth slice across her collarbone just below the hollow of her throat. If it had been a little higher … He stopped that thought, because the blinding pain it caused made it impossible to fly.

He concentrated on the objective. *Get her somewhere safe, somewhere safe.* The midplane. He had to get her to the midplane. Raven rocketed skyward with Nikki in his arms. The gash below her throat, nearly shoulder to shoulder, had started oozing a dark reddish-black fluid. Her blood, mixed with the poison from the slash, appeared to be burning her flesh where it leaked onto her skin. Her eyes were squeezed shut, and streams of tears trailed her face. He'd hoped she would be unconscious by now, have a respite from the pain.

She'll be safe in the midplane. Raven repeated the words in his head over and over. Partly because he so desperately wanted to believe it.

A lock of her hair caught the wind and fell across the wound. Nikki jolted and let out a howl. Raven took hold of the renegade strands and dragged them away from the cut. He couldn't tell how deep the wound was, and wasn't sure if it mattered. The skin around it had gone from peach to charcoal. If he didn't know better, he'd think she was being seared with a torch from the inside out.

The chills began and he prayed he'd get to the midplane quickly. Anything was better than this. "Hang on, Nikki," he whispered, as much to reassure himself as to encourage her. He tuned into the sound of his wings pumping feverishly.

Nikki's flesh had become clammy and he had to readjust her in his arms to anchor the slick hold. Every movement was excruciating, but her cries had become moans as strength left her.

She was paralyzed until they reached the midplane.

As soon as they entered the heavenly atmosphere, Nikki bucked, practically slipping from Raven's grasp. A long solid scream released from a throat tightened with strained muscles.

He nearly panicked when Nikki — writhing in his arms — reached for her wound in an attempt to claw at it. He wrestled her hands away from the cut and dropped out of the midplane. She calmed almost instantly.

Reduced to exhausted whimpers, she curled into a ball in his arms.

"I don't know what to do," Raven whispered, his voice sounding foreign to him. *If the midplane wasn't safe ...* He pushed tears from his eyes and sniffed.

Nikki had become a quiet shell.

"I don't know what to do," he repeated, rubbing a hand along Nikki's back. It wasn't to soothe her. Tearing his gaze from the small heap she'd become, Raven looked down at the world beneath them.

The sun glinted off something far below. From the distance, he couldn't make it out, but it beckoned, a searchlight, signaling the way home. He dropped from the sky until he saw the glow of the church's cross.

Impulse caused him to veer away, but he stopped and inspected the area where the fight with the seeker had ensued. The grounds were empty. The seeker was gone. The Halflings were gone, leaving a handful of cars in the driveway, and not much else.

Raven dropped to the parking lot beside the gargantuan church that somehow seemed even bigger now, more regal, more of a battle station than a sanctuary for lost souls. Before he could get to the door, it swung open and Pastor Layton emerged carrying a towel dripping with water.

"Press this to the wound. She won't like it, but it will help the stinging."

The pastor must have noticed Raven's frown because he explained before the question left Raven's mouth. "I had a feeling you would come back soon."

His words were a flurry as he told what had happened. "The girl with the bow ..."

"Glimmer," Raven said.

"She got her weapon after it dropped from the seeker's chest and sank about three arrows into the thing. Perfect shots, even with the wound on her cheek."

"Yeah, she's accurate. Did it kill it?"

Pastor Layton blinked. "No. You can't kill it. But it did run away. The others went after it."

Nikki moaned. Raven stepped to take her inside, but Pastor Layton blocked his way. "She can't be here."

What? Is he kidding?

"The intercessors are too exhausted. As weak as they are, the seeker could waltz right in the front door and take her."

Raven wanted to strangle the man, but steadied his hand instead. "What am I supposed to do?"

Layton dragged a hand through already messed-up hair. When he sagged against the doorframe, Raven realized how exhausted the man must be. He looked like he'd aged about ten years since they first arrived. "I tried to take her into the midplane."

"Burned like fire, didn't it?"

Raven nodded, and looked down at his pale angel. "It must have. She started convulsing. What can I give her to help?"

"There's no medicine for this. It's all internal, all spiritual. And a lot of the outcome will depend on her attitude. If her mind falls into darkness, her body will follow. She'll become a dark creature."

"What? How do you know?"

"Kaylyn's uncle was a close friend, a Xian who fought a seeker years ago. There were Halflings who helped him. When some were injured, it became clear deep wounds had devastating effects. Once I witnessed the horrors the infected were experiencing, I searched Scripture for information. It's all there, if you have eyes to see it. Believe me, Raven, if something isn't done, she'll awaken as a dark creature."

Raven's heart shuddered. *She'll awaken as a dark creature.* Vessler. This was just one more plot set in place by Vessler. "It's another way to turn her?"

Layton reached a hand to her cheek. "Yes. Some Halflings turn willingly, some have bitter blood forced into their veins. But those scenarios don't matter — she's being poisoned, Raven. From the inside out. I'm not sure she's strong enough to resist it."

"What can I do?" Even as he said it, the hopelessness pressed. All his work to keep her safe, only to see her body writhe toward darkness with no way for him to stop it.

"Keep her mind occupied on what is good — talk to her about anything that she loves or enjoys, anything you can think of that might remind her of the light. If you can get her focus on the goodness of God, that will help. I'm going to send you with an iPod loaded with worship music to maintain a heavenly atmosphere. Keep the music playing — at all times. It will help."

Raven took the gift, twisting it in his hand. "Thanks."

"Obviously, don't try to enter the midplane again. You have to find somewhere safe for the night — preferably behind water. And you have to watch her closely. Don't let her fall, Raven."

"I won't."

"I'll have the intercessors rest for an hour. Then we'll be in prayer, warring for you both. If she makes it through the night, she'll make it."

If she makes it. "But we can't stay here?"

"No. She needs to be somewhere beyond water so the seeker can't find her. By releasing poison into her veins, his ability to track has increased tremendously. But we can protect in other ways. Once Nikki is gone, the seeker has no authority here, and with it gone our intercessors can engage with full strength. We will battle, Raven. We won't let you down."

Raven believed him. The man had already shown his determination in protecting Nikki. He'd pray, he'd have the others pray — Raven could only hope it would be enough.

His gaze found the tall signage advertising the church. Did the people who attended here know what a warrior their pastor was? Probably not. In Raven's experience, most people chose to pretend there was no battle. *If you only knew . . .*

Raven was just starting to turn from him when the door opened again. An old woman with a cane stepped out and pressed her hand to Raven's cheek. "She will not die," the craggy voice spoke with such certainty, with such conviction it almost persuaded him even though his eyes saw Nikki growing weaker, the grayed wound across her collarbones evidencing her spiritual slide. He tried to utter something in agreement with the old woman's statement, but the words died on his tongue.

"She will live and declare the works of the Lord." The crepe-paper-skinned woman held out a Bible to him. "When it looks desperate, read her this. The passage is marked." She smiled, lines deepening on her face and wrinkling around her small, watery eyes.

As he held the worn leather, his destination became clear.

"We'll be beyond the waterfall." Before he could change his mind, he added, "If Mace comes back, let him know. He'll know what I'm talking about." His hand smoothed over Nikki's matted hair. "He should be with her too. Especially right now."

"Wait and I'll pack some blankets and food for you," Layton said.

"No time. Thanks for everything, though."

Once airborne, Raven jettisoned toward Missouri and the falls, pretending he held Nikki so tightly because of her inability to hang on herself, instead of in a death grip as a promise to not let her go. He couldn't lose her, not like this. He'd rather lose her to Mace.

He pumped his wings methodically while Nikki lay in his arms. *I should be thinking of ways to help her, not my stupid problems.*

The landscape changed to the telltale hills and lush forest of the Ozark Mountains. When he spotted the river, he dropped altitude and drifted into the valley, where the sound of rushing water filled his ears. It was so peaceful, soothing. Safe. "We made it, baby. We're going to be — " Raven looked down, where Nikki remained quiet, still curled into his chest like a kitten trying to stay warm. Her breathing was shallow. Touching down at the foot of the falls, he looked around for something to cover her as he entered the cave so she wouldn't get drenched. "Nikki," he whispered. "I'm going to lay you in the grass while I look around."

Her head lulled to the side as he removed his arm from beneath her, and she didn't respond as he placed her on the spongy green earth. Raven's chest felt painfully tight. What if she didn't pull through? Would Mace have known what to do to help her? A small voice murmured, "Soon, you'll need to let go," and he bit his lip hard to focus his mind on that pain instead.

Remembering the iPod, he removed it from his pocket and gingerly placed the ear buds into her ears before turning on the music. "This better be some playlist."

Now to find something to keep her dry. But after thirty minutes of searching, he'd turned up nothing but a small Ziploc bag with a few matches inside. The mouth of the cave mocked him, its waterfall doorway like a smooth sheet of glass. He needed to get her inside, beyond the wall of water, into the cave where the seeker couldn't see them.

And he couldn't waste any more time.

Raven tucked the Bible under his shirt and into the belt of his jeans then gathered Nikki in his arms. He tried to shield her with his body as he walked through the cascade. Nikki lurched as the cold water hit her. Still, Raven held firm and moved fully into the darkened cave.

The rushing sound of water echoed off the walls, its tone different, almost muffled inside the domed space. And in the quiet, Raven sighed and closed his eyes.

Safe.

He dropped his head to hers and let some of the anxiety melt from his muscles. But that was a mistake. The release of tension brought the first wave of the panic he'd staved off, causing his throat to hiccup. He squeezed his teeth so tightly, his jaw ached, but anything was better than considering the possibility of losing her. And as even the pain spread from his teeth to his neck and chest, that's what rushed his mind: a Nikki-less world. A world where he and Mace had failed in the only thing they'd ever teamed up to do. Or worse, a world where Nikki was a dark creature and their only option was to hunt her.

And then she'd truly destroy them. He and Mace both loved her too much.

Raven rubbed his cheek against her hair, wishing once again that he could take the pain away. She'd suffered so much already. If Nikki made it through this, it was time for the craziness to stop. Her entire world had been a whirlwind from the moment those hell hounds chased her in the woods to the moment she realized Damon Vessler was at the core of Omega Corporation. He claimed he'd created Nikki. That without her, his plan had no purpose. Vessler'd done insidious things to Nikki, but sending this seeker to hunt her down, to change her so painfully and against her will . . . It was inhuman. No matter what happened, Vessler would pay.

The hope Raven clung to was that for Nikki to be any good to her "godfather," she'd have to turn. If this attempt didn't work, the only way Vessler would succeed is if Nikki went to him willingly . . . which of course, was laughable. She knew who Vessler really was now. In fact, she'd nearly killed him in the plane crash, shooting him twice out of vengeance. No, Nikki would never let herself be influenced by Vessler again.

Fatigue sliced through Raven's biceps, but he wasn't ready to relinquish her yet. He stepped deeper inside, shaking the water from his hair. Strands stuck to his cheeks and his stomach rumbled. He ignored both.

Scanning the oval-shaped ceiling of the cave, he noticed a thin streak of light sifting through the rock. He laid Nikki on the ground and gauged the width of the cave. Yep, just enough to snap his wings open. A few gentle beats and he was able to reach the thin crack in the cave ceiling. Dirt filled the crevice. He touched it — dry. No water directly above. He clawed and scraped at the small crack, quickly creating a hole and letting in a bit more light. "Perfect," he mumbled, arms now caked with bits of mud. At least it would allow him to create a small fire without accidentally asphyxiating them both. Before leaving to get whatever dead wood he could find, he checked the iPod's volume and battery. *Still good.* With a deep breath he disappeared through the waterfall.

Within an hour, he had a fire blazing, with smoke curling into the air and out through the escape hatch he'd constructed. His clothes dried while he worked, but Nikki was shivering. He moved her as close to the flame as he dared, but her lips remained grayish blue and her skin cold and clammy.

Raven fitted himself behind her so his chest rested against her back. With the fire in front, and him behind, Nikki's chills subsided. In another hour, she was asleep.

He opened the book and read, "The Lord is my Shepherd …"

Chapter
11

Mace stood in the open doorway of a farmhouse in southern Indiana, still reeling from battle. He had led the group here once the fighting had ended; after finally working his way out of their grip at the church, the seeker had all but disappeared.

Mace's fingers gripped the doorjamb so tightly, he wondered if he'd leave indented fingerprints in the wood.

The house belonged to a Xian Pastor Layton knew, who'd offered to let them rest there awhile, as well as tend to the cut on Glimmer's cheek. While the hospitality was welcomed, Mace had found it difficult to find any respite since they'd arrived. His throat now constricted, angry with himself for letting the seeker slip from them.

His thoughts also lingered on Nikki. She was out there somewhere and injured much worse than Glimmer, the deep gash on her collarbone likely robbing the life from her body. And here he stood, surrounded by the long, rolling hills and the aura of perfect calm.

But that was what was meant to be, he supposed. Raven there with her and him here, constantly trying to catch up, always arriving as the cavalry and never the dashing hero. And he couldn't be angry with Raven for his actions — they had kept Nikki alive, and his results gave him every right to be the one who continued to run with her. Whatever kept her alive was what was best for her. In the time they'd been following Raven's trail, he'd had quite a bit of time to consider that very thought. Whatever kept her alive was best for her.

Or maybe whoever kept her alive was best for her.

He started when a cold hand touched his.

Winter smiled, dropped her fingers. "Sorry. Didn't mean to scare you. Feeling okay?"

Mace glanced over at her. "Yeah, just thinking."

Winter's hair lay in long dark sheets around her face, every strand still in place even though she'd fought as hard as any of them. Only the weariness in her eyes gave any hint to the events she had faced hours before. "Mace, thinking can be dangerous at a time like this."

"Tell me about it."

She quirked her head to the side. "Why don't you tell me?"

"Nikki's alive because of Raven. He's watched out for her and done everything right ever since they left Viennesse."

"And you think you wouldn't have done the same?"

"I don't know." He focused his attention outside, where a lone horse nibbled hay at a fencerow a few hundred yards away. "I don't think like Raven, that's for sure. I probably would have done the exact opposite and — "

"And how do you know that wouldn't have worked as well?" Winter brushed at a smudge on the hem of her white T-shirt.

"How do I know either way?" Mace turned to face her. "I've

never doubted that Nikki and I are supposed to be together. Never. Until now."

Winter stopped working on the stain and looked up. "Mace, you and Nikki love each other. Anyone could see that. When all this is over —"

He cut her off. "Over? This is never going to be over. Even once we find a way to beat the seeker, Vessler is still out there. He still wants Nikki, and everything he's planned hinges on her. Right after this battle, another will be on the horizon. This isn't even close to being over, Winter."

Tiny lines framed her mouth as she smiled. "Mace, you know in your heart that you are supposed to be together. Don't let your head get in the way."

"We'll see. She's okay, right?"

Winter tilted her head back. "It was a deep wound, but yes, I have faith that she's going to be fine."

"Me too." He placed a hand over his stomach. "Deep inside, I know she's okay. How's Glimmer?"

"She's good. Resting, doesn't want us to leave without her."

"Is the cut going to leave a scar?" They all had their battle wounds, and for the most part they wore them proudly. But a scar on Glimmer's face ... Mace didn't figure she would like that.

"No. I don't think it will leave a mark. It was superficial." Winter pivoted and looped an arm through Mace's. "Come on. Let's get you some food, then we can rejoin the fight."

He pulled from her. "You go ahead. I'm going to leap back over to the church in Philadelphia and talk to Pastor Layton again. See if he can remember anything about where Raven was planning to go next."

Winter stepped away from him. "Be careful out there."

He was halfway down the steps when she called to him again.

"And Mace?"

He turned to face her where she stood framed by the front door.

"Follow your heart. Not your head."

"You're awake," Raven said when Nikki stirred and rubbed her eyes with her hands. The fire had died down to glowing embers, with only a faint flame in the center of charred bits of lumber.

"Yes." Her voice was weak, but she was a fighter. She'd get stronger. "How long was I out? What happened?"

His arms and legs were asleep and aching because he hadn't wanted to move for fear of waking her. But now they screamed in protest as fresh blood raced to his extremities in a rush of needle pricks.

He moved to sit beside her and used one foot to kick at the fire. A flame erupted almost immediately, throwing dancing orange light onto the cave walls. "The seeker caught up to us at the church in Philadelphia."

Her breath quickened. Shallow, fast, each inhale growing deeper until her whole body shook.

"Calm down," he soothed. "It's okay. I got you out of there. We're safe here."

Her eyes darted around the cave wildly and she tried to rise to her feet. A moment later, her hands flew to her throat, grabbing at the healing wound until her hands became like claws ripping at her flesh.

Raven stared in shock at the nightmare in front of him. He finally fisted his hands over hers, wrestling her arms to her sides. "Nikki! Stop it."

She fought him, her spine twisting against his chest. "No! It's *in* me! I have to get it out, Raven!" Her tone rose to a shriek.

Talk about a fast recovery. For someone who was so weak moments ago, she was fighting — and slipping — from his grip in ways few opponents had ever managed to do. Frustrated, Raven clamped his legs around her lower half in an attempt to stop her momentum. To his amazement, it worked.

"There's nothing in you!" he yelled, but even he knew it sounded false. If Nikki could feel the poison, sense it, it meant she wasn't out of danger. Pastor Layton had given him some instructions. But right now, battling with Nikki, he couldn't remember a single word.

He dragged one of her wrists to the other and clamped her arms against his side, leaving his other arm free. "Nikki!" His free hand smoothed the hair from her face, where it had whipped across her cheeks and forehead. "Nikki" — softer now — "talk to me."

She bucked once more, but soon she calmed.

He pressed his mouth to her ear. "Talk to me, Nikki. Tell me about ..." About what? What had the pastor told him? *Get her to talk about things that bring her joy.* "Tell me about your artwork. You love to draw, don't you?"

The pause lasted for what felt like an eternity. Her eyes darting again, but not looking at the cave. This time they were searching for the memory he'd requested. Finally, she said, "No, I can't draw anymore. It hurts people."

Raven's heart stuttered. "Okay, well, um, tell me about ... your motorcycle."

"It's gone. Damon Vessler took it away, along with every-thing else I owned. He wants to turn me into a monster. But I think the seeker beat him to it. I can feel it, Raven. Something evil is moving through my veins." Her voice had dropped sev-eral octaves, as if she'd submitted herself to the transformation.

He needed a safer topic. Maybe concentrate deeper into the past. "You grew up with a great dog, didn't you? Bo. Tell me about Bo."

"A hell hound killed him while he tried to protect me."

Raven's heart sank a little more. *At this rate, I'll turn her in a few minutes.* He dropped his head against hers. *God, isn't there something in Nikki's life that doesn't cause her pain?* "Nikki, tell me about something that makes you happy."

Her words were a faint whisper. "There isn't any happiness for me."

He began to grind his teeth in frustration. "That's not true." Though much hurt, so many wounds had marred Nikki, maybe there really wasn't anything that could make her happy. Not that it would stop him from searching. "Come on. Let's talk about the night we met at the ruins. Remember? We rode my Harley all over Germany. I know it was a good night for me."

"I hurt Mace. He was so mad, and I lied to him about you."

"Something else, then. You're a Halfling. Tell me about that."

"If I was a Halfling, I would have wings. Do you see wings? No? Me neither. It doesn't matter what Will says. I'm still just a freak."

"You'll get your wings soon. Vine got his at a rock concert just a few days before Mace, Vine, and I showed up to protect you. You're worth protecting, Nikki."

She tilted away. For a moment he thought she'd closed

him out, but Raven quickly realized the truth. And it caused the backs of his eyes to burn. *Please don't make me do this*, he pleaded. But he knew it was the only way. This time when he spoke, there was a new authority in his voice, in part to mask the pain. "Nikki, tell me what makes you happy."

She shook her head, as if speaking was too great an effort.

"Tell me," he insisted. He clamped his hand on her chin and tilted to look at her profile. Her eyes were visibly darker, jolting him with alarm. "Tell me."

On a long breath, she uttered, "Mace."

Raven squeezed his eyes shut, trying to block the icy-cold dread, but there was no stopping the ice pick to his chest. Moisture rushed to his eyes. "Nikki." *Oh God, please give me the strength to do this.* "Tell me about Mace."

Her words came slowly at first, as if trying to remember a movie she'd watched a long time ago. "We had a picnic ... at Viennesse." As she talked on, deep into the night, she became stronger. He'd tried to route the conversation back to the stolen moments the two of them had shared, but each time he did, she became afraid, agitated, fearful. It was only when she spoke of Mace that she was peaceful.

His heart cracked further with every moment she described. Every look Mace had given her, every brush of hands ... or lips. And when she tried to trail off, because she was tired or felt embarrassed, Raven coaxed her on because he loved her too much to allow her to stop. Though it meant clearing his throat often to mask his sorrow. As the night wore on, he began to peek at her neck more and more, where the ash-black cut and graying skin of the wound was becoming like live flesh again. "That's good, Nikki," he said, stroking her hair with his hand. "You're doing great. Tell me more."

And she did. Sitting with Mace by the lake, watching the fog roll in and consume them both; working in the kitchen on the sailing yacht, where she would have broken every dish in the galley if Mace hadn't showed up and helped her store them just in time.

After awhile, the stories became dreamlike memories told with long pauses and breathy words. When she seemed very calm, he tried to alter the subject slightly. "Do you remember when we were in the woods and I was teaching you how to fight?"

Her body tensed. "I said some horrible things to Mace that day."

Raven's eyes closed. That memory had been his last chance — the day he'd fallen in love with her. And she with him. But now, to her that day was just one more time she'd disappointed Mace.

For Raven, it was like dying two deaths. He resolved himself to the reality that had always lived within all her mixed-up feelings. She loved Raven, there was no question. But Mace was her match. He was her soul mate. Raven slid a hand between them to press against his heart. It hurt so badly, he wondered if he'd find two separate halves.

By the time Mace stepped through the dark water at the mouth of the cave, Raven knew his days would continue. They had to, because it would be too humane for him to die.

Curled with a sleeping Nikki before the fire, Raven half expected Mace to become livid. After all, wasn't that what the two of them did? Get mad at each other for cozying up to Nikki? Instead, Mace came over slowly and dropped to his haunches.

But his eyes weren't on Nikki. They were on Raven. Those

weird blue-green eyes scanned his face a few minutes beyond uncomfortable. Raven gestured down at her with a nudge of his chin. "I think she's going to be okay."

Mace's eyes didn't leave him; he could feel them burning into his flesh and hoped the redness in his gaze would be mistaken for exhaustion. "So she is. I'm worried about you, brother."

Raven looked away, grateful for the slashes of light the fire created. Maybe it would disguise what he was feeling. "I'm good."

Mace drew a heavy breath and dropped a backpack down beside them. He busied himself pulling out a sleeping bag and some canned food. Raven took the cue and slid from Nikki without disturbing her. The two boys worked silently, and in a moment's time Nikki was snuggled into the sleeping bag.

Mace tugged at the neck of her shirt to reveal a section of the wound. He winced. "Looks bad."

Raven snorted. "You should have seen it before."

"Before?" Mace echoed.

"Yeah, before she started talking about you." Raven swallowed hard and reached for a couple cans of food. "Tuna and fruit cocktail? I ordered shrimp."

"Sorry. I guess I thought tuna and shrimp were about the same." Mace's smile was a flash of white in the dark cave, and it disappeared when he looked down to unzip a pocket on the side of the backpack. He handed a fork and can opener to Raven.

Raven nudged the tuna into the edge of the fire for a few moments, and for that span of time the boys sat with the sparks from the flame and the waterfall providing the only sound. He tested the sides of the can, found the temperature manageable, and took a bite. "Tuna on an open fire tastes pretty good," he lied. In reality, he could be eating last week's cafeteria special and it would have tasted the same. His mind was still reeling over the fact that he'd been wrong about Nikki all this time. Emotions were horrible things. He'd been right to avoid them before, and he never should have let himself feel.

He set the can aside. There was something else too. Something was tugging him in a different direction, pulling him from this journey. From her. He'd always felt as though his part in their mission was more about Dr. Richmond than Nikki. If he'd listened to his heart in the beginning and concentrated on Richmond, maybe he wouldn't be hurting so much right now.

Mace's gaze traveled to the tuna then back to Raven. "You should eat, bro."

"There are a lot of things I should do. But will I? People always assume I'll do the wrong thing. Maybe they're right."

Mace frowned. *What happened in here?* Something had changed inside Raven, and not for the better. "What are you talking about?"

Raven picked up the tuna can, but didn't take a bite, instead sticking his fork into the meat over and over until the prongs were filled like an overstuffed shish kebab. "What would you do if you knew something no one else knew, information that could change everything?"

Mace opened his mouth, but couldn't answer.

Raven chuckled. "Never mind. I know what you'd do."

It sounded like an accusation. "What do you mean?"

Raven's eyes trailed to Nikki.

131

"Raven, if you know a way to help Nikki and aren't talking—"

"Back off. It's nothing like that."

This wasn't going the way Mace had expected. "Sorry, Raven. I'm not following you."

"You know this is all Vessler, right?"

"What?" Mace had just opened the can of fruit cocktail, but he discarded it at Raven's words.

"If a seeker doesn't kill the target, it releases enough poison to—"

"To turn her? That's what this has been about?" He felt the urge to run to Nikki.

Raven stared him down and motioned him to stay put. "Vessler killed Nikki's parents, but when her desire for vengeance wasn't enough to get her to turn, he tried to lure her back, but that failed too."

Mace focused on the fire. "So he petitioned his god to release a seeker. Not to kill her, just to turn her. Unbelievable. We're back in the fight with Vessler again. I figured we'd get a little break while he recovered from the gunshot wounds Nikki inflicted, but I guess not." He reached for the tuna, slid most of the meat off the fork, and held it out to Raven again.

He rolled his eyes and took the can. Finally, he took a bite.

"Do you know of a way to stop this insanity, Raven?"

"No. I just think about all she's been through." Raven looked down at Nikki, and Mace followed his gaze.

"Yeah." Her hair lay across her cheek and feathered out around her, catching light from the fire.

"It's enough," Raven said.

"What do you mean?"

"She's been through enough."

Mace nodded in agreement. There was something very final about Raven's words, however, and if he didn't know better, he'd swear Raven held the power to end some of Nikki's pain. But that was crazy. How could Raven stop even part of her suffering? He stared at Raven, who was now poking at the flames. Something wasn't right.

Nikki stirred. They both turned to face her. Her eyes flittered open and she mumbled one word. "Mace?"

He moved from where he'd been sitting and reached to run a hand over her hair, her face. "I'm right here."

"I know what I have to do," she said, words forming on cracked lips. "I have to beat the seeker. I saw it in a dream. And you can't help me. Either of you."

Mace's gaze shot to Raven, who stared at her then shrugged. "I don't know what she's talking about."

Both boys leaned a little closer.

Nikki yawned. "I saw it. It'll come here to find us. And I'll fight it." She closed her eyes. "Promise me you won't intervene."

"There's no way on this planet that's going to happen." Mace's body tensed. "We fight together."

Nikki shook her head. "We can't. I saw that in my dream too. If we fight it together, it'll kill me."

Chapter 12

"I can't believe I'm even considering letting you do this."

Nikki sensed Mace's apprehension. He wiped a hand over his forehead, where tiny beads of sweat broke out.

Raven had left for the nearest town to get more food. But there was something in his eyes that Nikki couldn't place, couldn't understand. He was usually so easy for her to read, but a wall had closed him off, and for the briefest of moments she'd wondered if he'd return.

She examined the contents of the backpack, focusing on the monumental task at hand. "I have to kill it. Alone." Her hand went to her wound on her throat, fingertips running along the bumpy flesh.

"It's still healing." Mace took her hand and drew it away from the scar.

Would she forever carry the mark of the seeker? Probably. Just below her throat, visible to the whole world. If she had to live with it, she'd do it with pride. It was the mark of a girl who wasn't going to run anymore. She would fight. She'd fight alone. And if her dream was right, she'd win.

But there'd been another dream too. One where Mace and Raven intervened. In that vision, she died at the hands of the seeker. Her thoughts must have played out on her face, because Mace pushed the backpack out of her hand and pulled her to him. "Let's leave here," he said, the strength of his words tempting her to listen. "If you have to face it, let's do it on our grounds."

Nikki pushed away and looked into sorrow-filled eyes. "Why? So more Halflings can watch helplessly and have to stay out of the fight? No, Mace."

"You could have more time to heal."

"No. It happens here. It happens *now*."

He cupped her face. "You know I hate watching you fight."

A tiny laugh escaped her lips. "Yeah. No choice this time."

"Nikki, if I've ever made you feel like you weren't a good fighter …" His words trailed off. She knew what he meant. He didn't have to spell it out.

"You've always tried to protect me."

"I should have been helping you train. I never thought you'd be expected to go up against something like this."

Nikki reached into the backpack again and found a hunting knife. "I can do this, Mace. I have faith that I'm going to win."

Mace swallowed. "Me too."

So many emotions crackled in the cave around them. "Promise me you won't intervene."

Mace fisted his hand at the back of her neck and pulled her close enough to rest his forehead against hers.

She couldn't melt, not this time. "Promise me."

He closed his eyes. His breath, hot and sweet, fanned against her skin as he mumbled, "I promise."

"And Raven. Make sure he stays out of it too." She realized her pleas were killing him, but this is how it had to be. "You know how he is. All act now, think later."

Mace nodded. His eyes opened.

She studied him, dissecting the portions of his face with great interest. A face she could sketch by memory. Every quirk of the brow, every twitch of the cheek, they all meant something. And Nikki understood each one as they appeared, from his fear to his commitment to honor his promise. "Stay alive, Nikki."

"I will," she said, and knew the words sounded sure. She only wished she felt as confident. "When this is over, we need to talk about something." Nikki pulled her bottom lip into her mouth and bit down. She'd really like to stay lost in the moment, her and Mace together, but reality nagged her to speak. They'd approached the difficult subject before, only briefly — when she tried to kill Vessler. But Mace needed to know the truth before she left — their future relationship rested upon it.

"Sure, we can talk later. Right now, you just need to concentrate on beating the seeker."

He knew what she referred to, she could see it in his face, hear it in his voice. Just as she knew he wouldn't let her broach it when she returned. "Mace, I'm not the same girl you fell in love with." Now, after being on the run with Raven, that was even more obvious. Through Vessler's machinations, she'd changed into someone who frightened her at times, but who also felt more authentic than she ever had before. "I don't think I can pretend to be her anymore."

"I don't want you to, Nikki. Life is change. If any of us thinks we can stay the same, especially on a journey like this, we're fooling ourselves. With every step we take, we're growing into something new."

"What if the old was beautiful, the best I'll ever be?" She searched his face, willed it not to flinch.

"The new is beautiful too. Just different. You've learned so much already."

"Yeah." She rolled her eyes. "How to be a killer."

"You haven't killed anyone."

That much was true. Each time the opportunity to take a life arose — a life she'd deemed unworthy of living — something had stayed her hand. On the plane, she could have shot Vessler in the chest, but opted to aim the gun at his leg. She could have easily shot Keagan Townsend — the man Vessler had hired to kill her parents — until he took a wounded butterfly into his hands and tried to help it fly . . . She'd been halted by a stupid *insect*.

How long until she was able to make a lethal shot or slit a throat? Could Mace watch her do that?

Nikki couldn't change what she was becoming, and she didn't expect Mace to understand. Her "beautiful" changes made her dark like Raven — and that darkness was the one thing Mace loathed about his brother-in-arms. Now, poison from the seeker had been released in her system, and she had no way of knowing how that would play out over time. It wouldn't be fair to Mace to not warn him. Maybe he could love her or maybe he would loathe her. It would have to be his choice. Because right now, she was far from the innocent girl he'd first met.

A guttural scream echoed from outside. Nikki closed her hands over Mace's arms, heart hammering in her chest. The seeker was close.

Raven rushed into the cave. "You hear that?" He tossed a bag of groceries near the fire.

Nikki swallowed and refused to let her two protectors see her fear. "It's coming."

Raven grabbed her arms, turning her from Mace. "There's still time to get away, Nikki."

But Mace placed his hands over Raven's. "She wants to do this," he whispered, his throat catching on the words.

Nikki struggled to look at him directly. Mace had spent this entire journey trying to keep her from fighting; now, he was giving her the support she needed most, as well as his promise to stay out of the fray.

Mace cleared his throat. "Nikki's ready," he said, eyes boring through Raven. "We have to give her this."

Raven turned away and searched her. It was a long time before he answered. "We'll be right here when ..."

She took a gentle step back, causing Raven to release her. The boy's arms dropped and she reached for both of them, grasping his hands in hers. "You'll be right here when I get back." Raven's midnight gaze and Mace's blue-green one studied her, drinking her in, remembering in case ...

"I'm a fighter," she said. With a smile, she added, "And I'm on the winning side." She took several steps away from them and walked out to meet her fate.

Nikki stood near the edge of the cave and faced her enemy. Its large, bumpy, char-black body bristled as she stepped closer, closing the hundred feet of distance between them. It tilted its head back and released a half growl, half roar, in the process exposing a mouth filled with rows of teeth resembling a shark's. In its chest she could plainly see the scab from where she'd sunk the sharp tip of Glimmer's bow. Congealed blood — or whatever its life force was — cut a hardened stream from the puncture site to the center of its stomach.

"Everything has a weakness. What's yours?" she whispered. She chanced a look behind her through the waterfall, where Mace and Raven waited inside the cave. They'd promised to give her what she asked, but they remained ready to jump in if things didn't go the way she anticipated. *Please, please keep out of my fight.*

A hot sun beat down on her from above. She scanned the area. Trees and brush, soft grass to land on if this being knocked her off her feet. But what was the key to defeating it? And what things could she use as weapons if she lost her knife? A felled tree lay nearby, but it looked too large to wield as a club. The surroundings offered little help.

It screamed again, as if agitated. The creature drew a few breaths, sucking air into its putrid body through two concave nostrils. Its shoulders spread a little wider and it actually seemed to puff up.

"Like a blowfish," Nikki muttered, watching the display with growing curiosity and more than a little bit of excitement because . . . because this could be a key to her victory. "You want me to be afraid of you."

The thing growled, but didn't move closer. So Nikki closed the distance, running straight at it while raising the hunting knife in her hand. But one of the creature's tentacles lashed out and swiped her off her feet before she could get near. She landed with a thud, rolled, and hopped up quickly, knife still in her hand.

As she caught her breath, the creature puffed up again. "You really want me to be afraid. But I'm not." The realization brought power to her.

It hissed, leaning its head in her direction.

Nikki thought back to what Kaylyn had said about the creature using fear to home in on its target. "You *need* me to be afraid."

The long tentacle arms swished in front of her and one came slicing toward her face, but it moved in slow motion, making it easy to sidestep.

The seeker looked confused, white eyes darting in her direction but never really settling on its target. It lashed out again with the same tentacle, but it struck several feet away.

"You can't see me because I'm not afraid." The more she spoke the words, the more strength seemed to manifest within her.

When she said it again, she thought she saw the seeker get smaller. *I'm actually shrinking him with my words.* Boldness washed over her, propelling her a few steps toward the creature. They stood now less than twenty feet apart. Close enough for him to strike with his tentacles if he could get a fix on her position. "I don't fear you."

It growled and stumbled back, nearly falling into the lake.

Nikki's entire body tingled with awareness of her new power over the thing. She screamed, "I am not afraid of you!"

This time, the creature's tentacles shriveled and diminished to half their original size. Nikki pulled the hunting knife from where she'd slid it under her belt. She aimed at the creature's chest then drew back and threw, using the mark from Glimmer's bow as a target. The knife sank deep, with only an inch of the blade protruding from the flesh. The creature reeled back, but corrected itself and ran forward, using a razored arm to drag the knife from its rib cage.

Nikki froze. The thing fell forward onto her, pinning her to the ground. Blades snapped and clawed the ground around her as she tried to escape from beneath the weight of the seeker. The knife-wielding tentacle sliced closer and closer, sparking against rocks and chewing through the grass and dirt to get to her. On instinct Nikki grabbed the blade, feeling it carve into the flesh of her fingers.

The scent of fresh blood filled the air. The seeker drew long, quick breaths, as if frenzied by the coppery smell. Its mouth snapped at her, but she ducked beneath one of its arms so that the seeker bit into his flesh rather than hers. His grip on the knife loosened and Nikki slipped her fingers from the sharp blade to the handle. She snaked her other hand closer, and with all her might drove the knife into the seeker's side.

It screamed and flew off her. She scanned the grounds for additional projectiles and saw Mace and Raven running toward her. "No!" she screamed, holding her hand out to stop the two boys. Blood ran off her fingers. She gave it only a glance and yelled again. "No!"

They stopped, dividing their glances between her and the beast.

She turned and addressed the creature again, remembering her real weapon — the words. She had all but forgotten while she was wrestling on the ground. "I will not fear you." And again, it shrank before her eyes like a deflating balloon.

The authority she'd felt moments before settled around her like a cloak when the phrase passed her lips. A swirling, fluttery sensation caused her to raise and lower her shoulder blades. A pulling, almost tearing feeling skittered down either side of her back, but it wasn't painful. In fact, it felt ... free.

Nikki sucked a breath at the realization of what was about to happen. Anticipation caused her to stretch her arms out on either side of her body. She felt perfectly attuned to the rise and fall of her chest as she closed her eyes, and stood perfectly still even though she could hear the seeker moving closer. She willed her mind to calm, and before she could draw another breath, her wings snapped open. Instantly, she felt an updraft lifting her to her toes. She was barely aware of the seeker now, but knew he continued to come at her even as she left the ground completely. She pumped her wings once and felt the cool air sink into her feathers. *Feathers!* Nikki gave her wings a couple of quick shakes and yes, felt the breeze whistle through each pinion. Every movement, every stretch was met with a similar reaction by these new extensions of herself. *This is* amazing. She was alive — more so than ever before — and strong, like she'd finally tapped into who she really was. She was ... freedom.

Hovering a dozen or so feet above the ground, Nikki yelled at the seeker. "You have no power over me! I belong to the Throne. My name is Freedom. Go back to the pit and never return."

The seeker shook violently and lashed out with a desperate swipe. Nikki caught the tentacle and pulled, knocking the seeker off balance. It hurled forward at her, but she screamed, "I said, go back to the pit!" It started shaking again and, to both her shock and expectation, disappeared.

Nikki skyrocketed up, letting the currents carry her. If she'd thought being on a motorcycle felt free, it held no comparison to this. Air hissed past her ears as her shoulders moved in tandem with her wings. *My wings.* She paused in the air, eyes fitted on the brilliant blue sky above her, and now streaming with wind-triggered tears. She wasn't sure how far she'd traveled, but decided not to look down. After slowing a moment, gravity tugged and she tilted her wings so she would drop gradually. Soon she smelled the pine of the forest below and heard the rushing of the waterfall. Nikki chanced a look. The earth was a hundred feet below and Mace stood there waiting for her. Seeing him reminded her of the Halfling ritual he'd taken her to watch. She'd first thought they were giant eagles, the way the couple had rolled and tumbled in midair as the male caught branches tossed to the ground by the female. Mace had said the last branch always weighed the same as the female, and the male could only catch it at the last possible moment.

Retrieving the branch successfully meant the two were mated for life. And for Halflings, that was a long time.

Nikki wished she could find a branch the same weight as her; she'd lift it into the sky and drop it right now for Mace. Because love conquered all, didn't it? Even if she wasn't the Nikki he'd known, it didn't have to mean they couldn't have a life together. It felt like her wings had changed everything. What she knew — with all her heart — was that she loved Mace. And this would be her way of saying once and for all that she and Mace truly did belong together. Her mind trailed back to the ritual; the whole thing was based on the idea the male could catch the female if she ever fell ...

Nikki tucked her wings into her back and let the pull of earth drag her down. She heard Mace yell — a terrified sound. She couldn't bear to see his face, so she slammed her eyes shut as she rocketed faster and faster toward the earth.

Air whistled past her ears until she heard the flutter of wings and felt the warmth of his flesh closing around her. Her eyes opened just as they hit the ground. They landed hard, and the impact left her gasping for breath. For a moment they lay there, motionless, limbs intertwined, Nikki tucked into Mace. When she moved to get free, she realized he'd used every part of his body to shield her.

Mace spoke before she got the chance. "Why did you do that?"

"I needed to know you could catch me when I fall."

"I hope you're satisfied, because we won't be playing this game again."

She snaked a hand from where it had been trapped between them and lifted it to his cheek. "I'm satisfied."

"Did you see your wings?"

She wiggled her shoulder blades, and could still feel the sensation of something there.

"No."

"Come on, you need to see this." Mace unwound his limbs from hers and lifted her to her feet. Taking her by the hand, he led her to the edge of the lake. She looked down at the smooth water while Mace took a step back. "Snap them open."

Nikki bit her lip and searched his face. She hadn't opened them the first time — they had sort of done their own involuntary appearance.

Mace released a soft chuckle. "You can do it, Nikki. They're an extension of you. No one else is in control of them."

Nikki filled her lungs and spread her arms. Her wings unfurled beside her. Again, the wind grabbed them, forcing her to curl her toes and fight to stay on the ground.

From behind, Mace pressed gently on her upper back. "Now look."

Nikki tilted out over the bank of the water and stared down. A giant rush of air entered her lungs with such force she thought she'd pass out. Stretched out on either side of her were wings, as beautiful as any bird's and crimson as fresh blood. "Red?" At first she thought the light was somehow tricking her mind, but when she shook the feathers, the wind caused the water to ripple in long red waves.

"They're beautiful." Mace dropped one hand to her shoulder, using the other to press along the upper edge of her wing. She could actually feel his hand *on her wing*.

"Why are they red? *Blood* red?"

"I don't know, Nikki *Youngblood*. Why is Winter's skin ice cold? Why do Glimmer's wings sparkle?"

She glanced up from the reflection to look into his eyes.

"Whatever the reason, it's a gift, not a curse."

She nodded, finding strength in his cerulean gaze. "Okay. I can live with red."

He laughed. "You're going to have to."

From her periphery, she saw something moving at the edge of the cave. Nikki looked over in time to see Raven drop to a seated position by the mountain's smooth wall. "Nice," he mouthed, his face beaming, but somehow his happy demeanor shrouded something else, perhaps even sadness.

"Go," Mace said, pointing to Raven. "He kept you alive last night, and I don't think it was the easiest task. I'm sure he's anxious to talk."

When Mace turned to leave, she reached out and grabbed his hand.

He looked down at her grasp, almost surprised. "Don't worry. I'm not going far. And don't worry about how long your conversation takes — I get the feeling the two of you have a lot to discuss."

She watched as he rose into the sky, his wings carrying him over the treetops. Once he disappeared, she walked toward the cave, and whatever awaited her inside. Up close, Raven's eyes were red-rimmed and framed with dark circles. She'd planned on saying something catchy and cute, but the words died in her mouth. All she could do was drop to her knees and use her finger to trace the purplish half moon beneath one of his eyes.

"You did good back there." Raven reached up to grab her hand, his fingers closing around hers.

"You taught me how to fight."

"Not really. I just stirred up the warrior inside. Good to see Mace?"

"Yes."

"Good." His deep voice broke on the word.

She flashed a frown.

"I love you, Nikki."

She opened her mouth but he stopped her words. "Don't. Don't talk. Don't say anything. You need to hear this and I got one shot at getting it out." His voice cracked again, and she could feel her own throat closing up as he took in a long intake of air and continued. "This whole mess is twisted, you know? I never wanted to be in it. And until last night I didn't think I'd be willing to get out of it."

"You're sounding kind of morbid, Raven. Can we talk about something else?" His fingers traced a path on her palm.

"I'm not sure why it took me so long to see."

"See what?"

"Mace loves you more than I ever will."

She felt like she'd been punched directly in the stomach.

"Sorry." He shrugged. "But look at it. I went after you because it's what I wanted. I pursued you because it was best for me. I never thought about what was best for you. I told myself I did, but it tasted like a lie every time I swallowed it. Of the three of us, Mace is the only one who repeatedly put his desire aside to give you what you need. That in itself proves he's the one."

"I do love Mace, but you've always been there for me."

"That's not enough to base lifelong love on, Nikki. You deserve better than that. Mace will challenge you. He'll expect you to continue to grow, to become a real warrior for the battle ahead. But he will do it the right way, with what you need as the center focus."

Her emotions felt like a tangled mess. "You're the one who's always challenging me."

"No. I was doing whatever was opposite of Mace. I don't really know how to love sacrificially."

"That's not true." Her grip tightened on him; she would hold him here forever if she had to.

"Mace is your match. I didn't see it until last night. But now it's crystal clear."

"Why does everyone keep talking about last night? *What happened last night?*"

"You don't remember?"

"No!"

"Last night your heart spoke what your mind hasn't let you. Mace is the one."

With horrible clarity, she remembered talking about Mace. To Raven. Nausea roiled in her gut. Nikki was going to throw up.

"Calm down."

"Oh, Raven, I'm so, so sorry." And that sounded so, so lame. Memories spiked into her mind, each one a scalpel, cutting away her clouded emotions, cutting away Raven. The night's conversation rang with more and more clarity. She'd talked about Mace. How she felt, how she loved him. This was horrible.

Time stretched out before them as the words she'd spoken filled her head, sitting there like guilty little children. Trees fluttered in the breeze, water crashed on rocks. "Nikki, I'm headed in a different direction."

Her grip on his hand tightened as if the will in her fingers could stop him. "Please don't run away again, Raven."

He blinked away the hint of moisture. "That's not what I mean. After last night …" He made circles on her hand with his thumb. "When I realized, I felt like dying."

Nikki forced her eyes to focus. How could she have been so cruel — even if she was fighting poison? What kind of a monster does that?

He gave her hand a squeeze. "Let me finish, okay?"

She nodded.

"But then it was like the part of me that had just died made way for something fresh. There was a new — "

"Freedom?" she asked, barely getting the word out before she choked on it.

"Yeah." He smiled and pulled her closer, making a place for her to sit beside him. She tucked her shoulder beneath his arm, head against his chest. "There was a new freedom. You belong with Mace. And I *belong* somewhere else."

She tilted her head to look up at him, but he stopped her by holding her snug against his chest. The muscles beneath were rock hard, and she wondered if this was as difficult for him to say as it was for her to hear. A drop landed on her scalp in response. "Where, Raven?"

"There's still a journey for me that involves Dr. Richmond. I've known it since the beginning, and now it feels imminent."

Her science teacher. And the man who worked for Omega Corporation and Damon Vessler years ago.

She pressed closer into him. "Will you really go away?" She didn't think she could bear it. And yet, she knew she couldn't bear watching him hurt while she spent time with Mace.

148

"Who knows? Vessler's reach is far. Maybe we'll all be expected to help Richmond."

Nikki pushed back to look at him. "You think Dr. Richmond is in danger?"

"If not now, soon. But Halflings never work alone, so if the Throne is expecting me to get more involved in Richmond's life, the rest of the team is sure to follow."

"The other Halflings and Will?"

He nodded. "And you."

She hadn't considered that.

"You're a Halfling, Nikki. You've been drafted by the Throne, and have some pretty mind-blowing wings to prove it. You'll be expected to fight."

Her heart whooshed in her ears. For so long, everything had centered around her — keeping her safe, keeping her alive. Now, she was one more player on the field, and it was others whose lives were in danger. She couldn't decide if she wanted to whoop or scream.

"That's if pretty boy will let you fight."

Nikki frowned. "He's not in charge of me."

"Ah, that's the warrior I love to see."

She rolled her eyes. He'd baited her. Easily. "You said Mace would challenge me."

"He will, Nikki. He'll make sure you stay at the top of your game. Don't forget, you're not out of danger yet. Vessler is still out there. He still wants you."

She shrugged. "He gave his best shot and he didn't break me. I'm not a dark creature like he planned." A new feeling rose within her, a sense of supremacy, a strength she'd never known before. She *wasn't* dark. "He can't touch me."

Raven flashed a scowl. "Don't get cocky."

She shook her head. "Not cocky, just sure. What can he do to me? He tried everything in his power to get me to turn. I beat the seeker, Raven. That means I beat Vessler."

Concern closed over his features.

Nikki pushed off him, irritated that he'd be so quick to warn her after she'd just experienced such a victory.

Raven didn't speak. He reached out and stopped her from moving away. Then he gripped her arms and looked at her as if he stared into her soul. For a long time, they stayed like that, and Nikki felt her irritation melting. Once the last shreds had peeled away, Raven pulled her into his arms.

And there he held her for a long, long time.

Chapter
13

"Are you okay?" Mace asked as she folded the sleeping bag and tucked it into the backpack. She'd been cleaning ever since Raven broke their embrace.

Her hair bobbed in front of her as she nodded, but she didn't trust her voice to speak. Mace crossed the cave to where she stood and gently took the backpack. He dropped it on the ground and cupped her face.

"Your eyes are red from crying." He kissed her cheek on one side, then the other, and she melted into him. She didn't want to. She wanted to feel nothing. It seemed an even worse betrayal to Raven to relish Mace's touch. *Raven.* Her heart cracked yet again. *How could one girl cause so much damage?*

Mace glanced down the rock corridor leading deeper into the cavern. "Where is he?"

"Gone." She hated her voice. "He said he'd let Will and the others know the seeker is dead."

Mace's face troubled. "Is he —"

"Okay? I don't know." Nikki pressed her lips together, wanting, needing to tell Mace what happened. "He spent last night listening to me talk about you. How much I love you, how much I need you. And whenever he'd try to bring the conversation back to himself, I got angry." She watched as the horror registered on Mace's face. Raven must not have given him all the details.

He pulled her into his arms and rested his chin on her head. "Oh, Nikki. I'm so sorry. You didn't mean to hurt him."

She wrenched herself from him and attacked the backpack again. "I didn't mean to hurt him, but I did." She grabbed the empty can of fruit cocktail and took it to the mouth of the cave. Outside, the forest was a blur. She held the can beneath the rushing water then shook off the excess before dropping it into the pack. "Does it matter that I didn't mean to? Oh, sorry, did I just split that atom? Didn't mean to. Oops, did I just press the button and start World War Three? I didn't mean to."

He came at her. "Nikki, stop." His hands closed on her upper arms; his touch was warm, almost hot against her skin.

She stared past him to the crack in the cave wall where a line of ants marched. "You know the worst part of this?" Nice, straight rows of ants carrying tiny bits of dirt and food. "He said it gave him freedom, letting me go. And instead of being happy about that, I was hurt by it. How horrible am I?"

Mace's fingers twitched then loosened on her arms. "You're not horrible. You're human. Well, you're not completely human, but you have human emotions. They don't come with an on and off switch."

"If they did, this would have been a whole lot easier."

"You care for Raven, even love him on some levels." He raised the side of his mouth. "I've come to terms with that. So it's natural that you'd feel like you're losing him. And it's natural that your emotions would react to that."

She huffed.

"You know, for the very first time, I was beginning to wonder if Raven was the one for you. Then I came here."

"What a mess the three of us are. You wanting to give me up for Raven, me wanting to let you both go because all I seem to do is hurt you, and Raven giving me up for you."

"I guess we were all trying to do the right thing."

Mace caught her chin between his thumb and finger and forced her to look at him.

She tried to break his grip. "How horrible am I for talking to you about this?"

"Nikki, *deep* in my heart, I've always known you and I would end up together. Even though earlier, I was doubting it. Fact is, you're my match. And I've always known that you were scared for Raven, thought he wouldn't be okay if you didn't choose him."

"Am I so easy to read?"

"For me, yes."

She gave him the tiniest smile, her cheeks stretching and cracking after so much salt from the tears she'd cried. "I knew you could be okay without me. But I didn't know if Raven could."

"That's where you're wrong. I couldn't live without you, Nikki. You're air to me."

In that moment she knew it was all right for her to grieve for Raven, for the loss. That's what was so remarkable about Mace. His strength, his ability to cut through all the emotions to find the truth. She'd need a little time to heal, and Mace would give her that. No, he'd insist on it. Then he'd challenge her. He'd make her be a better person than she was. He'd force her to fly. "So, what do we do now?"

He put the backpack on his shoulder. "We can go back to the house on Pine Boulevard. Will had the entire group come to Missouri after the seeker appeared. We have to keep a closer watch on Vessler."

"Everyone's staying on Pine?"

"Actually, Will's going to let the girls sleep at their apartment downtown. Zero's back at the underground."

Ah, the underground, the mysterious place in Arkansas where Nikki first met the icy-eyed, sharp-tongued Halfling. "I bet he's glad to be home."

"You have no idea. And he's keeping busy watching Omega Corporation."

Which meant he was watching Vessler. For the briefest of moments it felt like there was something Mace wasn't telling her; the way his words clipped at the ends. She tried to brush it off but couldn't. "You going to tell me what's going on in that stubborn head of yours or do I have to guess?"

"What?" He seemed surprised.

"Whatever it is, you're avoiding saying."

His jaw twitched. "We confirmed Vessler is the one who sent the seeker."

She'd assumed it, of course, but to hear it said as fact made her a little dizzy. Vessler had tried to make her believe he'd cared about her — and on some insane level, she still believed he had — even though his version of love was twisted. But twisted enough to send such a vile creature to hunt her? She thought about it only a moment. Yes, that's exactly what Vessler would do. "Why does he want me so badly?"

"Nikki, Will thinks we should be close to Omega, but I disagree. I think the safest place for you is at Viennesse. We could go there—"

"And what, Mace? Hide until Vessler comes up with some other scheme? Some other monster from the pit? I'm tired of hiding. Will's right—we need to be close to Vessler and his operation. He can't get to me anymore. I defeated the seeker."

"That doesn't mean you're out of danger."

Ugh. Why did he and Raven keep reminding her of that? Couldn't they just be happy for two minutes that she'd won? "Mace, people have died because of me. To protect me."

"You mean the Frenchmen."

"Not just them. And others died by association. I won't go into hiding. I owe it to them. To avenge them."

A smile tilted one side of his face. "Nikki, the avenger."

She sank a punch in his arm. "Don't make fun of me."

"I'm not." His smile faded. "I honestly believe you'll bring Vessler down. You'll avenge the deaths that he's caused. Even your parents."

Her eyes left him and stared at the crystal clear water at the mouth of the cave. She couldn't erase the scene that played over and over in her head.

"What's wrong?"

"When I was hunting Vessler, I saw a man. He looked like my dad, but he was way too thin and just too old, I guess, to be Dad. Like the guy was a brother. He was meeting a man named Townsend and getting something—I think it was money—from him. Townsend left it in a trash can, and the guy looked really, really scared to be there."

"No wonder. Keagan Townsend is a marksman, Nikki, an assassin. He's Vessler's right hand guy. Zero said he probably pulled the trigger on the scientist we dragged from the fire."

"I just wish I knew who that other man was."

Mace took her by the arms. "You can't bring your parents back, Nikki."

His sapphire-tinged eyes bore into her. "I know," she mumbled.

"I realize you haven't had much closure where your mom and dad are concerned, but promise me you won't go snooping around Vessler or any of his men trying to find out things that won't change their fate."

Bleah. Does this whole "challenging me to be stronger" really have to start now? "But maybe I have an uncle."

His hands dropped suddenly. "An uncle who is meeting with one of Vessler's assassins. Not the greatest family member, in my opinion."

"But what if he was trying to find out what happened to me? There could be answers about my family."

"Nikki! Stop it. You *have* a family. *We're* your family now. Why do you keep reaching into the past?"

"Don't you ever wonder about your parents?"

"Every day. But it doesn't change anything. There's nothing but death back there for you. You said it yourself — you owe something to the people who died at the hands of the seeker."

And that was another thing she'd have to live with. "Why is one person's life more valuable than another?"

"We were sent to protect you. You're valuable to the Throne."

"Why?"

"Only time can reveal that. The important thing is you're alive."

She wasn't convinced.

"Nikki, I don't know what plan the Throne has for you. All I know is that he will go to no limit to keep you safe."

"But why me?"

"Do you think Zero is important?"

"Of course. Zero runs the network. He keeps Halflings connected all over the world. Zero is the hub and no one else can do what he does."

"Exactly. Zero's work is vital to Halflings everywhere. If he were to die, the whole network would shut down. Like you said, no one can do what he does."

"But I'm not Zero. I'm not anybody. I've barely learned to fly."

"But you still have worth beyond measure. When Zero was younger, do you think he knew how important he'd be?"

"I guess not."

"So stop questioning. Your worth will be revealed one day."

She gauged his words but still felt there were things he wasn't telling her. Things about her family, the world she left. For the moment, she'd let it go. "I have wings."

"Shall we go try them out? Take 'em for a test drive?"

She nodded and let the excitement drain the apprehension from her muscles.

Chapter
14

R aven! It's good to see you," Dr. Richmond said, using his body to hold the door open.

"You too," Raven returned, actually happy to be here. He wasn't sure why he'd come, other than it felt right.

Richmond's face dropped to a grimace as he inspected Raven's features. "Have you been ill?"

"Uh, no. Just not getting much sleep."

The doctor waved him in. The living room was filled with buzzing from a TV in the corner that no one watched. Some reality show with a girl dressed in clothes that had to be from the children's department, who was crying — mascara smeared her cheek. Doc Richmond shook his head. "I don't know why my wife likes these shows. I think they're all staged. No reality in reality TV."

"Well, reality is overrated."

The older man found the remote control and hollered toward the back of the house. "I turned off your show, hon."

A voice echoed from down the hall. "I'm doing laundry."

As she said it, the strong scent of detergent drifted into Raven's nose. Sometimes he wished things weren't so intense. Smells, his sight, everything a brilliant kaleidoscope of colors, scents, tastes, and feelings. Right now, he'd be thankful for the whole world to gray down.

The phone rang. "Have a seat, Raven. I'll grab that and make it quick, and we can chat."

Raven sank onto the floral couch and also to a new low, seeking consolation and friendship from a balding scientist. If he wasn't careful, they'd be joining a bowling league next and picking out matching polyester shirts. But when Raven heard the young female voice skating through the phone lines and out to him, his gaze shifted to Richmond, who stood at the edge of the hall. He cast a glance back to Raven and pointed to the phone. "My daughter."

Raven nodded and motioned for him to come and have a seat in the living room. Not because he wanted to hear her voice. Nah, couldn't be that. Yet she sounded so very alive and enthralling, and Raven tuned into her words as the doctor approached. Okay, so sometimes great hearing was a blessing.

Richmond dropped into his easy chair. "Yes, sweetheart, we're still going. No, not this weekend, next. Are you taking your medicine? Good girl."

That's right, Richmond's daughter was diabetic. He'd mentioned once he was worried she'd forget her daily insulin shots while she was off at college.

Raven heard laughter, and it sailed into his chest cavity, causing his heart rate to pick up. When he realized the reason why, he sank a little more. The girl sounded like Nikki. He closed his eyes and tried to ignore the sound.

Something drew his attention to the hallway. Almost commanded him to look. He obeyed, and there on the wall, mixed in with a ton of other photos, was a small snapshot of Jessica Richmond standing out like a firefly among moths. He moved toward it, coupling the voice with the face and body that wasn't Nikki's. He needed this, to separate the two girls in his mind, or the rest of his day would be plagued with that rolling laughter. That, he could do without.

Jessica was beautiful. More so than Nikki in every traditional sense. She stood on a beach in a bikini and dared the camera to look away. Her smile was bright and perfect, natural, and it too reminded Raven of the girl he'd just given up.

He growled and spun away from the picture just as Richmond ended the conversation with his irritatingly happy daughter.

Raven dropped back onto the couch.

"She's a card, my girl." Richmond sat the phone on the coffee table, by a large square book titled *Castles of Europe*. "All excited about her grade in Physics."

Raven nodded.

"No matter how busy she is, she takes time to check on us. We're going out of town for our anniversary and she thought it was this weekend." He brushed his hand through the air. "But enough about that. What's wrong, Raven? You don't seem yourself and you look like you haven't slept in a week."

"I've got a lot going on." *Am I really about to confide in Richmond?* Seemed so. "You ever think you know something only to find out you were way off?"

Richmond raised his hands. "I'm a scientist. That's a daily occurrence for me."

"Well, I'm not a scientist and I don't like being wrong. Besides, it's a little different when it involves people."

"Did someone betray you?" Richmond leaned forward to rest his elbows on his thighs. He studied Raven intently.

"Yeah." Raven laughed. "Me."

Richmond waited, lips pursed.

"Sorry, Doc. It's just that I thought this girl and I ..." No, he couldn't go through with it. Even total heartbreak wouldn't make him a share-your-feelings kind of dude. He stood and headed toward the door.

Richmond grabbed his arm and tugged him toward the pictures on the wall. "Did I ever tell you about the time I tried hair replacement?"

Raven shook his head to clear it.

"It failed miserably. You should have seen me. It looked like I'd sprouted miniature bean stalks on my head." The doctor dug behind the pictures that had been stuck in the frame edges of other pictures. Some were two and three deep. His sleeve caught the corner of the beach picture as he reached past it. Raven watched as Jessica Richmond tilted and dropped to the floor. From the tan carpet, she smiled up at him. He reached to pick her up. She and Nikki definitely shared a smile. Broad, soft lips, and white, even teeth. Raven brushed his thumb over the photo, half expecting it to be three dimensional, the colors and expression were so vibrant. He tucked it back in its spot inside a framed Christmas photo of Dr. Richmond dressed as Santa.

"Well, anyway." Richmond turned to face Raven. "The hair replacement was an expensive and utterly disastrous choice. But I had to try it, or I'd have always wondered."

And Raven understood. "Sometimes you have to give something a chance, even if it's ultimately the wrong choice?"

Richmond nodded. "You put it behind you, and move on. And you take what you've learned."

Raven stared at Jessica but saw Nikki. "It hurts, Doc." He was only marginally surprised when Dr. Richmond's arm came around his shoulder.

"I know, son."

"How long will it hurt?"

"I wish I could say. All I know is that another journey awaits you."

At that, Raven's attention snapped, eyes shooting to Richmond.

The older man smiled. "Life is one journey after another. Don't get trapped in yesterday's when tomorrow's is waiting for you."

Okay, that weirded him out until he realized Richmond wasn't talking about *journeys* — at least not the way Raven knew them.

Yet, there was something prophetic and profound in the words. It's the same thing Raven told Nikki: he was heading in another direction. And somehow, Richmond was involved. He'd felt it from the beginning. He'd always wanted to protect Richmond — always felt there was a need. Not surprising, since Richmond spent years working for Omega Corporation before he learned the horrible truth about what his breakthroughs were really creating.

The scientist released Raven and headed back into the living room. Before Raven could stop himself, he reached out and grabbed the photo of Jessica, tucking it into his back pocket. For a few seconds kept his hand over the photo. The photo that wasn't Nikki.

Nikki and Mace rose above snow-dusted mountains. She'd been in the air for a couple hours and her wings weren't even tired.

"You're getting the hang of it." Mace tilted, his gray-white wings angling just enough for her to tuck in closer.

"It's like I've had them forever." Even though he hovered nearby, she knew how much she could pump her wings to keep from bumping into him.

"You have. Are you tired?"

"We could take a break. I'm getting hungry."

"Follow me." He stretched to tilt one wing downward. There wasn't much below, just a lot of trees and the occasional curved road snaking around the mountain. A smattering of houses had smoky chimneys. Nikki wondered why there were never paintings done from this viewpoint. Maybe one day she'd do that — paint from the sky. Let the world see what it looks like from above, where all the dirtiness melts into a picturesque landscape.

They touched down in a small town somewhere in the mountain range. Nikki didn't know where they were and really didn't care. It felt so good, so free to just *be* without the immediate threat of a seeker or a madman or a hell hound at her back. She'd purposely forced everything from her mind except enjoying Mace, the day, and her new wings. Even if it was only for a day.

He took her by the shoulders and pointed to one mountain. "Do you recognize that?"

The rocky plateau did look familiar. Then she remembered. "That's the mountain where we watched the eagles — I mean, the Halflings."

He nodded, and before she knew what was happening he

pulled her to him, hugging her so hard she wondered if her ribs might crack. When he released her, there was an unusual light in his eyes, an illumination born of excitement or maybe expectancy. "Come, on," he said, and took her hand, leading her away from that particular view.

They entered a restaurant that looked like it was converted from an old train car. Nikki slid into the booth by the curved glass window and expected Mace to sit across from her. Instead, he slipped in beside her, nudging her over to make room. She accommodated him, relishing the feel of his warm body and the smell of wind and winter on his skin.

He nodded to the snow-capped peaks beyond the window. "Beautiful, isn't it?"

She noticed a winding path led up one mountainside. "Gorgeous."

"I bet you'd love to draw it, wouldn't you?"

Her gaze fell to the table. "I can draw things now if I'm careful. Will helped me learn, but he also warned me to be careful. Vigilant, I think he called it. It could open a door to the other realm."

"And let hounds through?"

She nodded. "So, no drawing for me. It's not worth the risk."

"I'm sorry, Nikki." He looked away for a long time, but his sudden change in posture held her attention. Nervous, maybe a little uncertain. Rather than look at the beautiful landscape beyond the window, she examined Mace.

He reached for her hand. "What if there was a way you could draw without worrying about opening a doorway for hounds?"

His hand was sweaty in hers. Very unnatural, and she could feel his pulse increase as he spoke. "If there was a way, would you do it?"

164

"What do you mean?"

He angled on the seat to look at her fully. "Nikki, we could leave the battle. We've found each other."

She shook her head. "What are you talking about?"

"You're a Halfling. When Halflings find their match, they're able to leave the war if they choose."

Now her heart pounded, matching the beat of his. "And what?" Was there actually a way out of this nightmare?

"We'd have to seek an audience with the Throne. If you're truly my match, he'll give us the option to leave the fighting behind."

"Where do we go?"

"We'd live on the earth as a married couple. From what I understand, our angelic side sort of goes dormant. We even age like humans. That's where a lot of Xians come from. They are Halflings who once found their match."

"You told me Xians were just humans who are aware of the spiritual battle."

"Some are. But some are Halflings ... or were Halflings."

A new kind of joy filled her, the spark of hope, of having a normal life again. "We'd leave all this bloodshed behind?"

He squeezed her hand. "Yes, Nikki. Leave it all behind."

They could be married and live a normal life. Have friends and go on vacations. Buy a house and maybe even raise a family. "Could we one day have children?"

Mace's face fell. "We could have one, but ..."

He didn't have to finish. "But it would be taken from us because we aren't human. And our offspring would be a Halfling expected to fight a war we ran from."

"Nikki, it's not like that. A Halfling baby is taken for his or her own protection."

165

"And we — the couple who created the child — walked away from the fight to let our child take our place?"

He brushed a hand through his hair. "We don't need to have kids."

She scooted toward the window, creating some space between them. "That's not the point. We would have run away from the war."

"No." His eyes pleaded with her. "You're looking at it all wrong. It's more like a reward. You know, for our service."

She worked to keep her breathing steady. "What service? What have I done? Nothing." Her voice rose as she spoke. "All that talk about how important I was to the Throne, and you're ready to just walk away? To let me walk away?"

"Nikki, I'm just trying — "

She held up a hand to silence him. "To protect me, I know." Would he really have her run? "Mace, I love being with you. Today has been great, but there's a war going on out there. We're warriors, not runners. We can't hide behind a human shell and spend the next sixty or seventy years pretending there's no battle. It would destroy both of us."

She could see the words drilling into his plan, cracking and shattering it. She had to make him understand. "You know why Raven left? He said *you* were my match, Mace. Do you know why?"

When his eyes came up to meet hers, the pain they held nearly stopped Nikki's voice. But he had to understand this, because right now — fresh from a victory and laden with wings — she was strong enough to face his hopes. But what about another day when she was weary and exhausted from the fight? On a bad day, he could easily convince her with a look much less wrenching. "Raven said you'd challenge me to be everything I can be. Instead, you're asking me to run away from my destiny?"

He opened his mouth, but she cut him off. "That's all I have left, Mace. I have the promise that my life — my actions — matter. That they'll make a difference. I won't walk away from that. Not even for you."

She pushed against him until he let her out of the seat. Hands fisted, Nikki walked to the restaurant door. Once she was safely on the other side, she broke into a run until her wings lifted her back to freedom.

Mace touched down on the mountaintop and breathed a sigh of relief when he saw Nikki tucked into the rock ledge. It was the same place they'd once sat and watched the elaborate ritual he'd hoped to share with Nikki.

Who was he kidding? She'd been right about everything. They were warriors, and warriors don't willingly leave the battle. They win it. Or they die trying.

The rustle of his feathers caused her to look over. Her hands went to her face and smeared tears in a feeble attempt to make them disappear.

"I'm sorry I'm such an idiot."

She sniffed. "You're not an idiot."

"Yes, I am." He closed the distance between them and motioned to the rock. "Can I sit with you?"

She slid over.

A cluster of trees moved with the mountain wind. Clumps of snow drifted from their branches and landed in heaps on the ground. *This would have been the perfect time to soar with her.*

She angled to face him. "Could you really have done it?"

He drew in a long breath. *But I had to make a mistake.* "I wanted to think I could leave this war. But I don't know. If it's what you would have wanted, yes."

"Leave Vine and Will?" Her eyes were red. "Leave Raven to his own devices? And what about Vessler? Just walk away from the chance to stop him? Vessler was planning to make wing-cuffs. Thousands of them to take – our *friends* — as prisoners."

And use Nikki's DNA to build Halflings he could control. A detail she still didn't know. And he wasn't about to tell her. But to think she could be the catalyst able to bring about his insane plan … that was more of a burden than even he needed. In truth, he'd reasoned that leaving the battle, and undergoing the change accompanied with that decision, could protect her. No angelic side, no DNA to turn dark.

Her gaze narrowed. "What is it?"

Mace looked away. "Nothing."

Beside him, he felt her angle closer, which normally he enjoyed. "Mace, tell me what's going on. You know something, don't you?"

"Contrary to what you might think, I know a lot of things," he tried to joke.

"Don't keep secrets from me. People have kept secrets from me my whole life."

He'd be no better than the rest if he didn't tell her the truth. *But can I deal with what that truth will do?*

"Mace."

He turned to her and took her face in his hands. "Nothing, Nikki. Really. I was just expecting to spend the evening catching branches you dropped for me. Instead, I'm having to think about going back to the battle."

"I'm sorry, Mace."

"Me too." Sorry he couldn't tell her the truth about her god-father. Vessler didn't just want to turn Nikki into a dark crea-ture. He wanted to cut her open and use what was inside to spawn an impossible number of dark creatures. Nikki wasn't just a warrior. She was an army.

Chapter
15

"Are you ready to go inside?"

Nikki chewed her lip. For some reason, the Halfling's house on Pine Boulevard looked different. It had been awhile since she'd been there, and well, a lot had changed. Mostly her. Being back in Missouri caused her to realize just how much had been altered in her life.

She tightened the muscles in her shoulder blades, felt her wings begin to respond, and smiled. Yes, quite a bit had changed.

She and Mace had left the mountain and the whole running-away conversation behind them. Neither had uttered a word until now. "Are you excited to show them your wings?"

She turned to face him. "No."

His brows rose. "No?"

"Not yet. I kind of want to keep it to myself for a little while. Is that okay?" It seemed her very life had been a book laid bare for all to see. Having this one thing to call her own, even for a short time, meant more than she could admit.

She saw the questions skate across his face.

"Or will they be able to see them, even if I keep them closed?"

"No, I don't think they'll see your wings until you open them." A frown now accompanied the questions.

"Then I'd like to keep it a secret. Just for a little while."

He nodded, but his face remained stoic.

"Two days. I promise I'll show everyone in two days."

This satisfied him. "Okay, warrior girl. Two days it is." There was a hint of a threat in his words. He may as well have said, "If you don't tell them, I will."

She tried to ignore the fact that he gauged her with untrusting eyes. "I'm not up to anything, Mace. I swear." Of course, she couldn't blame him for the suspicion. The last time she was at the house on Pine Boulevard, she'd escaped with the intention to hunt down and kill Damon Vessler.

Yeeaaaah. That'll cause a lack of trust in a relationship.

"Two," he repeated as if she needed to be reminded already.

"I promise."

Nikki settled into her room, the same one she'd stayed in after discovering she was half angel. The few clothes she owned rested in the dresser drawers. She was smoothing the wrinkles out of a T-shirt when someone knocked on the door. "Come in."

Winter and Vegan burst through the doorway and grabbed her in a tight hug, long arms clamping around her so quickly she barely had time to react. Winter stopped hugging first and her ice-cold skin left goose bumps on Nikki's arms.

"Hi," she said.

Winter stepped back a little more. "You're different." Her golden eyes narrowed, but the smile remained.

Vegan nodded. "There *is* something different about you, Nikki. What's going on?"

Huh, she'd forgotten how sharp these girls were. She concentrated on the T-shirt and tried to smooth the new wrinkles the hugs had created. "Nothing," she lied. "I'm just ... happy to be back."

Winter crossed her arms over her ribs, her wide gold-and-silver bracelet shining. "Uh huh."

Nikki blinked. "Really. And there's Mace."

Vegan sighed, hand to her heart. "You and Mace make a great couple."

Nikki bit her cheek. *Don't go there.* "Now, you mean." *Oops.*

Vegan tilted her head, confusion flickering in her eyes.

Nikki couldn't stop the words. Fact was, it wasn't that long ago that these two girls were agreeing with Glimmer that Nikki should go away. "We make a great couple now that I'm a Halfling."

The girls shared a look.

"I heard you. When we were at Viennesse and Glimmer was going on about how I should just disappear." Nikki pointed to Vegan. "I thought you'd come to my rescue, but you didn't."

Vegan's face fell. "I should have, Nikki."

Winter took Nikki's hand and led her to the edge of the bed. Nikki's other hand was fisted around the shirt that now had little hope of ever being wrinkle-free again. Winter sat and pulled Nikki down beside her. "We owe you an apology. We were all really scared for Mace, because of the penalty of falling for a human. It wasn't you, Nikki. We didn't dislike you."

She squeezed Winter's cold hand. "I know." How could

she possibly stay angry at these girls? They'd put themselves between her and harm over and over again. Running into battle to face hell hounds so Nikki could escape. Being angry at them, even for a few minutes, seemed one step beyond petty.

Winter and Vegan waited, as if hanging on her response. That was strange too, because she didn't feel she'd done anything to warrant their loyalty or their friendship. Yet her feelings mattered to them. She didn't quite know what to do with that, so Nikki fell back and let her shoulders press against the bed. Her shoulders. Where her wings were. A big part of her wanted to tell them. To show them, snap her wings open and watch their faces. But Vegan interrupted her thoughts.

"I have a present for you."

Nikki leaned up, excited.

Vegan held out a necklace like the one she'd presented the day they all met.

Nikki's eyes watered a little. *Gah.* "Vegan, I lost mine. I'd removed it at Vessler's house and he must have taken it."

Vegan smiled sweetly. "I know. I noticed you'd not been wearing it, and figured with all you've been through it must be gone. This works the same as the last one."

Nikki put the shell-shaped amulet to her mouth and blew.

Vegan and Winter clamped their hands over their ears, but Nikki heard nothing. "Okay, okay," Vegan said. "It works."

"Why can't I hear it?" Nikki blew it lightly again and listened close. Nothing.

"We've trained ourselves to hear it. We'll teach you, Nikki." When Vegan gave her the first necklace, she'd explained it would summon her, Winter, and Glimmer if Nikki ever needed their help.

Nikki nodded. Glimmer came screeching around the door,

golden-polished fingernails clamped on the doorjamb. She stopped, a look of expectancy on her face.

The girls inside the room laughed.

Glimmer inspected the group. "Did someone call?"

They laughed again. And for the first time in her life, Nikki felt like she belonged.

Glimmer huffed. "I probably smeared my polish. Thanks a lot."

Nikki lowered her brow. "If you didn't want to mess up your nail polish, why'd you grab the door?"

Glimmer lifted a perfectly pointed foot and wiggled her perfectly painted toes.

Oh. Nikki tried not to smile — she really should apologize — but when Vegan cracked up, Nikki couldn't help herself. Glimmer gave them a flat stare, but the edges of her cheeks twitched and soon she was smiling too. She rolled her eyes. "Let me go get my stuff, Nikki. You're hands are horrid."

Nikki hid her hands behind her back and prepared her protest, but Glimmer cut her off. "I only have gold polish, but you're way overdue, so don't even try to argue."

Glimmer wrestled her hands from behind her back, inspected her broken nails and damaged fingers. She made a gagging sound and spun from them mumbling about gangrene and something about hooves.

Winter chuckled. "Forced manicure. Have fun."

Nikki frowned at her nails. They weren't *that* bad.

Vegan tapped the necklace. "Guess you shouldn't have called her. Have fun at your spa party." She took Winter by the arm and headed for the door.

Nikki grabbed both of them. "Oh, no, you're not leaving me alone with her. You two can just settle in." Besides having

174

Vegan and Winter nearby as a support system, she hoped to talk to all three girls and see what they knew about Vessler's plans. Even if each one only had a bit of information, if she put it all together, maybe a clear picture would appear. Everything had been lost in a dark gray for her for so long, clarity would be a much appreciated change of pace. And if it came with a set of sparkly gold fingernails, she'd simply have to man up and take it.

Chapter
16

It seemed everyone was keeping secrets from her. Mace had on the mountaintop, and when Nikki questioned the girls, they too remained tight-lipped even though their body language demonstrated they had a story to tell. The whole mess was thinning her patience. So much for feeling like she fit in.

The only one she hadn't cornered was Zero, who probably had the most information of anyone because he ran the network and therefore knew everything. Yes, Zero would be able to help. She just needed to wait for the right moment to ask.

She'd briefly considered asking Will. But Nikki wasn't sure she could deal with his condescension when he told her it wasn't time for her to know. The last time she'd gone to him, questioning him about when she'd receive her wings, he'd patted her on the back like a child. Sure, he'd lived for millennia, but that didn't mean he had a right to treat her like that. No. She wouldn't go to him unless there was no other way.

And tonight, there seemed to be many other ways to get

information. All the Halflings except Raven, who'd kept his distance all day, had gathered for dinner at the house on Pine Boulevard. With everyone around, there was a big temptation to tell them all about her wings. Maybe snap them open in the living room and yell, "Surprise!" But a tiny voice in the far reaches of her mind cautioned her not to. Just like it whispered to her everything was about to fall apart. Again.

Nikki wandered to the back porch, where Zero was trying to light the barbeque grill. "How does this thing work?" He held the long lighter out to her.

She took it. "You have to hold the button down when you click it."

Silver eyes stared into her. "That's stupid."

"I didn't design it, Zero."

"What do you want?"

Ah, Zero … never one for small talk.

Nikki used the lighter to bring the grill to life. Flames flashed orange in Zero's mirrorlike eyes. "Who says I want anything?" The lighter dangled on her finger.

He snatched it from her. "Seriously?"

While Zero was a fount of information, the one drawback was he could always read right through her. He'd done it on the boat when she wanted information about her parents. He'd even done it when they first met at his underground bunker, where he'd examined her face so closely she could tell what kind of mint he'd just eaten. Peppermint Tic Tacs.

"Did you always know I was a Halfling, Zero?" No point beating around the bush.

"I suspected."

"How?"

He used a metal spatula to motion inside the house, where

Vegan and Winter sat laughing. "You look like *them*." He sneered the final word.

Nikki looked over her shoulder to the girls inside. "Like the females? Is that why you grabbed the light and examined my eyes while we were underground?"

He turned back to the grill, his only answer a slight shrug.

"Why didn't you tell anyone? Me, for instance."

"I always know stuff no one else knows. No big deal." He started placing the steaks.

"Not for you, maybe, but it's kind of a big deal to me."

He spun and held the spatula in her face. "If you're done scolding me, Mom, I'm kinda busy."

She huffed. He was right. What good did it do to relive the past?

"Nice necklace," he mocked.

Her hand went to it. But as he turned, she saw the flash of cord along his neckline too. Had Vegan given him one as well? Nikki bit back a smile.

As Zero poked and prodded the meat, she realized it was the perfect time to go in for the kill and ask Zero what he knew about her. What *else* he knew. Mace and the others had avoided the question whenever she approached it. "Zero," she began. *Here goes, whether I'm ready or not.*

"What?" he spat.

"I need to ask you about ... me. And Vessler, and my parents."

The sliding door opened and Will emerged with a plate of vegetables. "Is there room for these on the gr—" His eyes narrowed. He first studied Nikki, then Zero. "I'm sorry. Did I interrupt something?"

"No," she said a little too quickly after Will offered a belittling smile. *Breathe. Recover.* Nikki smiled back. "I was just going to tell Zero I like mine medium rare."

"Like I care." Zero poked one of the sizzling steaks with the end of the spatula. "This isn't a restaurant, ya know."

Nikki rolled her eyes and went back into the house.

She could get the information from Zero. She just needed to catch him at the right time. And here at the house, with Will constantly hovering, that right time might never come again.

But for the rest of the evening she watched Zero. Oh, he had answers.

The Halflings' network manager was a lousy liar but great at cooking steaks, even if he didn't know how to work a butane lighter. She'd eaten so much her stomach hurt. Fuel for the task, she told herself.

At least the good food meant the night wasn't a total loss, as thanks to Will's little interruption, she'd had to back off the inquisition. Will also seemed to be keeping an especially close watch on her now. Great. If he only understood she simply needed to know the truth. She couldn't stand not knowing.

And Zero seemed to be suffering as well. His gaze fired around the room every time Vessler's name came up in the conversation. He purposely avoided direct contact with Nikki. Guilty.

He did, however seem to welcome Vegan's attention, seemingly using her as a distraction from the guilt, as she'd sidled closer when he sat down. She'd brushed some lint from his shoulder, and at one point Nikki was sure the two were making googly eyes at each other. Until Zero realized; then he shot Vegan a dirty look and sulked off to brood in the corner.

While Nikki kept her focus on Zero, she noticed Mace was keeping a close eye on her too. He watched her while she interacted with the other Halflings, but kept his distance. Nikki tried to convince herself he was sharing her with them, letting her bond with her full brothers and sisters. Every time she looked over, he'd smile and nod. Weird, but kind of sweet. He was trying to help her fit in. Which, seriously, was finally possible now that she could spread her wings with the best of them, even if only she knew she had the ability. Nothing was holding her back. And at the same time, everything was. She just needed closure. Was that too much to ask?

Again, the voice in her head ... whispers, doubts. Wings or no, she still didn't feel whole. In the deepest part of her heart, she knew she was different from them. She wasn't one of the majestic angelic creatures surrounding her. Maybe as a child, Vessler gave her some strange drug in an attempt to mutate her into a Halfling. And perhaps Mace knew that. But right now, she couldn't think about Mace. Zero had the answers. The way he was acting, he must no more than the others. Of course he did; by his own declarations, Zero knew everything. She had to make him talk. But not here — too many curious eyes and too many powerful ears.

Zero knew her secret. And she knew the way to the underground.

"So, where are we going?" Nikki asked.

Mace could hear the excitement in her voice and it made his chest swell a little. For the first time in, well, forever, there was no immediate threat to her. No barriers or walls keeping her away from him, and no need for split decisions on who she was supposed to be with. And though he felt the twinges of threat hovering at the edge of their world, right now it seemed far away. He meant to enjoy this day. And to make sure Nikki enjoyed it too.

She grabbed him by the arm and shook it impatiently. "Where are we going, Mace?" She'd slipped into the front seat of his Camaro right after he put the top down, and had sat staring at him since he got into the driver's seat.

All he said in answer was, "Did you wear your boots?"

She raised one foot from the floorboard to show him.

Zero stared into the backseat, "Oh, you've got to be kidding."

Vegan stood on the passenger side and stared at the miniscule amount of space in the rear of the car. "You're just going to have to sit close to me. Sorry." But her voice was cheery as she used one hand to balance and hopped elegantly over the side of the car.

Nikki twisted. "Hey, I could have leaned forward."

"No problem," Vegan said, obviously delighted at the prospect of sitting so close to Zero. "I'm agile."

"Like a gazelle," Zero mocked, and got in the car after Mace hopped out and tilted the front seat forward.

All arms and legs — those two are quite cozy back there.

They would all be headed to Chadwick as soon as Will got into the Jeep in front of them; Vine, Glimmer, and Winter were waiting inside the vehicle for him. Vine, as usual, was passing out candy. He held up the bag and shook it at the crew in the Camaro.

Mace hollered, "No thanks. We aren't going too far."

"You *do* know where we're going. I knew it." Nikki crossed her arms over her chest in a pout.

"No, I don't," he lied, and fought a grin.

"You do too. Will had to have told you. You're driving."

Funny, but this morning it was easy to lie to Nikki. "He just said to follow him."

"Grrr." She continued to pout in the passenger seat.

Zero laughed. "Try a new approach. Growling at him doesn't seem to be working."

Nikki spun toward the backseat. "You must know where we're all going, Zero. You know *everything*."

Zero puffed out his chest. "So true. Yeah, I know. But I don't feel like talking."

Nikki's eyes narrowed on him. "Fine. And good, because if you don't feel like talking that means you feel like shutting up."

"Oooooh," Vegan said. "Someone's been taking snark lessons."

Nikki smiled and nodded her head. She reached and took Mace's hand in hers and used her free hand to rub his forearm. He knew she hadn't meant for that to *mean* anything, but it set his skin on high alert. Nikki was finally happy and so full of nervous, excited energy, it made her hard to resist. His gaze hovered on her, and she must have noticed. She turned to face him, and the intensity of the moment caused the smile to fade from her face. She blinked a few times, then slipped her bottom lip between her teeth and bit down. He fought to keep his breaths even.

She scooted around, growing uncomfortable. Conversation; they needed conversation to break the thick tension. "I want it to be a surprise. You're gonna love it."

"I don't really like surprises. Please tell me where we're going."

Right now, he'd give her anything. But if he told her, she'd stop the arm thing, and frankly, it was amazing. "I, uh, told Will I wouldn't tell." He cast a glance to her. Big mistake. Her golden eyes were pleading. Did she have any idea what that did to him? Probably.

Zero leaned forward and struck him on the shoulder. "I told you before, dude. Women are evil."

That announcement bought him a solid punch in the arm from Vegan.

"Ooooowww." Zero rubbed the spot.

Mace laughed. "We really have to toughen you up, Zero."

"I'm only going to give you one more chance to come clean," Nikki teased, making tiny little swirls on his bicep, causing goose bumps to spread across the tight skin. "Where are we going?"

He was toast. She'd spent so much time trying to stay away from him and trying to fight their attraction, her uninhibited attack was impossible to resist.

He turned to face her. With barely a thought, he clamped his hands around her face, pulled her to him, and pressed his lips to hers. At first, she tried to resist, but then she went soft at his touch. Her scent and her response shot through him with the force of a locomotive. As quickly as he'd grabbed and kissed her, he drew away. He left her stunned, mouth still opened slightly and eyes glassy. She blinked. And he knew he should look away, but wasn't able to abandon the series of emotions playing across her face. Finally, her lungs released a long breath and she closed her mouth. He was left with the thought she'd tasted like vanilla, hint of minty toothpaste, and … love.

Mace bit his cheeks to keep from smiling. "What were you saying?"

Her head shook slightly. "I don't remember."

And that simple fact alone made Mace want to bolt out of the car and skyrocket until his wings gave out. One kiss could render her speechless.

From the backseat, Zero said, "Now that I'm about to lose my breakfast, can we go?"

Chapter

17

Will stepped around the side of a large moving truck that blocked a section of the dirt parking lot. He was joking with another man, one Mace said he didn't recognize, but as the man and Will maneuvered toward the group of teenagers, their conversation ceased.

Vine pointed when the two men gave the Halflings their attention. "'Sup with the truck?"

Mace shrugged. "Dunno."

Nikki leaned over, hoping Will and his friend wouldn't hear. "Do you guys know him?"

Zero chuckled. He must have been standing right behind her. "Yeah. That's Will."

She turned and raised a fist, and Zero shrunk away, tilting behind Vegan.

Nikki laughed. "I know who Will is. I meant the other one."

They all shook their heads and mumbled about not knowing the guy.

Moments later that guy was standing before them. "Halflings," Will said. "This is Thomas Grayber. He needs our help today."

Nikki stared at Thomas's face. *Where do I know that name from?*

While she searched her brain for the answer, Will and Thomas were both grinning. Silly, excited grins, like they were in on a secret. Nikki'd had enough secrets and, suddenly, her irritation started to rise.

Thomas stepped a little closer. "I make motorcycles."

Suddenly it clicked. "*Grayber* motorcycles?"

"No," Zero said behind her. "Kawasaki." As soon as he said it, he ducked behind Vegan for safety.

The truck engine came to life and an unseen driver pulled away in *Extreme Makeover*: *Home Edition* fashion. Behind the truck sat eight beautiful new dirt bikes, the fresh paint shimmering like it did on the showroom floors of Grayber's shops. The pristine machines seemed slightly out of place on the dirt lot with the woods as a backdrop. They should be sitting on shiny marble floors with price tags hanging on them. Oh, who was she kidding? They should be out on trails getting the *new* worked off. Nikki felt a little gurgle of excitement. Thomas needed their help today? Eight bikes and seven of them. Eight including Will.

Thomas gave the bikes a long, appreciative look. "Normally, we test out the new line on closed courses at the plant. But, uh, I owe Will a favor, and he said the very best road test would be accomplished right here at Chadwick. That is, if we had the right riders."

Will crossed his arms over his massive chest. "You've truly shown your ability to work as a team. The boat, the train wreck, the seeker. I'm proud of you." His gaze went to Nikki. "All of you. I thought it was time for some fun."

Nikki's excitement swelled. She glanced over at Mace and whispered, "Does everyone know how to ride?"

"Yeah. Part of training as a Halfling."

"Training? You can *fly*."

"We can't always fly in and out of situations. We do have to be more discreet sometimes. Halflings train on bikes and in cars, along with a variety of weapons. We're pretty well-rounded, but we're not all as good on a motorcycle as you." He slipped his hand into hers.

"Speak for yourself, brother." The voice came from behind them, and Nikki spun because she thought it sounded like . . .

"Raven!" She started to run to him, realized how that would look, and held steady, gripping Mace's hand for strength.

Mace nodded over his shoulder toward Raven. "Go on, Nikki. We're all glad to see him." He gave her hand a squeeze, then released her.

Her feet propelled her to Raven, who was already surrounded by the other Halflings. As she stepped closer, Glimmer moved in front of her, blocking her access. Nikki halted just short of running into Glimmer's back. She hovered there a few moments, feeling foolish — and a little ticked at Glimmer, who'd obviously done it on purpose.

Nikki dropped her gaze. But then he was there, at her feet, his motorcycle boots kicking the toe of hers. "Too bad you aren't a guy," he said.

That forced her to look up.

His eyes were bright and sparkled, looking lighter and less exhausted than she'd seen in a long time. "If you were, maybe you'd be some competition for me on the trail." His face broke into a brilliant lopsided smile.

Her heart was pounding, but she cocked her head, eyes narrowed playfully on him. "And you need a lesson in manners. I'll be sure to give you one while we're out there. If I decide to let you catch up."

Mace joined the group, and he and Raven shook hands. "That's a dangerous thing, challenging a rider like Nikki."

"She doesn't scare me," Raven said.

"Yeah, well, you haven't ridden with her when a crazed maniac is on her tail."

"Anyone can ride fast when they're scared."

Winter folded her arms over her chest. "Boys are all talk. If you guys are so good, why don't you stop strutting your feathers and get on the bikes? By the end of the day, we'll see who's the best."

Nikki turned back to Thomas, who seemed to be enjoying their argument. He approached the group. "I think you need to lay down some ground rules. First man — or woman — to the river wins. The trail cuts in three directions, but all are the same distance to the river and have about the same number of obstacles. The western trail has more handlebar checks, but the eastern trail has a washboard that will rattle your brain out of your skull. The central trail, however, has its own brand of toxin thanks to a creek bed that's slick as buttered glass. Pick your poison." He pointed to the wide mouth of the trail. Through the brush you could see where it veered into three directions.

Nikki considered each and decided to go for the western trail. Handlebar checks didn't scare her — she barely slowed down for them. Her only real worry was the fact she hadn't ridden a dirt bike in years. She'd grown up on them, even did a little bit of motocross racing when she was in junior high, but karate had consumed her attention after she'd ranked in the top five at her first national tournament. At seventeen, she'd moved on to her street bike.

Thomas waited while the Halflings scoped out their plans. "Now for the rules. Wings or no wings?"

This question surprised Nikki even though Will had called them Halflings in front of Thomas. The man must be a Xian. She wondered if he was one of the ex-Halflings Mace had talked about — leaving the battle to spend life on earth with his match. There was a gold wedding band around his left ring finger.

Mace was staring at her. "No wings," he said.

"Wings are fine," she retorted and gave him a long look. A warning look.

Vegan spoke up. "No, Nikki. It wouldn't be fair to you."

"Fair to her?" Raven scoffed.

Nikki's gaze shot to him, her wide eyes giving a solid threat. He'd almost blown her secret. "No, seriously, I can still beat all of you. I mean, it's not like you're going to lift the bike and fly to the river." She laughed, stared at Raven, and watched the realization spark in his eyes.

"Well," Vegan said, trying to act tough, which for her was almost impossible. "Maybe Miss Super-Rider needs a lesson in Halfling ability. But to be fair, wings can only be used to slow down." She looked around the group until they all nodded.

"Fine," Vine mumbled. "Only to slow down."

Thomas went on. "You'll only be able to use them in the clearings anyway. It's too dense in the woods. But there are plenty of open areas and hairpin turns on each trail. If you take the western route, be cautious. The bridge is washed out near the end, and I don't recommend jumping the last hill. A few guys have tried it, but the woods on the other side are too close. Several bikes have ended up wrapped around trees. I'm serious. I want you guys to run these bikes full out, but please don't total one. That's really hard to explain to the insurance company."

They all nodded.

"Help yourselves to the gear in the truck. I brought samples of our new riding pants and leather jackets. We've changed the cut." He raised his arms shoulder high and drew his elbows together. "We added extra room at the shoulder blades to accommodate for long rides. I'd love some feedback. There are helmets for you guys as well."

After thanking Thomas, they all headed off to gather their gear. Nikki chose a black leather jacket and black leather pants. Her folks had never been able to afford high-end riding gear like this, and the soft leather was amazing against her skin. Not to mention she knew she looked awesome in the pieces she'd chosen.

She glanced at the others and found herself sizing them up. Nikki knew she had a competitive streak, but right now, she'd give her national karate trophy to beat Raven. *Maybe my competitive streak is a little deeper than I thought.*

She chose a bike and Mace settled onto the one beside her.

"I'll follow you?" he said, tossing his hair back and putting on the helmet. He looked good too.

"You'll *all* be following me," she joked, and gave him a wink.

"I mean I'll stay with you. Whichever trail you pick."

"You don't have to do that, Mace." Was he going all psycho protective on her again?

"No, I know. I ..." He looked down at the gas tank, and since she couldn't see his eyes, she grabbed the edge of his helmet and jerked it so he had to look at her. He laughed. "I really enjoy watching you ride, Nikki."

Oh. She dropped her hand from the helmet, because something about the way he said that sent a fierce spike of hot lava into her belly. Her cheeks burned so she hid inside her helmet by shoving it on quickly. "Okay, then."

"Western trail, right?" He kick-started his bike and it rumbled to life.

"How'd you know which trail I'd choose?"

"I know *you*, Nikki."

Her heart fluttered, and she wanted to scream at him because she really needed to keep her attention on beating Raven, not going all girl-mush. To lessen the effect he had on her, she revved her engine until it shook the whole bike.

"Raven will take the washboard trail. Uses his wings to lessen the bumps."

She sucked in a breath. "That's cheating. He can only use his wings to slow down."

"Trust me," Mace said.

Raven slid to a stop beside them, having taken a small lap to test out his bike. Already, fresh clumps of dirt spattered the tires and frame. "Who's up for the washboard?"

Nikki's mouth dropped open and she resisted looking over at Mace. "I have a different plan, but I'll see you at the finish line."

Raven gunned his engine hard enough to make the bike fishtail. Dust settled as he disappeared into a nearby patch of brush.

Before she went to the starting line, which really was just a wide opening to the trail, she waved at Thomas, who'd produced a clipboard and was making notes. "Have fun," he yelled.

Will stood poised at the line, using a shop towel as the starting flag. The second he dropped his arm, eight motors revved then whined as each fought for pole position on the dirt track. Nikki slid into third right behind Raven and Winter, but she pressed toward them as they slowed once they neared a section of ruts and protruding rocks. Nikki gunned her bike and didn't slow until she felt the first stone beneath her tires. This put her in second with Raven, who'd needed to back off a bit as the path narrowed before opening to the separate trails.

She cut onto the western trail as Raven took the eastern. Casting a glance behind her and past Mace, she saw Glimmer and Vine both veering to the washboard route and Vegan and Zero — who seriously was going so slow a toddler on a tricycle could fly past him — take the central route.

Nikki concentrated on the path ahead, easily navigating a creek crossing and climbing a hill that offered a panoramic view of the woods around them. She paused at the crest while she decided which path down to take, as Mace came up close behind. Several narrow trails scarred the hillside: some shot straight down, while others were less steep and cut curved lines into the valley below. She made her choice and shot a quick glance at the surrounding scenery. It was her idea of beautiful, thanks to all the mountains and valleys dissected by motorcycle trails. Heaven, she decided. This was heaven.

The far-off whine of engines snapped her back into focus, as their rumbling echoed off the mountains and valleys. She had a job to do — beat Raven to the river. Enjoying the view would have to wait for another ride.

She started down the slope. Her lips were quickly covered in a dusting of dirt, and when she licked them she tasted it. It shouldn't taste good, but it did.

They navigated the drop to the valley, and Nikki entered the woods again with Mace close behind. Climbing another hill and pausing at the top gave her a view of the washed-out bridge Thomas had talked about. The problem was obvious: to garner enough speed to jump the river below, you'd have no choice but to slam into the tree line. If she wanted to survive in one painless piece, that wasn't an option.

She was pretty certain the other riders were behind her, even if they were on other trails. Their engines sounded far off, at least, and she could see the finish line past an open field and beyond the bridge — no other bikes were approaching.

As she contemplated her next move, Mace caught up and skidded to a stop beside her. Beneath her bike, the ground rumbled. Nikki shot a look to him, then inspected her front tire, where dirt was separating from rock. "Mace, we have to get away from here! We have to — "

A rock the size of a basketball gave way beneath her front tire, causing the bike to shift. Nikki gunned the engine in an attempt to outrun the rockslide, but one rock became several and her bike was caught in the debris careening toward the ravine below. She fought to keep the motorcycle upright as stones materialized and disappeared once tossed by gravity's pull. A rock struck her ankle, but the leather of her riding boots cushioned the blow. By the time her bike stopped at the bottom, Mace was off his bike and hovering in the air above her.

"You okay?" he yelled down as dust settled around her.

"Good," she said, but her heart was pounding. "That was intense."

He chuckled. "Glad you liked it."

"How'd you get down here so quick?" But a look to the hilltop, where his bike lay on its side, answered her question. "Go get your bike. I'll wait for you."

"No. You go on and I'll catch up. You've got a race to win."

Nikki lifted her hands from the handlebars and crossed them over her chest. "Some things are more important than winning races. Now go. I'll be here."

Mace's blue eyes filled with some deep appreciation that made her ears burn in a strange but good way. This was what it meant to be a couple. To be in it together. It was an odd, new sensation, but as she waited at the bottom of the hill, hearing other bikes sail past her as they moved closer and closer to the finish line, she realized she loved it. It was better than winning. Winning was solitary. This ... this was complete.

Chapter
18

Mace pulled ahead just slightly when they reached the drop to the river. "I'll check out the best route on this side, you check the other?"

"Why don't I meet you at the bottom?" she asked. Nikki'd been doing some calculating in her head. The jump across the bridge was possible only if she had a way to slow her stop before hitting the trees on the other side. But no one has breaks in midair. Except her. And she was going to use them.

She paused at the crest of the hill and looked down into the clearing below. The other Halflings were already there. Why hadn't they crossed the clearing and passed the finish line? The only reason Nikki could think of was they'd decided to run out the last bit together in a sprint race to the end.

"All right," Mace said, and started down one of the trails to the bottom.

Nikki recalculated one last time. If she jumped the bridge, she'd sail right over the Halflings waiting in the clearing, land on the other side, and cross the finish line ahead of all of them. The temptation was too great to resist.

Mace pulled to a stop beside Raven, who looked behind with a shrug of one shoulder. "When's your biker chick planning to join us?"

"We separated at the crest of the hill. She's headed down the side where the ..."

"Where the what?"

Mace didn't answer. *She wouldn't.* He turned to stare at the washed-out bridge and the hillside beyond it. He could hear the whine of Nikki's bike engine; it sounded wide open, which meant —

Less than a heartbeat later her bike crested the final ramp that would send her airborne over their heads.

"Look!" Raven yelled.

Nikki took the ramp like a pro, tires straight and smooth, and a second later she was above them. All seven Halflings watched as Nikki sailed over. But awe quickly turned to panic when Vegan yelled, "Nikki! The trees!"

Nikki snapped her wings open, and gasps filled the air around Mace. Stretched out alongside her bike were the most brilliantly beautiful red wings trapped between sky and sunlight. She angled them, and the momentum of her bike slowed as her feathers fought the wind.

Vegan was now screaming excited words that got lost in the others' jumbled yells. Behind Mace, Winter's voice broke through. "I knew it. I just knew there was something different about her when she returned."

Nikki landed on the other side and slid to a stop just short of the tree line and a good fifty feet from the finish line. She removed her helmet and shook out her hair before turning toward the group with a "What did you think of that?" glint in her eye.

Glimmer clapped wildly, Zero gave her a thumbs-up, and Vegan was off her bike, jumping up and down squealing.

Nikki's face broke into a sunbeam-strength smile.

A grin Mace understood. She finally felt like she belonged, like she was a part of their group. Maybe now she could move forward with her life and ditch the whole idea of poking into her past. Mace hoped so, because one thing he knew: Rummaging around in her past would bring nothing but pain and offered nothing but death.

Early the next morning, Nikki took Mace's car and drove down County Road 182. Though nearly forty miles from home, she knew these back roads from motorcycle trips last summer. Gold-polished nails — compliments of Glimmer — winked at her as they caught the sunlight. The ride the day before hadn't wrecked the prissy manicure like she thought ... which was both good and bad, because she sort of liked looking down and seeing golden jewels at the end of her fingers but sort of hated how girly liking them felt. Kind of the same divided feeling she'd had after the ride yesterday — being on the bikes had been awesome, though at the end of the day, there were still questions that needed answers. Late last night she'd decided it was time to take a road trip and confront Zero.

The first time Mace took her to the underground, she'd

slept most of the way. He'd covered her eyes when they left, but not before she got a good glimpse of the area.

Sneaking out of the house early this morning proved no easy feat due to Will keeping such close tabs on her. But she'd managed, and now, after making ridiculously long circles on back trails, she arrived at Zero's lair.

A big part of her wanted to turn back. Answers often meant consequences, and she was still getting used to the idea of being a Halfling. It wouldn't be easy to deal with being a mutant. After all, isn't that what they'd said the horses at Vessler's lab were? Genetically mutated creatures. Maybe that's why her wings were blood red when they showed up. She'd also being thinking a lot about her childhood lately. Nikki was positive her mom and dad weren't Xians — she'd never gone to church or even cracked a Bible before meeting Mace and Raven, so if the Throne had chosen them as her caregivers, he'd made a big mistake. They also didn't look like Halflings at all. And yet Halflings came from Halflings, so if she was her parents' child, she must have started as a regular baby. Then there was the fact her name had been in the database Zero recovered from Vessler's lab. Too many things pointed in the same direction. Vessler mutated her into a Halfling — it was the only thing that made sense. And that meant she wasn't a Halfling at all.

She navigated the underground's stairs and tunnel without bothering to turn on the lights. Each metal step clicked as she descended, tiny little warnings to turn back. At the bottom, she mustered her courage and knocked on the metal door. She waited, knocked again. And again and again for a full five minutes until Zero answered.

"Did you think I would just eventually give up?" she asked, stepping past him before he offered her entrance.

He wore shorts with ducks all over them and a rumpled T-shirt with a roll of toilet paper on it. Emblazoned across the chest it said *Just how I roll*.

She looked him up and down. "Nice," she mumbled, a smile tugging at her lips.

"Sorry, I already bought Girl Scout cookies." He continued to hold the door open. "So, thanks for stopping by, and maybe try my neighbor about three hundred miles west of here."

"Cute, Zero. Don't you want your present?"

She reached into her backpack and shook the package at him. "Juice boxes."

Zero licked his lips. His hair was a mass of white-blond sprigs sticking out everywhere.

She rattled the gift again. "The newest flavor. Watermelon Zinger."

Zero lurched at her but missed. He crossed his arms in a huff. "What do you want?"

She dragged a box from the package and tossed it to him. "Answers."

He snagged it in the air, tore off the straw's plastic covering, and shoved the straw into the small hole. Pink liquid squirted onto his arm. He grumbled and lifted the drink to his lips. "I'm sworn to secrecy."

She dropped into his computer chair and spun it around to face him. "So there *is* more to the story."

He held up a finger. "Didn't say that."

"I'm not a real Halfling, Zero." Hearing the words from her own mouth, Nikki fought the onset of tears. Her cheeks tingled. She busied herself with a juice box. She slid the straw in easily and handed the drink to Zero, who'd just finished the first one.

"Of course you are."

"No, I'm a freak."

He choked on a laugh, and Watermelon Zinger spewed from his nose. "We're all freaks, baby girl. Take a closer look." He leaned on a counter opposite her. "Besides, what makes you so special?"

"What?" she said.

"What's wrong with being a Halfling? We're kind of cool. I mean, yeah, sure, we may rot in hell for eternity once our time here is done."

She felt queasy.

"Sorry, I, uh, didn't think about ..." He lifted his hands, dropped them. "You're kind of immortal now. Well," he corrected, "unless someone kills you."

Her head pounded. It was too early in the morning for talk like this.

"Look on the bright side," he said.

Her eyes found his. "Which is?"

He gestured toward her but didn't speak. Moments passed, his hand still hanging in the air. Finally, he dropped it. "You're right. Stinks to be you." He snagged another drink, wrestled with the straw, squirted more liquid, and handed her the sticky mess. "Why don't they invent a better system for these stupid things?" He swiped his hands on his duck-emblazoned shorts. "Look, you want answers, Will has them. Talk to him. Let him know you're ready."

"Ready?"

"To hear the truth. You can take it. You're a big girl."

Her eyes narrowed playfully. "I thought I was a baby girl?"

"Nah. Not so much."

"I just can't talk to Will."

"Why not?"

"He makes me feel really ..."

Zero motioned with his hand for her to continue.

"Childish."

He laughed out loud. "He is sort of older and wiser than you. Like reeeeaaaally older and —"

She pressed a hand to her throbbing temple. "I get it."

She'd been stupid to come here. He wasn't going to talk. She'd have to pin Will down, and the crazy thing was she might have known that all along. Maybe she'd avoided talking to Will because once she asked she'd actually have to know. Nikki chewed her lip. "Is it bad, Zero?"

"Is what bad?"

Ugh. Did she have to spell it out? "You know, the truth about me."

He took a long drink, stared at the ceiling. "Yeah, it's bad."

Something dropped in her stomach. *Okay, time to go.*

Zero pointed to her throat. "Vegan give you that?"

Her hand fell lovingly to the amulet. "Yes. She's a special girl — uh, Halfling."

Zero tugged at his collar and produced a similar trinket. "She really is."

Keagan Townsend perched on a hilltop above the rocky country road. Nikki Youngblood's head fell into the scope of his sniper rifle. "I have a visual on the target, Mr. Vessler." Seeing her again caused a sensation that coursed through his body like a Tabasco cocktail. It was the familiar hunger for fresh blood. He willed his breathing to slow. Fingers trembling, he licked his lips, hoping, praying that Vessler would change his mind and let him take the shot.

Through the headset, Vessler's voice hummed. "She's a good girl, our Nikki."

Townsend barely heard. The girl filled his vision. He imagined hovering over her lifeless body. He envisioned hunting her, chasing her, and, finally, the sweet reward of death.

Vessler's angry tone snapped Keagan's attention to the present. "Did you hear me, Townsend? Leave the girl. She has to come to me by her own will."

Townsend sneered and dropped her from his scope.

"Just pick up the bait," Vessler ordered.

Chapter
19

W hat now?" Zero yelled through the metal door. He'd just drained the last juice box and wished he had a few more. Watermelon Zinger might be the best flavor yet.

Nikki knocked again, this time harder. He shuffled to the front door, mumbling, "Annoying females. Don't they know a guy needs his privacy?" The thought of females brought Vegan to the forefront of his mind.

Hand on the knob, he smiled. Vegan would bring him a case of Watermelon Zinger; all he had to do was ask. She'd breeze through the front door and drop her brows when she noticed all the frozen dinner boxes. Then, she'd always say, "It's time for you to get out of here. Get some air! Stretch your wings!" And she'd grab his hand and tug, dragging him to the river to wade. One day, he was going to get in the water with her.

Bang! Bang! Bang! The pounding on the door startled him so much his hand flew from the knob. He pulled the door open. "Look, Nikki—"

Keagan Townsend stood there instead with a sadistic grin. "Were we expecting a playmate?"

Zero slammed his shoulder against the door, throwing all his strength into the movement. Just before the heavy metal sealed shut, he caught a glimpse of the shock registered on Townsend's face.

Keagan Townsend: one of Vessler's favorite hit men. Zero and Vegan had found his name and photo in an unprotected file they jacked from Omega Corporation.

Zero bolted the locks while Townsend's voice filtered through the cracks around the door frame.

"Think, think," Zero said to himself, heart hammering in his chest. "Come on, you've run a thousand drills for this." He stopped, closed his eyes, and drew a deep breath. As he exhaled, the plan rushed into his mind.

Bang! Bang! Bang! Sounded like Townsend was throwing his own weight against the door.

Zero shoved clothes and trash off the trunk by the computer desk. He grabbed the giant magnets inside the crate and rubbed them across his work center. *So much work. So much time lost.* But erasing the hard drive, files, everything would send an instant alert to anyone logged into the network. One that only lasted a few seconds before fading to nothing. He'd wired the network to shut down three seconds after infiltration or — as in this circumstance — compromise. Thinking back on it, he wished he'd built in a little more time. Five seconds. Maybe ten. One minute. What if no one was on the network right now? He forced his mind to the task at hand and threw a glance toward the entrance.

Townsend would eventually get through, but not by slamming a fragile human shoulder into sheets of metal. "Keep it up, moron," he said when Townsend pounded again.

From the other side, he heard a scream. Townsend yelled a stream of curses.

"Do you kiss your momma with that potty mouth?" Zero chuckled while his hands trembled at the keyboard. From the sound, the fool had probably just dislocated his shoulder. Good. That should buy a little time.

Two minutes later and exhausted, Zero did a mental checklist. Yep. Everything gone. He carried his laptop to the bathroom, dropped it into the toilet for good measure, and headed back to get the Mac. Gunshots erupted, echoing off the tunnel walls. The door dimpled and finally swung open.

Zero snapped his wings open to leap, but was stopped when a metal wingcuff zipped around his midsection. It clamped down, squeezing his lungs. He wrestled against it, trying to thread his fingers beneath the metal. He'd heard about these weapons but had never been in one. The thin titanium sheet spread about sixteen inches wide, designed with the purpose of keeping Halflings from snapping their wings open. No wings, no leap, no escape. *Man, at least Superman got Kryptonite, a rare* alien *material.* Titanium was so easily accessible, humans were making everything from jewelry to cell phone covers from the stuff. The Halflings already knew Vessler was shipping loads of it stateside. They'd intercepted a couple of those loads. But still, there was probably enough titanium to make a wingcuff for every Halfling on the planet. The thought scared him more than the inability to move.

Townsend rubbed his upper arm and entered the building, casting narrow-eyed glances around the room.

"What's the matter? Scared of a locked-up Halfling?"

He spat in Zero's direction and continued his cautious steps.

"Don't worry, I work alone." Zero rocked back on his heels,

watching the scared little human, and opted not to focus on the gun dangling from the end of his hand. "Did you hurt your shoulder?" He tilted his head, sarcasm lacing his words. "Ah, that's too bad. You humans are just so" — he grinned — "easily broken."

One man posed no threat to a Halfling. One man holding an automatic weapon with armor-piercing rounds did. Zero knew he should tread carefully. Too bad the desire to do so escaped him. "It was nice of you to drop by." He plastered a phony smile on his face. "But I'm afraid I already made a donation to your organization."

Townsend's brows drew together.

"Your organization." Zero knew he'd hooked Townsend. "You know, the one for men who are too stupid and ugly for even their mothers to love."

Townsend closed the distance, drew back, and swung.

Cold metal struck the side of Zero's face. He'd seen it coming, but with arms locked beneath the titanium, there was nothing he could do. He didn't try to lean away from the hit; instead, his head slammed to the side. He ran his tongue over the inside of his bleeding cheek. When his eyes shifted back to Townsend, he grinned again. "I guess you don't know much about Halflings," he mocked. "We're tough. Don't get me wrong, I'm sure you've been practicing, but that felt like a nasty bee sting." He thought a moment. "Maybe not a nasty sting … more like a kiss from a sweat bee."

The blow fell again, this time with more force. Zero smiled past the pain. He wouldn't dare give Townsend the satisfaction of knowing it hurt.

Townsend dragged him from the lair and into the light. That stung his swollen eye. And as they left his compound behind, Zero realized he needed to get a message out somehow. The whole three-second network warning seemed a really stupid idea at this point. But it was all he had. Unless he could think of something else.

He tripped once on his way to the yellow Hummer and went down hard, landing on his knee. Pain sliced up and felt like it split his leg in two. He realized just how human titanium could make him feel. He'd watched football players and guys on soccer fields fall and overreact, screaming and grabbing their legs after a knee injury. Now, he understood.

Townsend tossed him into the backseat, clamped a chain around his ankles for good measure, and locked it by running the chain through the door handle. So much for jumping from the car. If he did, he'd be dragged. Zero wasn't vain or anything, but the idea of having his flesh peeled by asphalt just didn't have an appeal.

Before long, they arrived at the Omega Corp laboratory. Zero knew more abuse was sure to follow and tried to brace himself.

The interior of the lab was about what he'd expected. He knew they'd have state-of-the-art equipment and hadn't been wrong. Everything from computers to medical apparatuses dominated the space — all shiny new and gleaming with the slightly futuristic look of gear that wasn't on the market yet.

As a way of saying hello, they'd slammed him around and locked him — in titanium brackets, of course — onto a slab of a table. Scientists poked and prodded him, then injected something into his arm that caused everything to go a little dreamy. His eyes blurred and he fought it, but his vision refused to locate any specific object, choosing to pulse to a total haze then return to semi-focused details. People in white coats, medical equipment on metal poles, all a foggy distortion. Zero fought panic as the white-coated personnel then dragged him from the examination table and tossed him onto the floor where a trio of thugs — whose waist size and IQ probably hovered around the same number — beat him mercilessly. These weren't scientists, just Vessler's hired muscle.

Wounds healed; some quickly, some taking time. But with each passing hour, Zero worried a little more. What if he'd missed something? If information about the network leaked, it posed a threat to every Halfling on the planet. He tried to retrace his steps but blows to his head caused a haze of memories that he wasn't sure were real or imagined. He'd dropped the laptop in the toilet. That he remembered with vivid clarity. The rest, who knew?

Around him, a hospital-white room held computers, medical equipment, and long counters. White-coated, clipboard-cradling science dweebs oohed and aahed with each bone-crushing blow like he was some new species just discovered ... which to them, technically he was. Occasionally, they would make notes on their clipboards or on a computer screen.

These guys are sick.

"I bet you're just upset that you didn't win the beauty pageant," he said when the middle guy paused to catch his breath after a battery of blows. Zero figured his ribs must be broken, because the words came out in a whisper and it felt like a knife blade jutted from his side.

The man answered with a kick to the thigh.

Zero clenched his teeth to keep from groaning. *Ugh. That hurts like flying full force into a mountainside.*

A ringed fist caught his jaw. He squeezed his eyes shut and concentrated on Vegan. Her face, her scent. Vegan preferred to go barefoot, and she kept her toes polished with soft colors.

Often, they walked the woods to the lake's edge. She'd roll up her pant legs and wade carelessly through the water. From the bank, he'd watch tiny fish swim up to her, drawn by her heavenly essence. They'd bump against her ankle and she'd giggle and wiggle her toes, then beckon him to come out with her. But he'd always said no. Even through the cloud of excruciating pain, he could see Vegan's warm smile and hand beckoning to him on the bank.

When another punch landed in his neck, tears welled in his eyes. Not that the humans noticed. They were busy finding the best ways to pummel him, their sweat sprinkling him like their own personal Total Gym. The stench of body odor filled his nose, replacing the scent of Vegan and all that was good in the world. Bits of their perspiration dried on his cheeks. Good. He didn't want them to know he'd cried.

Halflings *could* die. It was possible. The bad thing about his body having self-healing ability was that just when he thought he couldn't take any more, he'd heal and they'd begin the assault all over again. He was too wounded to snap his wings open, and when they'd realized that they'd removed the wing-cuff, allowing for more body targets. It didn't matter. He was too weak to even move.

He wasn't sure if he'd die here or not. If he did, at least he'd protected the network.

Zero runs the network. He remembered the day he'd received the commission.

Zero runs the network. He relished the memory, the honor. Another tear blurred his vision. If he made it out of this place alive, he planned to do two things:

He'd run the network.

And he'd wade in the stream with Vegan.

Chapter
20

"Y ou love him, don't you?" Nikki said, lifting one of Vegan's newly crafted necklaces to inspect the design. Vegan had set up a makeshift workspace in Nikki's room — which Nikki hadn't minded at all, because it was fun to watch Vegan work the cords and beads into jewelry. Besides, Nikki wanted them all to believe she was settling in to her new home . . . her new life . . . her new species. What she didn't want was everyone wondering if she'd run away again to go after Vessler. The Halflings trusted her, of this she was certain. That didn't change the fact she wanted answers about her past, her parents, and, well, on more than one occasion she'd acted impetuously and had left the Halflings out of the loop, especially occasions concerning her godfather. Vegan hadn't answered her query, so Nikki spoke again. "You love him, right?"

Vegan's eyes rounded and her cheeks flushed, a nice compliment to her rosy-colored shirt. She slipped her feet from her sandals. "Who?"

"Zero. I see the way you look at him. How he looks at you."

Vegan stood and paced. "Oh. We're just friends."

"Right."

"He looks at me like an annoying kid sister." She traversed the room a few times, then sank onto the bed with a frown.

Nikki sat beside her. "When you're not looking, he gets all mushy-eyed."

Vegan gasped. "He does?" She tucked her feet beneath her.

"He's toast." Nikki held up her pinky. "You've *so* got him wrapped around your finger."

Vegan giggled. The sound was like a thousand fairy wings flittering in an enchanted forest.

Nikki glanced down and was aware of her sloppy posture compared to Vegan's regal one.

"What?" Vegan leaned closer. "What's wrong?"

Nikki motioned toward her. "You. Not *you*, personally. Just … you, Glimmer, and Winter. You're like perfect heavenly creatures. I don't even have decent posture."

"But you do have wings." Vegan smiled. "You're one of us."

She tucked her hair back. "Uh, yeah, right. I'm more like the hillbilly cousin no one talks about."

Vegan laughed. "You make me smile, Nikki. And I'm proud to have you in my family. I'm proud to call you sister."

Proud. Really? What had she ever done to warrant that? Nikki's eyes puddled. "But I'm not." She reached for Vegan's hand. "Don't get me wrong, you guys have done everything in your power to welcome me. But Vegan, I know there's something really dark about my past, though I've yet to figure out what that is. And no one seems to want to talk about it. I was going to ask Will, but every time I start to, I clam up."

Vegan swallowed, gold flecks flickering as her gaze dropped.

"You know, don't you?" Nikki tightened her grip on Vegan's hand. "Please, tell me."

"It's not my place. Will—"

Nikki sprang from the bed. "Will this and Will that. I'm tired of waiting for Will to decide for me, and I'm too much of a coward to ask him." Her hand covered her heart. "My parents are gone. Dead. And now I have you guys, but everyone knows more about my past than me."

Vegan brushed her hand back and forth across the bedspread.

A long exhale escaped Nikki's lips. "You aren't going to tell me, are you?"

"I'm sorry," Vegan whispered, her eyes begging forgiveness. "Besides, does it really matter? I mean, look at *us*. We're orphans, but we're not. We have parents, but don't get to know them. What I'm trying to say is, embrace who you are *now*. Not who you were. You've been chosen for the great war. There's no higher honor in this world or any other. You, Nikki. Chosen by the Throne. Don't you think that's what should matter, rather than the pieces of your past?"

Nikki dropped onto the bed again. "But then what?" With bent knee, she pivoted to study Vegan's face. "What happens after ... you know."

"After we die? Well, we don't have a writ like the humans do."

"A writ?"

Vegan smiled. "Oh, sorry. A written word. A covenant."

"Yeah, they're safe and we're dogmeat." It was hard for Nikki to imagine a being who would call someone into service then reject them. And yet Vegan seemed so sure about the future, so confident.

"It's not like that. Some spiritual laws pertain to every living creature."

"What do you mean?" Nikki asked.

"Things like seed time and harvest, sowing and reaping. You don't have to coax a seed to grow. You plant it in the ground and everything around it works in harmony to produce a plant — that's seed time and harvest. A sunflower seed won't produce an apple tree — that's sowing and reaping."

"Okay, thanks for the lesson on spiritual laws. It's good to know." Nikki grabbed her by the shoulders. "But Vegan *what happens to us?*"

"We've made a choice to serve the Throne. In knowing his nature, we assume that on the Great and Terrible Day of Judgment, we'll be allowed entrance into heaven, though we may never be able to enter the holy city or the Throne Room because of our ancestors."

"Wow, hillbilly cousin again." Nikki's hands dropped to her sides.

"No. Heaven isn't like that, nor is the one who created it. He made room for us. I'm sure he did, Nikki. Just as sure as I know a seed will grow if it's placed in the ground." She paused a moment. "At the same time, he can't go back on his word. That would make him a liar. Our ancestors, the fallen, were never to enter the Great Kingdom again."

"Are you telling me God found a loophole in his own contract?"

"He flung the stars into the sky and told them to stay, and they do to this day." Her eyes glistened with an adoration for this being that Nikki couldn't quite grasp. "No. He didn't find a loophole. He knows the end from the beginning. I think he made the concession at the beginning of time when he was still measuring out the waters of the seas."

"You're saying he made a concession before one was needed? That sort of staggers the mind, doesn't it?"

Vegan's eyes widened. "Indeed. His desire is that none perish. Even the hillbilly cousins. But there's a delicate balance he has to maintain as well. The Fallen mated with human women in an attempt to destroy the bloodline."

"Destroy it how?"

"Maybe *destroy* isn't the right word. It's more like *infect it*. The fallen angels wanted to corrupt the human bloodline by introducing fallen blood. God could have just wiped them and all their offspring off the face of the earth. But he didn't." Vegan smiled. "Because he knew one day Nikki Youngblood would be born. And he already loved her. He made a way for us, Nikki. He called us into service because he loves us. We're the ultimate army."

"Thanks, Vegan. I've never looked at God like that." Silence followed while Nikki contemplated the goodness of a creator who would make concessions for offspring of the very beings sent to destroy his plan. "I just don't understand why God created people if he knew what a huge mess they were all going to end up in."

"Because they're worth it."

Nikki'd had enough of this conversation. It was too much to try to grasp when she was still so new to all of it. "Have you talked to Zero today?"

"On the phone early this morning. I plan to stop by later."

"Be sure and take a package of Watermelon Zinger juice boxes. He loves them."

Vegan's brows rose. "Did you try to bribe him?"

"Yeah, snuck out this morning."

"And?"

She shrugged. "And nothing. He's as tight-lipped as you."

"Remember, Nikki, concentrate on who you are now. Not who you were." Vegan rose and slipped her dainty pink toes into her equally delicate sandals. Who would ever guess at the immortal weapon she actually was? Gliding across the carpet as if she were floating, Vegan left the room.

Nikki sat alone in the quiet space. Though the other girl's suggestions about leaving the past alone rang true, the desire to know outweighed it. Damon knew the truth. But no matter how desperate she became, she'd never go to him for the answers. He'd hurt her for the last time.

A sound interrupted her thoughts. A ringing that came from the corner where her backpack sat. Nikki frowned and took a couple steps toward it.

It stopped momentarily, then began again. She dug inside and found a cell phone, and wondered where it had come from. She'd ditched her last one eons ago. When she could stand it no longer, she answered. "Hello."

Vessler's voice crackled through the line, and Nikki nearly dropped the phone.

"We didn't get to finish what we started, Nikki."

His voice crawled through the receiver, setting her skin on alert. Twinges danced and tingled across her shoulder blades. "I have nothing to say to you." Her voice was flat. Dead.

"Really, my lady? Don't be cross. We have much to share. And there is still much work to be done."

"How'd you get this phone into my backpack?" The idea that Vessler had access to her was more than unnerving. Instinctively, she shot a look to the window and the world beyond as if he'd be there, on the other side of the glass. Fury erupted in her gut. "How are your legs?" She just couldn't resist the reference to their last encounter, when she'd incapacitated him with two well-placed bullets.

"Practically healed."

Nikki worked to keep her voice steady as her body began to shudder. "Gunshot wounds don't heal that fast."

"Ah, the miracles of modern medicine."

No, it was impossible. She'd watched as each shot sank into his body, creating a spurt, then a wide wet section of blood down one pant leg then the other. The wounds had nearly drained his lifeblood. No way — even with the very best medicine — could he have healed. Raven had once suggested that Vessler was on some kind of hyper-powered steroids. Maybe he was right.

She started to hang up, but a whimper in the background caught her attention. "What is that?"

"What?" Vessler asked, innocently. "Oh, that sound? That's Zero. He says to tell you hello, and the next time you want to come visit, don't. You're much too easy to follow. He says to bring drink boxes — the Watermelon Zinger you bought this morning at the grocery store would be wonderful."

Her heart sank into her stomach and the blood drained with it, leaving black splotches before her eyes. No. *No.* What had she done?

Muffled words echoed through the phone line. "Don't tell him anything, Nikki. He can't hurt me."

"Can't hurt you? Really?" Damon said with a grunt.

Zero yelped in pain.

Her hand flew to her mouth, where she stifled a cry. Her heartbeat intensified until it drowned Zero's voice. Slamming her fist onto the bed, she pleaded, "Damon, let Zero go. Please, he can't help you." She chewed her lip, gripping the phone with both hands. "Look at him. He's the weakest Halfling alive."

From beyond Vessler's phone, she heard Zero's weak voice. "Thanks a lot, Nikki."

"True," Vessler conceded. "He's weak. Not like you. You possess the strength of an army."

"So, you'll let him go?" Hope dared enter her heart.

"Sure. If you'll come and take his place. And if you tell the others, I'll kill him."

Nikki's breathing matched her heart rate while her mind spun, searching for solutions. Zero ran the network. His life was worth more than ten of Nikki's. He's the hub, the link that keeps Halflings connected all over the world. Zero was gold … and she was paper.

Her eyes slid shut. "Yes," she agreed. "I'll come."

Chapter
21

I'm just saying that male Halflings are stronger than females. That's all." Vine shrugged and took another bite of a hot dog.

Winter sighed. If Vine thought he'd convince the three females, he was clueless.

Will chuckled and turned the meat on the backyard grill. "Vine, I'm going to give you a piece of advice. Having lived for thousands of years, I've learned one universal rule that has transcended eras and ethnicities. Never tell a female she's weaker." Glimmer and Winter both nodded agreement from their sunny perches, stretched out in chaise lounges.

The girls spent most of their waking hours on the back porch now, or congregated in the living room or backyard with the other Halflings, waiting for the faintest scent of trouble. Winter, even though she was better with patience than the other two girls, was starting to feel somewhat like a caged animal — no battle, no hell hounds to fight.

Vegan caressed a wilted plant in a terra-cotta pot.

The enemy had been extremely quiet. And that fact didn't bode well with Will, Winter could tell. He'd been around too long, seen too much, to look at this as a reprieve.

"That's the stupidest thing I've ever heard." Glimmer stood, took a hot dog Will offered, and dropped her free hand onto a cocked hip.

Uh-oh. Vine was about to get a lesson in girl power. Will stifled a grin and shared a *poor, innocent Vine* look with Winter.

Vine shrugged. "It's obvious males are stronger." His attention was on his lunch, and with his head down he smeared the bun with ketchup.

Glimmer's eyes leveled on him. "Is that so?" Her voice deepened to lethal.

The tone brought his head up with a snap. A storm swirled in Glimmer's gaze.

Hot dog half hanging from his mouth, he chewed quickly and swallowed hard. "Uh." His eyes flashed an SOS to Will.

Will raised his palms as if to say, "You got yourself into this, get yourself out."

Vine set the rest of his dog on his plate and rose. "I didn't mean anything by it. It's just that —"

Glimmer stepped closer, cutting off his exit. "That what?"

He stumbled back a step. Off balance, he plopped into the chair. "Um. Just that ..." His gaze darted around the back patio looking for help. But Glimmer, Winter, and Vegan outnumbered him, and Will was neutral. Vine's only possibly ally, Raven, had disappeared inside to get a root beer.

"Well, males were originally angels. And the females were human. So, I mean, it makes sense. Angels are stronger than humans." His flashed a quick smile, hoping he'd diffused the situation.

"So true," Glimmer agreed, sweetly. She batted her eyes, just before they turned to ice. "Let's go out in the yard and put your ideas to the test."

"I wouldn't," Raven said, stepping onto the patio with a half grin on his face. "Don't let that little-boy-lost demeanor fool you. Vine is an expert warrior. One of the best I've ever seen."

Vine threw him a grateful look that replaced the deer-in-the-headlights one.

Vegan, who'd been watering the nearly dead potted plant, placed the greenery on the porch. "Glimmer is a marksman. With bow and arrow, she can nail any target from over a hundred yards away."

Raven laughed and dropped into one of the deck chairs. He popped the top on his root beer. "That's got to be helpful in hand-to-hand combat," he said, wryly, and slurped the liquid from the can. "Which, by the way, is what we're involved in nine times out of ten. For those of us who've *seen* much battle."

Glimmer drew a quick gulp of air. "We've seen plenty of battle. Haven't we, Winter?"

"Like Will, I'm staying out of this one."

Raven's lips curled into a sadistic grin. "I'm sure you've seen plenty, Glimmer. From your safe hundred-yard distance. Look, we've seen you fight. Honestly, you could stand to brush up a little."

Vegan faced off with Raven, Glimmer with Vine. Four perfect bodies, taut and ready to fight. Will shook his head while electricity crackled on the patio. If anyone were walking by, they'd swear an actual storm brewed around the Victorian home. Will heaved a breath. "Teenagers," he mumbled. But the skirmish was interrupted when Mace threw the patio door open. "Has anyone seen Nikki?"

Winter stood. "Yes. Two hours ago she told me she was going to lie down for a while. She's in her room."

"No, she's not."

Zero wouldn't cry again — he'd promised himself. For countless hours, they'd taken turns beating him and he could feel life slipping away. He tried to wriggle his fingers. *Yes, still working.*

A cold, concrete floor inside a jail cell-sized cage was his new home. The entire room had finally emptied of people, and he was alone. He tipped his head up in an attempt to assess the extent of his injuries. Every muscle ached with each breath, but he willed himself to draw the next. He could taste blood through lips too swollen to be his own. His limbs were bruised and maybe some were broken. Wounds took longer and longer to heal. *This is worse than death.*

After the last beating, he'd been thrown behind the thick metal bars. Titanium, of course. Sitting on the floor beyond the cage, and just beyond his reach, was a glass of water. He scooted painfully to the bars, lugging his dead weight. He couldn't move his lower body, so he pulled himself forward with his hands, dragging his legs behind him like a kite tail.

Am I paralyzed? He forced the terrifying thought from his mind. *Zero, the gimpy-legged Halfling.* As if he wasn't enough of a misfit already.

At the bars, his head fell forward until it was resting against the cool metal. He could feel the titanium zapping what strength he had, but the water was so close. He squeezed his eyes shut and tried to concentrate on Vegan. He couldn't access her face. Or her laugh. With his eyes closed, all he saw was fist after fist coming at him, paired with the clatter of bones cracking and breaking, and the scent of blood.

A chair scraping the floor drew his attention. He turned his sore neck toward the noise.

Expensive, pointed-toe shoes. Perfectly worn-in jeans. Until the guy squatted — putting himself at Zero's level. *If only I could raise my head enough to make out a face.* The guy must have been in the chair until he'd come closer, quietly sitting there watching the Halfling suffer. Now he was about five feet away, sitting on his haunches and studying his captive.

"We haven't been properly introduced. I'm Damon Vessler," the man said, hands planted on his knees. His gaze roamed over Zero. "Oh dear. It would seem as though my boys got out of hand. I'm terribly sorry." He smiled as if apologizing for bumping into someone at the grocery store. "Now" — he tilted back slightly — "you must be the one they call Zero. I hear you run the network."

Zero swallowed dry, sandpaper air and glanced at the glass of water.

"Would you like that?" Vessler pointed. "Tell you what, share a bit of information with me and I'll give you the water."

"Give me the water," Zero rasped. "And I'll use the glass to slit your throat."

Vessler's nostrils flared. "You're not playing very nice." He pulled a gold toothpick from his shirt pocket and slid it into his mouth. "Doesn't *Zero* mean *nothing*?" Vessler's eyes flashed. "One minus one?"

"Yeah," Zero said in a hoarse whisper. "And you want

information from me. What does that make you?" He chuckled, winced. "Oh, I know. Less than Zero."

Vessler shoved off the floor. Smooth leather shoes stepped toward the glass of water. Drawing back, he kicked it at Zero.

Glass shattered when it hit the bars. He closed his eyes in time to avoid the shards as they flew at him. Water and bits of broken glass splashed his face.

"What was all that computer equipment doing in your underground space? Is that where you run the network?" Vessler demanded. "And what's the network's purpose?"

Zero sucked the bits of water from his lips. "Computers? Is that what those were? I thought they were just bulky paperweights."

Vessler erupted. "Don't play games with me, boy!"

Zero grinned. "That's Lost Boy."

Vessler strode to the bars, grabbed Zero's arms, and yanked. Zero's head clanged against the titanium, sending a shock wave through his already-aching system. Again, he tried to conjure the image of Vegan.

Vessler grabbed him by the throat. "Tell me what you know."

Choking, Zero tried to pry his fingers beneath Vessler's powerful hand. Vessler squeezed harder.

Black spots materialized before his eyes. Everything started to fade … fade … "All right," he said, words barely a whisper. "I'll tell you."

Vessler dropped to his knees to look Zero eye to eye. "What do you know?"

"I know …" Zero rubbed a hand across his throat. "I know …"

Vessler's gaze was wild as he visibly held his breath.

"I know … zero." He slid back from the bars before Vessler could grab him.

Vessler roared and thrust his arm through the bars. Face wedged against the titanium, he managed to snag Zero's collar and the necklace beneath, using both to drag him back to the bars. After manacling Zero's wrists, Vessler dropped to the floor, pressed his feet against the cage, and jerked Zero's head into the bars again and again.

Slam after slam, Zero felt metal smash his face and collarbone. Finally, Vessler stopped, focusing with terrifying steadiness on the necklace from Vegan. Zero began reconsidering his vow not to bawl, because if Vessler knew how to use the necklace, Vegan could be drawn into this pit as well. Zero couldn't let that happen. He had to protect her.

"What's this?" Vessler asked, back to his sorry-I-bumped-into-you-at-the-grocery-store voice. "Did your mother make that for you?"

Zero's face, arms, and shoulder hurt so bad he thought every bone must be shattered. But how could he resist such an opportunity? "News flash, Einstein. We're orphans." He coughed. Searing pain jolted him with each movement. "Gotta hand it to you on the beating, though. You're pretty strong. Bet you're taking steroids." He tsked. "Nasty thing, those steroids, but I hear all Halfling wannabes do them."

Vessler shook with anger.

"Hey, I don't blame you. If I was just a human, I'd be upset too. Can't leap, can't fly. No ability to heal yourself. It's okay that you want to be like us. It's just sad that you never will. Sorry, poser."

Vessler's nostrils flared.

"Poser. You know, someone who *poses* as something they're not. Halfling wannabe. Or should I just call you Wannaling?"

Vessler's veins began popping from his neck and arms. He

grabbed the necklace from Zero's throat and threw it to the floor. "You know nothing of my plan."

The pearled amulet broke. Thank the Throne; Zero would rather die than put Vegan in harm's way. "Really, Vessler? I know you're genetically altering horses."

"And do you know why?" Vessler dragged the chair over and sat. "Technology is a dangerous partner. It can let you down if you become too dependent on it."

Zero glanced behind Vessler, where a line of computers and medical equipment sat at the ready. "For a guy who doesn't like technology, you certainly have enough of it surrounding you."

"For a purpose. Technology is destined to implode. And do you know what will matter most when it does?"

"Enlighten me," Zero said, coughed, then pressed a hand to his ribs to block the pain shooting through them.

"Whoever carries the biggest sticks."

Zero rolled his eyes. "Right. And mutant horses can carry really big sticks. Do you want to call the loony bin or should I?" Every inch of him hurt, but if he could keep Vessler talking, maybe he'd reveal his plan.

"The horses will carry my army of Darklings."

Zero scoffed. "*Darklings?* Are you kidding me?" But on the inside, his heart dropped. This is how Nikki fit into Vessler's plan. And the horses made some sense, in a way. But Vessler wasn't telling all his secrets, because horses against tanks ... well, no chance there. His mind went back to the technology statement — how it was destined to implode — and with terrible clarity he saw the other end of Vessler's plan, how the electromagnetic studies the Halflings had uncovered on the Omega computers played into the world domination agenda. All at once, he felt sick and frustrated by his helplessness. *Just keep it together, Zero.* "That sounds like a bad sci-fi movie title, dude. I think you better lay off the He-Man drugs. They're affecting your brain."

Before Vessler walked from the room, he ground his heel into the necklace. The bits of glass crunched until only powder was left.

After he left, Zero tried to reach the dust that remained. Pressing a shattered cheek into the bars, he stretched, but his index finger barely touched the broken leather cord. "Come on," he whispered. And tried again. But just like Vegan, the necklace was out of reach.

Finally, he gave up. Hopelessness overtook him. He dropped his head and let the tears fall.

Chapter
22

When Nikki arrived at the lab, a guy dressed in black pants and a black dress shirt stopped her as soon as she entered the parking area. Big surprise there. The wind hit her from the east, carrying the scent of horse manure. Then she caught a glimpse of the magnificent animals Vegan had talked about. She stopped and stared in awe until her escort shoved her forward, prodding her with something hard.

She flashed him a dirty look. "Give me a second, okay?" Nikki pulled two pencils from her back pocket and threaded them through her hair to trap the runaway strands at her nape.

Moments later, they entered the lab. They snaked through a long tunnel punctuated with light from windows along both sides of the passageway. She glimpsed the laboratory rooms beyond, painted stark white and containing computers that twinkled from the four corners.

For the first thousand feet or so, the rooms looked like what she'd expect of any lab. But as they walked deeper into the monster's belly, rooms glowed with strange lighting, and scientists actually became *creepier* looking.

They passed one room where she viewed a row of cages. *Human*-sized cages. She looked away quickly. She couldn't be sure, but from the corner of her eye she thought she saw human remains on an examination table in the corner of that room.

Finally, they stopped. "Arms out," he said, and when she obeyed, he patted her down, obviously searching for weapons. The gorilla-sized guard in the dark clothes pressed his right wrist to a glowing blue square on the door. *Click*. It slid open. As far as Nikki could tell, this was the only door that operated like that. The others had an open entrance — something she'd made a mental note to remember in case she got a chance to escape.

Vessler greeted her with a smile. "My lady," he oozed, sitting behind a granite desk.

Anger rushed through her; his lies and phony affection boiled beneath her skin. She pulled in breath after breath, praying for peace. She couldn't lose it right now — it wouldn't help anyone. With that thought, the peace she'd requested flooded her consciousness like water to a sponge, saturating her to the very core of her existence. *I can do this. I'm on the winning side.*

"They've ruined you," he said with a sneer. "I can see that pathetic attempt to stay calm when you should be trying to kill me." He leaned forward, pressing his elbows onto the desk. "But it's a lie, Nikki. The only peace is revenge."

"And you're nothing but a liar. So I guess you'd know."

A half smile tilted his hardened face. "We could sit and debate this all day long. It doesn't change the fact that you're a poor, pathetic orphan."

Pride surged within. "No I'm not. I'm a Halfling."

He folded his fingers together and rested his chin on his thumbs. "About that ... I'm afraid you don't know the whole story."

She felt the blood draining from her face. Vessler saw it too. He always knew how to get to her. This was it: the answers to the truth about her childhood. She sank into the chair across from him.

He took such pleasure in her weakness. "Years ago, oh, I suppose nearly twenty now ..." He paused and unwrapped a gold toothpick.

She steadied herself by gripping the chair arms.

"Time sure flies, doesn't it? Seems like only yesterday we were at my beach house. You loved that home, didn't you, Nikki?"

She recalled the soaring ceilings painted with splashes of shadows as the sun tilted, the miles of white sand kissed by the sea, the explosive sunsets displaying every color in her artist's palette. Yes, she loved it there.

His chair creaked as he leaned back. He stuck the toothpick into his mouth. "Of course you did. Who wouldn't? I'd rather hoped to give it to you."

She crossed her arms. Was he actually going to try to bribe her with a house? "I don't want anything from you. You're a monster, Damon."

He laughed. Long and loud. "No, my dear, I'm not. But you are." His grin faded. "You want answers. And I'm the only one who can give them."

How did he always know?

"When we first became reacquainted, I said you didn't have a poker face. The questions are killing you, aren't they? Not

228

knowing? Don't worry, I understand your inquisitive nature. It's how I engineered you. Lucky for you, I'm more than happy to unfold how my vision for you began two decades ago."

She nearly gave in, but something surged within her. Something new and fresh and full of power. Vegan's words echoed in her head. She sprang from the chair. "You overestimate yourself, Damon. I *don't* want to know. Because what I was in the past doesn't matter. It's what I am now that counts. Save your pathetic words. I'll never be suckered by you again."

Vessler's nose twitched. Irritation flew off him in glorious waves. No, she wouldn't make it easy on him. And she wouldn't be a victim. Not ever again.

"Enough of the past, then. Let's talk about the future, shall we?"

Her interest sparked and she knew he'd seen it. "The future you have planned for me will never happen, Damon."

He leaned his weight on the desk and narrowed his gaze until his eyes were cold black slits. "But don't you want to know why, for seventeen years, I've had you trained to be a warrior? Made sure you knew how to defend yourself and had the abilities to kill anyone that gets in your way? Even the motorcycle. What decent parents let a seventeen-year-old have a street bike as her only means of transportation?"

She sat down and remained statue still. Her knuckles soon ached from the grip on the chair.

"Your eggs will be harvested. They'll provide the DNA for an army. You, Nikki, are special. Worth more than a thousand other Halflings."

Deep and penetrating horror enclosed her heart. "Who — who knew about this?"

"Everyone in my employ." Then his eyes widened and he leaned back in smug satisfaction. "Oh. You meant your new friends. Well, they were able to access a good portion of my private records." He sat quietly, clearly letting this new realization settle in for her, letting its uncertainty torture her. Then he shrugged. "I'd guess they all knew."

Nikki tried to swallow. Tried to breathe.

"I suppose they wanted to keep it from you. Figures. Self-preservation and all."

"What do you mean, self-preservation?" *They knew. Mace, Will, all of them. This was the giant secret they were keeping from me.*

"The army you and I create will easily have the power to destroy every Halfling on the planet."

"No. You're talking about DNA and creating more Halflings from eggs ..." Nikki stood, shook her head violently. "No. That would take years."

"Actually, not as long as you would think." He stood as well and walked around the massive desk. Barely a limp in his walk. "My scientists have developed a way to rapidly age humans — or Halflings, as the case may be. Once you're on board, we can look at the completion of our army within about five to six years."

Nikki's voice lowered, and she felt it turn deadly. "There is no power on this earth that would make me join you."

Vessler motioned behind him, and a barrel-chested man dressed in black stepped toward her. Before she could react, he slung a metal vest around her chest. She struggled as the clamps tightened. Her arms were free, but she wasn't able to fight. Nikki tried to flex her shoulder blades in the same manner she had a thousand times since she realized she had wings as a way of making sure they really were there, were really hers, and wouldn't disappear. But the metal squeezed so tightly she couldn't move a single muscle. It was excruciating, knowing she lacked the ability to unfurl her wings. It was almost like being shoved into a room that was too small and being trapped inside as the walls squeezed in.

"Sorry about that. Can't have you leaping to safety," Vessler said. He wiped the gold toothpick on his sleeve then stuck it into his shirt pocket.

She stared down at the metal surrounding her midsection.

Vessler came around the desk and propped his weight against it. "I guess you're wondering how we got that on you so quickly. Titanium." He reached to touch her, and she flinched. "It will keep your wings from opening. And as a surprising benefit, that amount of metal slows your reflexes. Since you're destined to be difficult, I can't take any chances. Would you like to go visit your friend now?"

A chain dangled from the front of the wingcuff. He grabbed it and jerked her toward the door. She felt like an animal at the circus. No — circus animals got better treatment than she was likely to receive.

Nikki clenched her teeth to keep from crying out when she saw Zero. One eye was swollen shut, his mouth had a dark line of blood streaming from it, and every inch of his exposed skin sported different shades of purple, yellow, and red. Never had she seen someone so badly beaten.

Damon and his goon dragged her through the lab room to the far wall, where Zero lay on the floor of the cage. By her estimation, she was in the last room of the entire lab. Damon threw her in with Zero and slammed the door shut.

She spun to the bars. "Damon, let him out." She rattled the

cage and pleaded. Too late, she remembered the bars were made of titanium, and she felt her energy wane. "On the phone, you said I could take his place." Panic threatened to overtake her. Vessler had no intention of releasing Zero.

He stopped and turned back to face her. "See, that's the problem with trusting the bad guy. We lie." He shrugged and cast a pitying glance at Zero, who lay curled in a fetal position on the floor. "I hope you'll choose to work with me. Zero, he was quite uncooperative. But you, my lady, it would be a shame to mess up such a perfect face." As the implication settled in, a slow burn rolled down her throat. He'd torture her if he had to. He'd use whatever means possible to twist her into the monster he needed. Getting her here was one more attempt at turning her into a dark creature. And once again, she'd have to find a way to fight.

"Wait," she said, not bothering to hide the quiver in her voice.

Vessler anxiously turned to her. His cold black eyes scanned her while bits of hope sparked in his gaze.

"Why *me*?" She squeezed the bars tightly between her fingers, eyes pleading for him to come closer while wishing the wingcuff wasn't so tight on her ribs. At least her arms were free. That was good. She was going to need them. Now, if she could just divert his attention, ease him into a false sense of security … There was a time when Nikki was Vessler's weakness. Maybe she still was.

"Why, Damon?" she whispered.

She could almost see him drooling.

He maneuvered a step closer. "Because most Halfling females can only bear one offspring."

He was close enough now she could smell his sickening aftershave. It once comforted her; now it made her gag.

"You are the culmination of my dreams. My plan. You are perfect, Nikki. I created a perfect, pure young blood. The fact that you beat the seeker only shows what I'm capable of."

A perfect young blood? Nikki tried to force the thought from her mind. *Youngblood*. Her name.

"Damon," she murmured, drawing him nearer by the soothing tone of her voice. Though her hands were wrapped around the bars, she partially unwound her fingers, reaching for him. "The Halflings knew this all along, didn't they?"

His eyes narrowed, as if he was gauging each word carefully.

"That's why they came for me, took me in." She pressed her lips together. "It was for their own protection."

His resolve was crumbling. "Ah, Nikki." He closed the distance and rested his hands atop hers and gently squeezed. "You just can't trust them."

A tear swept her cheek. She pressed her head to the metal and tried to blow stray strands of hair from her eyes, but the wisps tangled into her lashes and caused her to blink repeatedly.

He reached in and brushed the wisps away.

She pressed against his touch and tried to ignore the feel of the bars. They didn't cause her pain, just drained her strength — strength she was about to need.

Vessler quivered and Nikki was sure he had to fight the urge to reach into the cage and soothe her.

Her eyes fluttered open, and she tried her best to look innocent and lost. "You prefer my hair down, don't you?" she whispered softly, wanting, *needing* to draw him even closer.

"Yes." Beads of sweat broke out across his brow.

She could actually hear his heart hammering. He was

breathing hard now, and his palms had gone sweaty against her skin. Slowly, she reached behind her head to tug her hair free. The palm of each hand landed around the two pencils. With a smile that could liquefy glass, her body stiffened. Her hands lunged forward and she planted the pencils deep into his chest.

Chapter
23

Vessler screamed and reeled back, gasping for air. One pencil protruded from his chest cavity, the other had snapped off and rolled, bloody, across the floor.

The commotion caused the group of lab employees to converge on Vessler at once, yelling for help. Scientists in white and men in black sprang into action, hurrying through the wide door. A gurney was rushed in while Vessler screamed orders and tried to keep pressure on the wound.

Nikki sat down on the concrete floor, careful not to touch the bars. She watched the uproar she'd generated by trying to kill Vessler with her pencils. She'd failed, but she'd certainly left her mark. Once Vessler was wheeled out, one of his men stopped at the cage door. He pulled a short wooden baseball bat from behind him.

Nikki swallowed hard.

"For you," he mouthed, and smiled sadistically. He tapped the bat against the bar. "Soon."

Nikki turned her back to him, refusing to let him see her fear. She moved across the floor and settled in next to Zero.

"Nice move on Vessler," he muttered. "But I think you missed his heart."

"Too small a target," she said.

Zero's shirt was ripped and his necklace was gone, but his fingers kept going to his throat as if searching for it.

His gaze fell on something outside the bars. Nikki turned to see. The cord was all that remained of his necklace.

"Zero, I'm so sorry." She started to touch him, but was afraid of causing more injury. There was nowhere to place her hands — every inch of Zero was already swollen or bleeding. "What can I do?" But her words were as hopeless as her question. Nothing. There was nothing she could do for him.

"Did you bring any juice boxes?"

A tiny laugh escaped her throat.

Then, Zero did something unexpected. He reached for her. Nikki responded by sitting on the floor and drawing him closer, and even gently placed his head on her lap. When one tear fell from her cheek to his face, she brushed it away. "You look terrible," she said, pushing his white-blond hair away from his silvery eyes. Clumps of blood caused some to stick, but she worked them free and smoothed the strands.

"Difficult to kill a Halfling." His breaths were heavy, labored. She listened to him inhale, exhale. There was a gurgling sound with each intake of air. "Have you read about the death and resurrection? Will gave you a Bible, right?"

She frowned. She didn't want to hear Zero talk about death.

His lips cracked and bled as he continued. "It says that the Son gave up the ghost. The essence of heaven had kept him alive beyond what any normal man could endure. I think he finally asked death to take him. I never understood it. Until now." Zero's eyes closed. "It was a beautiful sacrifice, wasn't it?"

She nodded, though with his eyes closed, he couldn't see. But Nikki didn't trust her voice to speak. Zero would hear her uncertainty. She needed to stay strong for him, and a broken voice wasn't an act of strength.

He pulled a few more breaths. "Hey, I liked your hair with the Jinsu pencils."

"I learned that from Raven."

"I've never known Raven to wear pencils in his hair."

Nikki grasped the edge of his T-shirt and gently tugged the material away from one of the cuts on his throat. "No. He taught me to drive through. I should have spent more time working on it. But after I almost planted the pencils in Raven's chest, I didn't really want to try it again."

"Until now," Zero croaked.

"Until now."

"Remind me not to make you angry, 'kay?"

She pressed her hand gently to his head and smoothed his hair again. "I'd never do that to you, Zero." More tears followed, and they dropped from her onto him.

"Enough with the water works," he whispered. "You're getting me all wet."

"This is completely my fault. If I hadn't come to ask you about my past and what Vessler was planning, you wouldn't be here." Hopelessness stole through her system, followed quickly by anger. "Everyone warned me to stop poking into my past. To leave it alone, concentrate on who I am now, but I wouldn't listen."

"Yeah, you're stubborn that way."

Nikki nodded. Her stubbornness may have killed Zero. But then his upper body tightened and his hand rose to grasp hers.

His bloody fingers trembled so much Nikki slid her hand into his to help steady him.

He took a moment to inspect the room beyond the cage. Two scientists were clicking away on computers and one of Vessler's bodyguards hovered nearby the men. The room beyond the cage was fairly large, but Zero leaned closer as if to keep anyone out there from hearing.

"Listen to me, Nikki." His voice was slightly stronger. "Stop blaming yourself for everything. You tried to take my place. I'll never forget that as long as I live ... however long that might be." He grimaced, then gestured above them. "There's an air vent in the ceiling."

Nikki glanced into the rest of the room to make sure no one was watching them. The adjacent room off to the right — visible through a window behind the scientists — held Vessler. Nikki's eyes followed Zero's gaze. Across the ceiling, the bars were spaced farther apart. In the right corner a vent took the place of a small section of ceiling.

"You're thin, Nikki. You can fit through. When the chance comes, I want you to run."

"If I can fit, so can you."

He chuckled. "Yeah. Good luck getting me up there."

She considered the vent for a few seconds. That was all it took to know she'd never take the coward's way out. Of course she could go for help. But she knew Vessler. If she left, even through a skinny air vent, he'd kill Zero. That, she'd never allow. "No. I just need some time to think. Time to pray. When we go, we go together. There's no way I'll leave you here."

He squeezed her hand. "They can't hurt me anymore. Run, Nikki. Run." He passed out on her lap just in time to miss the creaking of the cage door.

Vessler's men dragged her out. She caught a glimpse of an exam room adjacent to her cage, where a doctor stitched the wound in Vessler's chest. When they took her from the cage, she saw Vessler smile.

She'd assaulted their boss, and in doing so had assaulted their livelihood and manhood. If they beat her, so what? At least they weren't focusing their attention on Zero anymore. The first few blows were to her face, causing spikes of pain from her head down through her body. With the wingcuff secured to her midsection, keeping her from bracing herself in any way, each strike was unlike anything she'd experienced since tapping into her Halfling power. But Nikki'd been in karate tournaments where the abuse was nearly this bad. She could take it. She had to. She needed to protect Zero.

Vine shut off the barbeque grill for Will while the other Lost Boys — and Girls — shared what information they had. Nikki'd been gone for nearly two hours. Vegan had just told them Nikki had also snuck out earlier in the day to visit Zero, who now wasn't returning her calls or texts. Vine ran inside the house and tried to log on to the network. Zero was always reachable there.

He tapped his foot while the computer booted up. Something wasn't right — about any of it. When the computer screen flashed on, he sprang into action, tapping in his personal access code.

Vine swallowed the thick ball of apprehension when a blank screen appeared. He tried again, slowly this time, making sure he entered every letter accurately. Again, a black screen. The network was down. That had never happened. He ran outside, sliding through the patio doorway.

He started to tell Will and the Halflings what he'd discovered, but his words stopped in the moment he reached the backyard. Everyone was looking at the sky. Vine looked up as well, but the sun shot straight into his eyes. He slammed them shut for a few seconds, and when he reopened them it was darker, and a sound much like a tornado became louder as moments ticked past. He realized the sky was filled with wings, enough to block the setting sun. There had to be twenty Halflings, all descending on the backyard like a great flock of birds.

Vine searched out Will on the back porch. "Who are they? What are they doing here?"

Will didn't answer, just stared at this new group as they sailed toward the house.

As they neared, the wind smacked with such force, it blew over the patio table. Chair cushions swirled into the violent current of air. Winter and Vegan's hair flew in all directions, while Raven, Mace, and Glimmer seemed to be bracing themselves against the onslaught.

Vine's gaze shot around the patio, then back to the sky. They were outnumbered by more than two to one. Mace stepped forward and stood a little in front of Will. Mace always took the lead now, and if these Halflings were here for a war, he was ready. Unlike the rest, who were still shell-shocked, with their clothing plastered to their bodies like they were all trapped in a wind tunnel.

Vegan and Winter finally began to move, and both girls worked to cluster and hold their long hair away from their faces. Vine's heart kicked up and adrenaline sluiced through his system.

As the twenty-some Halflings touched down in the back-yard, one took center stage. His flock of giant, graceful winged creatures all fell into place behind him.

Vine instantly disliked the guy. And after a quick sizing up of the Halflings on the porch, the strange leader's gaze lingered a moment on Vine. The dude's face said the feeling was mutual.

For a short stretch of time after they returned her to the cage, the room was blessedly quiet, giving Nikki time to examine Zero's wounds, hold him while he rested, and pray. "Please, see Zero safely out of this. I don't really want to die either, but if dying will protect him, I will. No matter what my future after that holds. I don't want to live on this earth as a dark creature. Whatever Vessler has planned for me, please, give me a way out. Even if it means drawing no more breath." She prayed all of this silently, not wanting Zero to hear and be tempted to give up hope. Nikki wasn't giving up, though she reasoned it could sound like it. She was a fighter. And right now, this was the only way she knew to fight.

The exam room door opened and Nikki stood. When Vessler came closer with the short baseball bat in his hand, she placed herself between the door and Zero.

"Your spirit is good, but your aim is faulty. You didn't pierce my heart, only my flesh."

Nikki spread her stance. "You're supposed to be my teacher, so why don't you give me one more shot?" The strength of her voice surprised her, and the contempt it held for the man who'd once been her guardian made her proud. She wished she could think of something more cutting and clever to say.

"There's no edge to gain, Nikki. You can't win. That is, until you join me."

She leaned forward. "I'll never join you."

He laughed. "Of course you will. You've already secured that future by coming here. Now, it's just a matter of time. And, sadly, torture. Disobedient children have to be punished."

Vessler's men opened the door and dragged her out onto the floor, where Zero's blood had already dried and stained the concrete. Vessler took the first few blows, using the bat to pummel her thighs and shoulder. When she could no longer stand, he had his men hold her up. After several strikes, they thrust her to the ground.

Boots stepped into her peripheral vision, the wooden bat swinging to and fro like a pendulum above them. She buried her head between her arms and whimpered in anticipation. The blow made a thud as it landed across her back. She screamed, the nerve endings beneath her skin erupting on impact then radiating outward. Her muscles bunched violently beneath her damaged flesh. She cried out again, the sudden stiffness tearing her bruises apart. Then Vessler yanked a light toward her face to inspect her eyes. He did this over and over while Nikki silently prayed for God to help her. *Please, please don't let me turn.* And over and over again she knew Vessler was angered by the fact that her eyes remained filled with the light of heaven.

He finally tossed her back into the cage. Once he was gone, Nikki rose onto her knees and bent forward in a prayer posture. "Give me grace," she whispered. "I can't do this without you."

Chapter 24

They continued to remove her from the cage and batter her. Her stamina had waned over the prior beatings, making her easy to knock to the floor. Each time she dropped to her knees, she staggered back to her feet in agony, in defiance. Her bruised knees became a constant reminder from her foe to stay down, to submit to the torture he offered. To succumb to the dark.

But she fought him. She fought him until she no longer could.

She opened her hands. Splayed them flat on the floor. Ten bloody fingers, ten shards of pain. She swallowed, the metallic taste of blood coating her lips and throat.

Streams of hair hampered her vision as she struggled to lift her head. Her gaze shifted, left then right, but her enemy wasn't nearby. Her head sagged, and her eyes filled, forcing her to blink them clear. Tears of blood fell to her hand, raining her life onto the floor. Releasing her from his cruelty. But not soon enough.

A noise. Behind her. To the right. The sound of her tormentor stepping back preceded the strike, soon paired with a crunch as the impact of his boot to her ribs buckled the bones. She gasped, bolts of pain exploding through her as lung and fractured bone made contact.

For a few moments, all was dark.

Inside, something stirred ... some fierce entity that wasn't her yet was somehow a part of her. She'd felt its presence before. When she stood in the park ready to kill the man named Keagan Townsend. When she'd nearly killed Vessler on the plane loaded with titanium. The presence fought for control inside her, prodding her to seek vengeance for her parents, to never walk away without knowing her past.

She rolled to her other side just as one of Vessler's men grabbed an examination tray from a nearby table and used it to land a powerful blow to the side of her head. She felt a rush of anger disperse through her body, cradled by pain from the hit.

They'd removed her wingcuff long ago, but her prone state proved it hardly mattered. She flexed her shoulders and felt the tingle that came before her wings emerged. It comforted her — reminded her who she was. But there was no strength to snap her pinions open and escape. Reassurance that she was still a Halfling was the only comfort she'd receive. But it was enough.

She wished she'd listened to Mace. If she had, she wouldn't have gone to Zero, wouldn't be in this lab, and wouldn't be fighting the darkness that was threatening to overtake her. She knew the darkness's methods. When the seeker slashed her collarbone — no doubt aiming for her throat — she'd felt the poison spreading through her being, the same clawing urgency she felt now. It was life and death rolled into a seductive package.

A thought struck her that she hadn't considered before:

maybe she could control it. If she gave into the darkness, perhaps she could possess the strength to control it.

Just then, Vessler dragged her by the hair, dragged her into the cage and shoved her to the ground.

"I'll be back soon, my lady. I thought I would give you some time to think."

Nikki reached through the bars after he'd gone and dragged the dented exam tray to her face. Her eyes had darkened, but not completely. She squeezed them closed. Control evil? No, there was no controlling the darkness. It was all-encompassing. It devoured everything it contacted.

Nikki clasped her hands together and rested on knees that screamed in response. "God, please, don't let me turn. I can't turn. Now that I know who you are, I can't walk this earth separate from you. I want to live my life fulfilling the purpose you have for me." The lab around her dimmed and blurred, forcing her to prop herself against the cage bars. "Take anything you want, but please don't take your light from me. Take anything else. Take my life. Take ..."

But what did she have to offer? "Take ... my wings." It was all she had, and the one thing she possessed that held worth. Pain pierced her heart. She let out a sob. "Take them, God. But please don't let me turn."

A short time later, Vessler returned. But rather than fear his arrival — and the abuse he was sure to give — Nikki felt strong. The poison in her system was gone, and the desire for vengeance replaced by the strangest peace, even though he beat her with such vigor she started to wonder if he was even human.

As the blows layered pain atop excruciating agony, the only thing she didn't feel was her wings. As he beat her, she sobbed for them. They had still been as new and fresh to her as

Christmas morning gifts, yet they had become so much a part of her—and now they were no more. The pain of the loss was unbearable, and as time dragged on, she began weakening, not to the darkness but to life itself. Everything dulled around her, and it seemed the only comfort would be in closing her eyes to never awaken again.

More than once, Nikki prayed for death to take her.

He was average height for a Halfling, probably around six foot three. But nothing else about him met Halfling standards. Long black hair graced his shoulders, falling in smooth sheets around his face like a cloak. His blue eyes were too dark—and penetrating when he spoke. "The network is down."

Vine allowed himself a few moments to inspect this new Halfling and the twenty-some who'd just landed in the yard. Dark-haired guy was definitely in charge. When one of the others stepped forward to say something, he quelled him with a look.

"Zero's been abducted."

Vine's heart dropped. "What makes you think so?" He'd already known the network was down. But Zero abducted? He hadn't even considered that.

Vegan's hands flew to her face. Vine knew she'd been trying to get in touch with Zero for a couple hours. He hadn't returned any calls, but, hey, that was normal.

She shook her head. "No one other than us knows the way to the underground. And I know for sure Zero was there. Nikki went to see him this morning, and …" Her face clouded, and she didn't seem able to finish her thought.

Vine watched as Vegan put the pieces together, then said, "Someone could have followed Nikki."

Mace clenched his fists. The smell of battle rose around him, practically wafting into the air. "Then whoever has Zero probably has Nikki too."

The black-haired Halfling spoke up. "I don't think so."

Mace's eyes narrowed. "Why?"

In almost a whisper, Vine heard Will say, "I recognize this young man. I can't access the memory, but something dark ... very dark about his past."

"Because we found tracks at the underground bunker. Gunshots in the door." He paused when Vegan grabbed the railing to keep from collapsing. "Two sets of footprints leaving. Zero must have been dragged part of the way, by the looks of the tracks."

"Then where's Nikki?"

The guy shrugged. "I don't know who that is. All I know is that if she went to see Zero, she compromised his cover. Now he's gone. Or dead."

Vegan moaned, and Glimmer and Winter ran to her side.

"What kind of car tracks were outside?" Mace demanded.

The dark Halfling glanced at him sharply.

"If you could determine Zero was dragged, and it looks like he was taken by force, then you must have seen some vehicle tracks too."

The leader sniffed. "Looked like the freshest tracks were made by a Hummer."

Mace slammed his fist on the railing. "Vessler." He turned to the group. "I'm going up to Nikki's room to see if there's any clue about where she may have gone. If Vessler has her, they could be anywhere."

The fact that Nikki and Zero might be in Vessler's clutches heightened the already tense atmosphere. Once Mace disappeared into the house, Will stepped forward and addressed the group of Halflings on the yard. "How'd you know to come here?"

The dark one shot a piercing glance at Vegan. "She's Zero's match."

Vegan blushed.

"I petitioned our caregiver to help us find her. Heaven whispered, and here we are."

Will crossed his arms and regarded the newcomer thoughtfully. "You're Viper, aren't you?"

The Halfling bristled.

Vine snorted. *Riiiiight, the guy doing everything in his power to look different doesn't like being singled out. You sort of stick out like a sore thumb with your dyed hair, Lost Boy.*

The dark Halfling answered after a long pause and a silent war between himself and Will. "Yes."

Vine could only wonder what that was all about, but there was definitely some history between Will and Viper. Will had also said he couldn't access the memory, which was weird in itself, because in all the time Vine had known Will, the heavenly angel remembered *everything*. Every missed trash day, every dollar Vine spent on candy, every promise Vine made to clean his room.

Another spot appeared above the treetops, catching Vine's attention. The dude flapped his wings while his body jerked around awkwardly, pelican style. "Uh-oh, uh-oh," he said.

Vine stared. *Is this guy for real? He was worse than a newbie flyer.* Maybe he was drunk. Vine had never seen a drunk Halfling before, but figured it'd look something like that.

When the Halfling finally touched down, he hit hard, landing at the edge of woods and rolling to a stop. He popped up and hollered, "I'm all right, y'all." He waved a hand and grinned widely, shaking leaves and twigs from his feathers and brushing them from his puff of sandy-brown hair. Despite his efforts, a stick remained wedged in the tip of his right wing. He reached, couldn't quite get to it, and began a series of circles like a dog chasing its tail. He swatted at the stick, but it remained lodged.

Viper's lowered his head into his hands. He turned on the other Halfling, black hair flying as he moved. "Crash, you're an *idiot*."

The twig finally fell, and Crash waved with his now free wingtip. He smiled like he hadn't just been yelled at and like everyone was really happy to see him. Eyes bright, he looked around at the crowd. "What'd I miss?"

Will nodded to Viper. "You're caregiver is named Temperance, right?" It was obvious to Vine that Will didn't fully trust this Halfling yet.

"He goes by Tempy, but yeah." Viper shifted his weight. "I don't mean to be rude here, but we're in a hurry." His eyes fanned to the Halflings on the porch. "Are you interested in going after Zero or not?"

Five sets of wings snapped open so loudly, so quickly, that had a human been standing close, he'd have suffered a busted eardrum. About that time, Mace ran back through the door. "Cell phone. I found it in Nikki's room."

"What does that tell us?" Will took it, inspected it.

Mace shook his head. "Nothing. Except this whole thing is a setup created by Vessler." Then his gaze narrowed on Viper.

"We aren't working for Vessler, so back off, Halfling. We're going after Zero. If you want in, fine. If not, fine too."

Raven stepped closer the edge of the patio. "And if you think we'll let you leave here without us, you'll have a fight on your hands."

Will pressed a hand to Raven's chest, then turned to face Mace. "Viper's telling the truth. But to do this, you'll need to work together."

Vine watched Mace swallow his anger then nod.

Will continued. "Before you go off to storm Vessler's domain, don't you think it might be a good idea to have a plan?"

Mace faced Will. "Vessler's got Nikki. I'm not going to stand around and wait."

Will lifted his chin. "Uncovering a cell phone doesn't mean that Vessler has Nikki. What would be the use of kidnapping her? He can't make her turn now, unless ..."

Vine grabbed a sour gummy from his pocket stash. "Unless Nikki went to him by her own will," he said.

Will shook his head. "She'd never do that. Vessler wants to use her to create an army. She'd never go to him willingly."

Mace dropped the phone from his hand. "We didn't tell her, Will. I didn't think she could handle it. Did you tell her?"

Will shook his head, his large, expressive eyes mirroring the desperation in Mace's. "I was waiting for her to ask. She never did."

"Hey, can someone explain what's going on?" Viper yelled.

I'd appreciate that too. Vine swallowed the gummy, but didn't reach for another. *I really need to get a handle on this emotional eating problem.*

Will drew in a breath. "Zero was probably bait to get to Nikki Youngblood. Vessler wants her. If he can get her to turn, then he will use her dark DNA to build an army of Halflings who swear allegiance to him."

Raven gripped the rail. "That means they're at the lab."

Glimmer grabbed Raven's arm. "The lab where the horses are? Vessler has it fortified. There's no way in."

Raven pulled from her grasp. "We can get in, but it won't be easy. And getting out will be even worse. The timing will have to be perfect."

"Wait." Winter floated over to Raven, and when she placed her hand on his shoulder, he didn't flinch. "Aren't we making a lot of assumptions? We don't even know Vessler has Nikki."

"Vessler's entire plan rests on Nikki. Without her, he's got nothing. And since she defeated the seeker, there's only one way to turn her. Like Will said, she has to go to him willingly. Then she has to choose evil."

"*Choose* evil?" Winter shook her head. "She'd never do that."

"Once she's gone to him willingly, he can use any means possible to make her turn."

"Like what?" Winter said.

"Whatever he thinks will work. He attacked her on her lawn and nearly turned her, maybe he'll try that again." Raven's expression grew grim.

"Nikki's a fighter," Mace interjected. "But she's stronger than she's ever been, now that she's full of faith."

Raven's jaw twitched. "Everyone has a breaking point."

Glimmer's eyes misted. "Then it's hopeless."

Mace's fists clenched at his sides. "It's not hopeless. She overcame the seeker with faith and courage. She's smarter than Vessler gives her credit for. She's tougher too."

Raven put his hand on his shoulder. "Yeah, but for how long? Vessler's ruthless. Nikki isn't."

"Raven's right. We have to go now." Mace snapped his wings open.

Viper's eyes narrowed. "Lead the way."

In the distance, a police siren grew louder. Will cast a glance to the small stretch of road visible from the back porch. "Don't try to leave yet. We need to discuss this inside. I have a feeling breaking into a fortified lab will draw even more attention than a yard full of winged teenagers."

Mace grabbed him. "Will, we don't have time."

"Mace," he countered, "we have no choice. You think Vessler won't be ready for a swarm of Halflings coming down on his lab? Take time to get your plan together or you'll be putting Nikki in even more danger. We only get one shot at this."

"Quiet!" Vegan yelled, throwing a hand in the air to hush them. The other she cupped around her ear.

Glimmer and Winter slid a hand to their ears as well and tilted their heads at varying angles. Winter pointed west. The other two nodded.

"Nikki's calling for help!" Winter said.

Chapter
25

Raven knew Mace was about to explode, and pacing the living room floor wasn't lessening that urge. Mace didn't like Viper or his two wingmen, Steel and Shadow. But Will was right: if they weren't in this together, they had little hope of success. Vessler would be ready for them. That advice would be easier to follow, however, if these three dark Halflings made any attempt to seem like team players. At least they'd arrived after tracking down Vegan and getting help for the rescue. But that's where the appreciation ended. There was too much wrong with all three of them. Viper was a control freak, and once a plan was made, he'd try to take the lead. No one would be heading this mission … but Mace. Raven knew Mace would take the lead as soon as the moment presented itself. That meant his poor brother also had to cooperate with Will's infuriating instructions.

Like a freshly caged tiger, he looked around the room until he saw Raven, who crossed the space to stand by him.

"We'll get her, brother," Raven assured.

But they both knew what Nikki faced. "He won't waste any time. Raven, he could do anything to her."

"I know." He cleared his throat, because it would help for Mace to hear the fear in his tone.

"We need to go now."

Raven tucked his hands into his pockets. "You know I'm never one to sit around and wait. But, Mace, I think we have to this time. Vessler has all the cards. He's got Nikki and he'll be ready for us."

Various conversations filled the room around them as they discussed the best strike time. They'd all agreed they would depart at five in the morning, which according to Raven's prior research was an hour before Vessler's morning crew arrived, which also meant the nightshift patrol would be tired by then. But that opportunity was hours from now, which meant waiting patiently. Raven didn't like sitting around, and neither did Mace.

"Raven, promise me we'll get to her in time," Mace choked.

"I promise." But the look in Mace's eyes showed the words were just that — words. His brother was fighting the urge to focus on the worst scenerio.

He couldn't blame him.

Raven knew the lab. He just hoped he wasn't lying about being able to get to Nikki.

Nearly thirty Halflings filled the large, Victorian living room as they plotted out the exact rescue plan, and moved into three groups based on Mace's instructions.

Glimmer turned to Raven. "Can we leap inside?"

"Probably not." He ran his fingers through his long side bangs. "The lab is a long tunnel lined with rooms. From what

I've seen, few of them are large enough to allow all of us to enter at once. And leaping in one at a time puts us at a disadvantage — they catch one of us, and the rest are target practice. Besides, I have a feeling the walls are fortified with titanium."

Mace paced the available floor space near the stairs. Halflings were sitting, standing, blocking most of the area, but Mace had carved out a path.

"We *could* draw them out," Glimmer said.

Mace immediately rejected the idea. "Vessler won't fall for it. We have to go in."

Raven agreed. "He'd lock down the cell where he's keeping Nikki and Zero."

"You think they're together?" Mace asked. "Seems like he'd split them up."

"Seems like," Raven said. "But I did a little recon awhile back, remember? Vessler has only one cage fully lined with titanium, so it's by far the most fortified. It's big, and it's at the farthest corner of the lab. Difficult to reach and even more difficult to infiltrate. That's where we'll find them."

Mace's eyes narrowed on him. "How do you know all this?"

"You kind of pick up a few details when you stake out a lab facility in order to distract yourself from reality. But to fully answer your question, I had Zero run some files awhile ago. I know the amounts of titanium Vessler's mined in the last few years and how he's using it. Even found a blueprint for the cage."

"So Vessler owns titanium mines?" Mace said.

Several Halflings shuddered.

"Plus, we know he's got a ton of wingcuffs. I just don't know how many. Everyone will have to be careful." Raven's gaze drifted from one to the next. "And remember, don't kill any humans."

"Speak for yourself, Lost Boy," Viper said. "Some of us are already doomed. If corporal punishment needs to be carried out, we'll do it." He waved a hand, encompassing himself and two other Halfings. "Steel, you stick close to the group stationed outside. Dispose of any stragglers that try to flee."

Steel shot him a frightening smile.

Raven took several steps toward Viper. "Look, by murdering humans, you could implicate all of us."

Viper fisted his hands, puffed his chest, and squared himself. "Shut up and stop your hand-wringing. You'll be judged for your own acts, same as always. *We're* not afraid of the punishment we'll receive. But we won't let Halfling killers go free. If you don't like the plan, don't go."

When Raven stepped closer to Viper, Mace put a steadying hand on Raven's shoulder. "We're all in this together. If you choose that path, Viper, we won't try to stop you. But we also don't approve. What matters right now is saving Nikki and Zero." Mace's eyes leveled on Viper. "Don't take any unnecessary chances."

Viper's bright, white smile contrasted sharply with his jet-black hair. "Never do." He motioned to the third Halfling in the dark trio. "Shadow, stay with group two. If we have to fight our way through the tunnel, they'll need a backup who isn't afraid to do what he has to."

Visibly shaken, Winter stepped to the center of the army. "Those who live by the sword —"

Viper put a hand up to silence her. "Yeah, yeah, we know. Die by the sword. We've already killed, chicklet. So back off. It's too late for us to worry about it."

Mace stared at Viper a moment before he took a deep breath and addressed the crowd. "Group three, we'll need to infiltrate the deepest cavern of the lab. I'll lead, and try to draw the first fire."

"No." Raven pivoted to face his brother. "I'll lead. You follow me in. You need to get to Nikki and get her out while I draw fire, and Vegan and Vine can get Zero. Once everyone is out safely, I'll leave. First in, last out."

Mace didn't like it, Raven could tell. Maybe because he still considered Raven a loose cannon. Or maybe it was something else entirely. Whatever, it didn't matter. Raven planned to make sure Mace was the one who rescued Nikki.

"Promise me one thing," Raven said to Mace. "You'll get them out. No matter what."

For a moment of time, there was only Mace and Raven, two brothers — not by blood but by choice.

"Promise me," Raven repeated.

Mace nodded. "I'll see them to safety."

Good. Because Raven was working on a side mission. Once he got the others inside and he knew Nikki was on her way out, he'd put his plan into action. "Now, all we have to do is wait."

Raven scooted the cold latte to the edge of the table. The waitress kept trying to catch his attention, and it was testing his nerves. He should have gone somewhere else. Somewhere private. Problem was, the house was out of the question — too many eyes would be curious about why he was drawing a detailed diagram of the lab. And every other location he could think of meant larger crowds and thus more nosy strangers.

The girl in the green apron paused at his table again. "Can

I take this?" Fingers reached for the cup. Her red polish was chipped.

He nodded but didn't look up.

"I can get you some paper if you want it. Those napkins must be awfully hard to write on."

"No, I'm good." *Please, just leave me alone.* She smelled like too much vanilla. She'd probably gone to the back and bathed in it while he let his latte get cold.

"Did you not like your drink?" She let out a soft laugh. "I can make you anything you want — on or off the menu."

Can you make yourself disappear? "It was fine."

"Okay," she said.

How can she not get the hint? He felt her lean closer. "Looks like a cool building. You an architect student? Guys like you are always sketching on napkins, bits of paper." She cocked her hip, as if settling in for a long conversation.

Out of habit his gaze clawed its way up to her face. Blue eye shadow that was way too dark; slick, glossy lips in a shade so bright you could see it from space, and a flirty smile that proclaimed she was trying too hard. He almost felt bad for her. "No. I'm not an architect. I just have to sketch something out, and came here because at home people kept *interrupting me.*"

Her smile disappeared, the twinkle left her eyes, and her chest deflated. She spun from the table and nearly sloshed the drink on him in her rush to leave.

Raven heaved a breath. He'd barely gotten back to the drawing when he became aware of the three walking in. He rubbed a hand over his face. *Great. Now all I need is a neon sign proclaiming I'm up to something.* Keeping his back to the door, he folded the small piece of paper and slipped it under the table.

"What's your plan, Halfling?" Viper dropped into the chair

across from Raven. Steel and Shadow moved where he could see them, but chose to stop at the bar near the barista, who'd quickly recovered from his rejection. She was running her hand up and down the counter, and they looked like they wanted to swat her like a pesky fly. Raven assumed they thought having all three sit at his table would show too much respect, too much of a "let's be friends" attitude. Well, he wasn't really in the market for more friends, though he did appreciate them drawing Pesky Girl's attention.

"Plan? I don't know what you mean."

Viper leaned his weight on the table and stared at Raven. "I recognize the look in your eyes. It's called desperation, and it is usually followed by action."

Raven tilted back. "Dude, you don't know me at all."

Viper shrugged. "Maybe. But I know that look. You're working on something. If it has to do with going after Zero early and ditching this whole take-time-to-plan idea, we want in."

Raven chewed on the inside of his cheek, considering the offer. "It doesn't. And I work alone."

Viper laughed out loud, causing Raven to blink. The Halfling flipped his hair back, jet-black strands catching the light. "Sorry. It's just that usually people who say that fail."

Fail. Not an option.

"Look, we owe Zero." Viper nodded for the other two guys to come over and sit. An act of compliance? Showing they'd let him be in charge? If Raven let them in on his plan — and that was a big if — that's the only way it'd go. Some things weren't negotiable.

Silence dominated the space around them. They weren't going to beg; also good. He didn't need a bunch of wimps on his side.

Viper stared at him, waiting.

And Raven let him wait. He glanced over at Steel. The guy looked capable. In fact, all three seemed pretty tough, and pretty determined to save Zero. But would they do the same for Nikki?

Shadow rubbed his hands on his jeans. "You going in early at the lab? We were thinking it could probably be done if we went in the middle of the night."

Raven's eyes narrowed. If these fools thought he'd trust Nikki's fate to three Halflings who he just met, they were as stupid as they looked. Especially Viper, with his weird dark hair and dark eyes. Raven wasn't sure he should trust them at all. At the same time, if he succeeded in getting his plan together, he'd need others on board. Mace would never go for this. And there was no way Raven was going to get Vine messed up in this. If anything went wrong — and with a plan like his, that was pretty likely — humans could die. *Three doomed Halflings is the best I can get ... and I could end up doomed as well.*

"Look." Viper leaned back. "We care about Zero. If you care about Nikki or Zero half as much, you know we're all in for the win."

This guy could never understand how much he cared about Nikki. Raven chuckled. "All in for the win, huh?"

Viper shrugged, and one side of his face creaked into a smile.

The tension in the air changed, now charged with anticipation.

"I'm not going in early. But I'm also not planning to leave the lab standing after we get Nikki and Zero out."

"Explosives?" Shadow asked, and the other three gave him wide-eyed stares. He shrunk back a little. "Sorry. Guess that's obvious."

Raven pulled the paper from under the table and spread it out for them. "I need enough to blow the whole place. Problem is placement. We need to give people time to get out."

Viper shrugged one shoulder. "Why? They aren't letting Zero and Nikki out. Why do they get any consideration?"

Raven folded the paper and pressed his hand firmly against it. "I'm not going to intentionally kill humans. If that's what you're here for, forget it. Too much can go wrong, and you may be willing to gamble with your eternity, but I won't gamble with the other Halflings'. We're *all* going into the lab. And despite what you proclaimed back at the house, that means we may *all* be held accountable for what happens as soon as we enter the lab." Raven waited while Viper and his two minions digested his terms. One wrong comment from any of them and this discussion would be over.

Steel shook his head. "How are we going to get all the people out before the blast? If your diagram is right, it's a huge facility."

Raven removed his hand from the paper. "It is huge. But everything runs off this main hallway. When we storm the building, most of the humans are going to try to escape through the front doors. Even Will knows we need to keep the front clear of Halflings so they can get out. The fewer humans inside, the easier it will be to find Nikki —"

"And Zero," Viper said.

"Yeah, and Zero."

Viper reached for the paper. "So we need to encourage the scientists and guards to leave. That shouldn't be too hard. But it *will* take time."

Shadow rested his weight on his forearms, scrutinizing the drawing. "Why not multiple blasts?"

"Huh?" Raven pushed the paper toward the guy. He liked where this was headed.

Shadow turned the paper to face himself. "First blast in the very back of the lab right after Zero and Nikki are safe. That way any people in the lab will rush out, head for the main door or any door that will take them outside. If the blast is near the back, we won't risk catching people in a crossfire. What's this?" He pointed to the last exam room at the end of the long main corridor and the smaller room beyond it.

"That's the titanium cage."

The other three visibly shuddered. "It's much bigger than I thought it would be," Viper said, and actually leaned away from the paper. Raven swore the guy went pale.

Viper drew several deep breaths. "Is that where they're keeping Zero?" The distress in his voice, though he tried to hide it, was evident to Raven. For the first time, he wondered if Viper was up to the task.

"That'd be my guess. Nikki and Zero are probably both there. No telling what Vessler's done to them." Raven had already run all the scenarios in his mind, but Viper's reaction could tell him how viable each might be.

After a few moments, Viper yanked a hand through that ink-black hair and focused on Raven. "Okay. We'll have to set the charge near the cage to destroy it. Titanium is tough. We're going to need exact measurements for the explosives and the building size. And we have to make sure we give the other Halflings plenty of time to get Zero and Nikki out."

"No joke. Especially if we're thinking of setting off multiple charges," Raven said.

"So, we're in?" Viper's brows rose.

"Yeah, you're in."

Viper nodded. "Good. I've always hated waiting around doing nothing. You have a connection for this much explosive power?"

Raven rubbed the back of his neck. "I sort of planned to tackle one detail at a time, and the first detail was figure out if this was even possible."

"So you don't have any way to get the charges we need?"

Raven swallowed and tapped his pen on the diagram. "Anything can be found, dude. You just gotta know where to look."

"And you need the *time* to look. Which we don't have." Viper spun the paper and considered it while the seconds ticked past. "I know somebody. He can help us."

So why the hesitation? One minute Viper was tough, the next he seemed to be playing at being bad. "It has to be someone you trust. Someone who knows explosives."

"It is. He's totally trustworthy, but, uh …"

"But what?" Raven pressed.

"He's a little quirky. Kind of odd. Maybe even a little crazy."

"Guy works with explosives, so yeah, you'd have to be a little on the crazy side." Raven thought a moment. "Is he good?"

Viper nodded. "He can drop a twenty-story building and leave a brand-new car untouched across the street. He's the best. Just don't let his personality get to you."

"I don't care if he sucks on a pacifier, as long as he can get us what we need."

"No problem, then." Viper flashed a white smile. "Let's go. Faster we talk to him, the faster we can start blowing that lab to bits."

They all stood. Raven moved to face Viper. "How far away is he?"

"Not far by air, but we need to take a truck. I don't know what explosives we'll need or how much room they take up, so we better be prepared to drive it all back. If we can carry it in packs and fly back, we will. It's about a four-hour drive from here. It'll probably take him a couple hours to get everything together for us."

"Can we call ahead so he can get started?"

"No. Andy doesn't believe in phones. He thinks they're all wired to record conversations."

"Four hours back if we have to drive." Raven ran the calculations in his head. "That gives us just enough time to get to the lab before the Halflings invade."

"Not a lot of room for error," Viper said.

"Never is." Raven headed out the door with the other three on his heels.

Chapter
26

"Don't open that cupboard."

Raven pulled his hand away from the door handle. Viper had warned him Andy was a little odd, but seriously? The guy answered the door with a monocle over one eye. He'd then inspected them by pulling each one into his house individually and slamming the door on the others. Once satisfied, he allowed everyone entrance and offered coffee. He currently was leading them into the kitchen while Viper explained what they were doing.

Andy peeled the paper away from a candy bar and took a bite. "I've always liked Zero. I'll help anyway I can."

Raven wasn't convinced the man was all there. He watched Andy place the half-eaten candy bar on the table. Which wasn't too weird, except there were two other half-eaten bars nearby — one on the counter and one by the coffee pot.

Raven pointed to a row of coffee cups on the counter.

Andy nodded. "Yes, those are fine."

Raven took one and filled his cup while Andy yammered about being rushed. Raven reached for the sugar jar and was stopped by a blood-curdling scream.

"Don't open that jar!"

His hand stopped midair.

Andy grabbed the jar and held it close to his chest. "There's sugar in the fridge."

"Okaaaay." Before pulling the refrigerator door open, Raven looked this supposed genius over carefully. Andy nodded as if confused by all the fuss over opening a door. He still cradled the sugar jar.

They went into the living room and sat down. Steel reached for a magazine and Andy yelled, "Don't open that!"

Raven's patience was running thin. Andy walked to a nearby bookcase and grabbed a different magazine and lobbed it at Steel. Rather than read it, Steel stared at Andy.

"I can't be too careful," was all Andy offered by way of explanation.

Viper placed a paper on the coffee table. "We worked the numbers on our way here. From what Raven says, these are the dimensions of the lab. He's estimated each room, but figures he's within a couple feet on all of them."

"Good, good, good." Andy put his monocle on his eye and studied the page. "I know just what we need."

Raven looked at him questioningly.

"A candy bar. Do you happen to have a candy bar?"

Anger started to boil in Raven's gut. If he just wasted four hours coming to talk to a nut ball who was scared of open cupboards and magazines, he'd kill Viper. Raven stood and headed for the front door.

"Because a candy bar will blow the lock off the titanium

cage," Andy continued. "You should be ready for that in case you can't access the key."

Raven turned to face him.

Viper explained, "Andy created an explosive device that fits into a candy bar wrapper."

Maybe dude wasn't so crazy after all. "That's the reason for all the half-eaten candy bars?"

"I hate to waste them, but I'm so sick of chocolate I could scream. I actually tried screaming one day, but it didn't help."

Raven nodded. "Can you hook me up with a candy bar, Andy?"

"Sure. But that's nothing compared to what you'll need. I've been working on a new project. You're familiar with C4, right?"

Raven said, "As much as any Halfling is."

"Well, my new baby is smaller, more stable, and easier to use than C4. And it packs a heavier punch."

Viper took a drink of his coffee. "Have you field-tested it, Andy? We can't take any chances. This is a one-way mission."

Andy blinked and the monocle dropped from his eye to dangle on its gold chain. "I've tested. It's a go."

"What do you call it?" Viper asked.

"Andy Soup," he said proudly.

Raven leaned forward. "It's a liquid?"

"No. It's a solid, but it's a little of this and a little of that, so ... Andy Soup. I thought about calling it Andy Lasagna, but it just didn't have a poetic ring to it. My baby's brilliant, though. You'll be able to carry it in on foot. One gym bag will haul it all."

Raven nodded. "Is it easy to set the charge? And how does it detonate? Wire, remotely? Can we set a charge with a digital detonator, and is there any way to stop it if something goes wrong?"

Andy stared at the ceiling and counted off the questions by raising his fingers one at a time. "Yes. Either. Yes and it can be manually stopped if detonated digitally, but you have to be at the timer and it takes a full twenty seconds."

Raven took in the room around him and realized it looked right out of a steampunk movie. Old World charm mixed with various pieces of copper and wire bundles that complemented the space. Andy's monocle made more sense now. "So if the timer reads fifteen, run."

The explosive expert's face broke into a smile. "Exactly."

Raven threw his hands in the air. "What can go wrong?" He started to drop his hand on a hat rack in the corner of the room.

Andy waved frantically. "Don't lean on that. It's wired."

Raven stopped cold and stared at the piece of furniture. "Out of curiosity . . ."

Andy nodded. "Yes, the cupboard and the magazine are wired too."

Raven's heart froze. "Seriously?"

Andy stood and dropped his hands to his hips. "I can't be too careful. Do you know how dangerous this is? If my stuff fell into the wrong hands . . ." He shook his head.

Within an hour they were loaded and ready to leave. Raven, Steel, and Shadow had been careful not to touch anything else. Viper, on the other hand, had floated around the house comfortably, never worrying about opening a cupboard filled with explosives. He and Andy must be pretty close friends.

Whatever; Raven didn't care. As long as they got to the lab in time. Saving Nikki and destroying Vessler's place was all that mattered. And finally, he had the firepower to do it.

On the way back, he'd lay out the details of the plan for Viper, Steel, and Shadow. Each could take a specific amount of

Andy Soup into the building. Placed around the lab and detonated at specific times, the entire place would become one giant pile of debris. The first explosion would be small, used to drive the people out of the area. Once the place was clear, he'd detonate a bigger charge, able to destroy the titanium cage: Nikki's prison.

Though her head throbbed, her hands were numb, and her back burned from the strikes from the baseball bat, Nikki's eyes were clear and light. They had not faded to black. And that meant Vessler couldn't win.

But neither could she.

In all the attacks she'd suffered, they'd avoided her stomach. She knew what they were protecting. Nikki knew from biology class that a woman was born with all the eggs she'd have during her entire lifetime. She wasn't a true baby factory. But now she understood why her name had appeared with the words *Genesis Project* on the computer she and Mace dug from the fire so long ago. Later, Zero had admitted to her the name *Nikki Youngblood* also appeared in another file from the Genesis Project, along with the word *surgery*. Vessler planned to operate on her and remove what he wanted once they were overtaken by her fallen DNA. Only one thing kept his plan at bay: she hadn't turned into a dark creature.

And that's where logical thought ended. When she wasn't being beaten, the most precious moments of her life entered her consciousness as hazy shadows. Her mom and dad on Christmas morning, running with her dog, Bo, on the tennis court, watching the eagles soar with Mace. Everything that had once mattered was reduced to flecks of images she could barely see. Barely recall.

Each time Vessler left the room, the assailants became less cautious. A few kicks landed in her lower abdomen. Since she'd suffered little abuse to her stomach, the blows sent a fresh round of pain through her.

After what seemed an eternity, they dragged her back into the cage with Zero.

The two lay there like newborn kittens abandoned by their mother. Helpless, unable to move, but unlike kittens they were also unable to die.

"Nikki," Zero whispered.

She tried to turn her head toward him, but the movement shot pain down her spine. "Wha?" she mumbled.

"You're okay for a girl."

But the fear in his voice was unmistakable. Did he think she was about to give up? Death would be a welcome rest. Blackness enveloping her like a warm blanket, closing out the pain. Closing out the hurt.

"Nikki!" His urgency caused her eyes to flutter open. "Did you hear me?" He'd scooted closer and shook her shoulder. "I said you're okay for a girl."

She tried to open both eyes, but one was matted shut with bits of dried blood. She attempted a smile. "So are you."

He sighed relief. "You're gonna make it out of here. We both will."

"Zero ..." Her words weakened. "When they weren't looking, I blew into the necklace and called for Vegan."

Silence. Zero sighed. "That's good. She'll come. She'll bring an army."

But Nikki just wanted to sleep. The dimness pressed. "I'm an army," she whispered. "Damon told me."

"Nikki, you're just *one* Halfling."

"You can count how many seeds are in one apple. But you can't count how many apples are in one seed."

"What?" Zero shook her harder when her eyes closed completely.

"It's better this way," she mumbled, giving in to the deep, quiet peace, allowing its comforting arms to wrap around her. "I'm the key. To his plan. It's better. If I die."

Zero clenched his teeth and shook her. "No," he gritted, fighting tears.

Her breathing turned slower, slower. Soon, it would all be over for good. Zero had improved over the hours, but he hadn't been as badly wounded as her. He stroked her hair and whispered to her. "Don't give up, Nikki. Don't run. They're coming to get us. I know they are."

But she was floating on a shadowy cloud.

Zero's voice slid farther and farther away from her. "No, Nikki," he said, panic fresh and hot in the words.

This time, it was Zero who offered soothing touch, placing her head in his lap. She tried to smile. "You don't understand. How much. Power I have."

"What are you talking about?" But she could hear the urgency in his voice. He wanted to keep her talking. Keep her alive.

"I'm the key ... to the Genesis Project. Vessler ... will harvest my eggs. Use a cold process ... rapid — rapidly age the offspring. Five — six years, enough dark Halflings to ... destroy ... your entire race. But, you've known ... all along, haven't you? So smart. No wonder ... Vegan loves you."

"Nikki, listen to me." His hands clamped on her shoulders. "You haven't turned. You won't be dark."

She forced her eyes open. "I will, Zero."

"No." He shook his head, and blond hair floated around his face. "They've beaten you practically to death and you haven't turned."

"But they haven't been as ... violent toward you."

Zero's hand dropped from her shoulders. Since Nikki's arrival, they'd left Zero to lie in the cage and left his body to mend.

"I know Vessler. He'll ... look for the way to gain ... the advantage. And when he accepts beating me ... has no effect, he'll turn his attention on you. I won't let him do it, Zero. I'll turn ... so I can fight him."

"No, Nikki."

"He's won."

"Vegan will come. We just need to wait."

"Yeah, that's what I ... thought too." She'd called for Vegan hours ago. "If she hasn't come ... by now, she's not coming. Do you recall ... telling me about the death and resurrection?"

Zero clamped a hand over his mouth, his fingertips digging into the skin on his cheeks. He kept the anguish at bay for Nikki's sake.

Her eyes closed one last time. "A beautiful sacrifice, remember?" Nikki closed her eyes. And everything became dark and quiet and nothing.

Zero cradled Nikki in his arms, rocking her lifeless body back and forth until Vessler's men realized what had happened.

They stormed in and carried her to the examination table, the same one where Vessler's chest had been stitched.

Scientists hooked her up to several machines, ripping her clothes to place electrodes on her upper torso.

The heart monitor read a flat line. No heartbeat. Zero hugged himself, sitting on the floor in the cage alone. Beyond him, doctors gave her several injections, then stared at the heart monitor and waited. A long straight line streamed across the screen where her pulse should be. *This … this isn't happening. She can't be dead.*

Zero cried. And prayed. And cried. Because he knew she'd willingly given her life to save them all. Without her, Vessler had no hope of creating his army. With her dead, there was no possible way of turning her then harvesting her Darkling eggs. And the harshness of that fact caused Zero to love her all the more. She'd been aware of exactly what she was doing. Nikki was the bravest Halfling he'd ever known.

He'd been lost in his own thoughts until he heard the screams. Vessler, running through the door and stopping by Nikki's bedside. "*No,*" he yelled and folded forward, throwing himself over her body. Between his anguished screams, he sobbed.

Genuine love seemed to ooze from Vessler. It sickened Zero that he and this man shared the same grief of losing Nikki. Zero shrank away from the bars he'd pressed close to while trying to stay near Nikki.

After several minutes of crying, Vessler pulled the monitor wires from her and slowly lifted her in his arms. Her hair fell in soft waves as he carried her out.

That's when Zero heard gunshots.

Chapter
27

The sounds of chaos rumbled through the sterile room and into Zero's cage, charging the atmosphere. "Bolt the door," one of the black-clad thugs hollered. Another had disappeared with Vessler — and Nikki — through a side door. The lights flickered. The white-coated flunkies stared at the ceiling. The bulbs flickered again. Then the room went black.

Zero watched the pathetic scientists and tough guys huddle together in the darkness, shifting their weight, eyes wide and fearful each time a boom permeated the air. When the computer screens glowed green, all eyes fell to their digital displays. Across every screen in the room, a banner flashed:

Zero runs the network. Zero runs the network. Zero runs the network.

Zero's small, sad smile split the cut open on his lips. Vegan had come. But she was too late.

Several scientists roamed from computer station to computer station, clicking buttons and rattling cords. Again, the screens went black, blanketing the room in darkness. Tension rose like a hot air balloon with too much fire.

Beyond the door to the room, Zero could hear a battle. With each pounding jolt and scream, the skirmish drew closer, and the room's population — including him — jumped with each sound. Someone managed to produce an emergency light. Excited chatter began, discussing if they should remain inside or try to escape. Zero overheard two of them whispering about Vessler's secret exit, though it became clear neither knew the code to open the door.

He knew he should keep his mouth shut, but he just couldn't do it. "Hey, science guys, how does it feel to be a rat in a cage?"

Frightened eyes shot to him. They must have forgotten he was there.

"Do you know what Halflings do to humans?" He thought quickly, trying to conjure the most sadistic action he could imagine. "We string them alive and peel the skin from their bodies." He stifled a weak snicker.

People screamed beyond the door. The pathetic scientists searched the room and grabbed for anything they could fashion into a weapon. One even broke a rickety metal chair and clasped the leg like a club. The guard cradled a short club and pitched his weight from one foot to the other.

"That's a toothpick for a Halfling," Zero taunted. "When that door opens, they'll wrap it around your neck like a noose and allow just enough oxygen past your windpipe to keep you alive. Then they'll dangle you from the ceiling until your neck snaps."

The man dropped the chair leg like it was on fire. The guard struggled to pull a gun from his holster. His hand shook as he pointed it at Zero.

"A .22? Really? What are you going to do with that? Those shells simply bounce off Halflings." It was a lie, but the guy didn't know it.

Another crashing boom and the door flew open. Zero saw the .22 barrel flash and looked down. Blood gushed from his leg. And was that Raven running toward him?

It was. Soon other Halflings were stopping the scientists, but Raven was carrying a . . . He must be hallucinating. Raven stripped a wrapper from a candy bar and pressed it to the cage lock while he screamed for Zero to get back. Then he disappeared through the same door he'd entered.

Five seconds later, the candy bar exploded and blew the door open. *Definitely hallucinating.* And weak. Zero could feel his life force draining from his leg. It was okay. He didn't mind dying.

Then Vegan walked in, and he remembered what he had to live for.

Vegan entered the cage and went to work on Zero's leg. She ripped a strip of material from his shirt and tied it off quickly. "I'm getting you out of here," she said, and dropped a kiss on his cheek.

Mace followed her in. "Where are they keeping Nikki?"

Halflings were routing the scientists out until his brothers and sisters were the only ones who remained around him, and this brought a rush of safety—a sensation Zero'd wondered if he'd ever feel again. From the corner of his eye, he saw Vine searching the adjacent rooms.

Mace dropped to his knees beside Vegan. "Zero, where are they keeping Nikki?"

Zero shook his head. How could he tell him? "She's, she's gone."

"Gone where?" He grabbed Zero's shoulder.

"She's gone, Mace. She's dead."

Mace's hand became a vice on his collarbone. Vegan had to pry his fingers away. "No! She can't be dead. Vine, keep looking!"

"Mace, she died in my arms."

His head shook, refusing to believe.

"They put her on a heart monitor. I saw the readings. No life. Nothing. Just a long, flat line. She's dead."

Mace flew from him and hammered his fist into the titanium bars with such force the metal groaned and shook under the pressure.

Vegan was crying. She dropped her face into her hands, and Zero reached up to stroke her cheek. His hand was slick with blood, and when she looked at his fingers with wide eyes, she sat straight. "Mace, we have to get Zero out of here."

Mace turned, his eyes glassy. Vegan showed him the blood still pouring from Zero's wounded leg. With a jolt, Mace ran back over and scooped Zero into his arms.

Chapter
28

Nikki was caught up on wings of eagles and carried to a hillside. Below her, steps led to a meadow, where colors as vibrant as oil paints fresh from the tube surrounded her, making her feel like she'd stepped into a living masterpiece.

And the pain. The pain was gone. She glanced down at her clothing, pristine, as if the nightmare at Vessler's laboratory had never happened. But it did happen. It was as real as ... the landscape she now saw.

This couldn't be earth. Her gaze fell to flowers that seemed to smile as she glanced their way. Far off, she could see a city, its glory shining like a diamond in a field of emerald grass.

"Is it beautiful?"

The deep voice neither frightened nor surprised her. When she looked at him, her breath caught. He was the most perfect man she'd ever seen. Pure devotion seeped from a gaze so deep, she thought she could stare forever and not understand the depths of his adoration.

"Beyond imagination," she said. "Are you …" But she knew. No human alive emanated such love. Such life.

A sash crossed from his collarbone to his hip and shone like diamonds. Then he smiled, and the entire realm seemed to swell with grandeur as if his very pulse gave life to the world around her.

She drew a breath of pure oxygen. So clean and clear, it cooled like mint as it permeated her lungs. It felt so good to breathe. She stretched, allowing her shoulder blades to expand. Nothing hampered their movement. And she felt no wings.

He gestured to the road and took a step. "Walk with me, Nikki."

Her feet answered with movement before her mind responded. A feeling of peace rose with each footfall. She had no wings, but right now, wings didn't matter.

His eyes were like mountain glaciers as he observed her. "That is the city of my Father. Do you know of it?"

The first sparks of panic set in. Vegan had told her something about the city of God, about Halflings never being able to enter it.

His smile melted her tension, and when he locked his hands behind his back and continued to walk, she continued too. "That is my Father's kingdom. But my kingdom is my people." Again, he stopped. "Do you understand?"

"Yes," she answered, wondering where this clarity of thought came from. Fear quickly replaced comfort. "Humans," she whispered. "You're kingdom is the humans."

Which she wasn't.

"My heart beats for mankind. I love them beyond comprehension. I died for them."

She drew in a slow breath, then another, but her heart kept speeding. She wasn't a human.

She hadn't been granted his love.

And she wouldn't be able to enter the city. Her hands started to sweat and her mind spun. He wouldn't bring her here — allow her to experience his beauty, his glory only to send her to hell. Would he?

"Peace," he whispered. His breath, the breath of life, blew across her face, erasing the panic.

Nikki had never felt more loved.

"Halflings have captured my heart," he said simply. "Will, he has been a good caregiver?"

"The Lost Boys' devotion to him and his to them humbles me," she said.

"And are you pleased that you were in his charge?"

Were. Everything in past tense. She was undoubtedly dead. "Yes."

"What may I grant you while we're here talking?"

"Uh." She stumbled over words. Her mind raced. What should she ask for? Something for Mace? To feel her wings one last time? But with her brain reeling, the only person she seemed able to concentrate on was Will, her caregiver. "There is something," she said, tentatively.

He waited for her answer, those eyes of peace coaxing her to continue.

"I know that Will was once a great general in your army. And I know he was demoted to being a caregiver for Halflings."

"Yes, this is so."

"I would like you to restore his place of honor."

He stopped and turned to face her. "Of all the things you could ask? And all that is in my power to give? You ask this?"

She swallowed. "Yes."

"Though your life hangs in the balance, you ask for forgiveness for another?"

Mace rushed to her mind. She'd never see him again. Pain followed a tear down her cheek, but she stood firm. "Yes."

His smile lit the sky, chasing her anguish away. A hand fell gently to her shoulder. "Daughter of man, Will was restored to his position long ago. When offered the army, he chose you. He chose to serve Halflings rather than lead angels. And his decision is pleasing to me."

Nikki nodded slowly, and wondered if she'd ever comprehend this new world she'd been thrust into, its every element at war with the principles she'd grown up with. Yet with each passing moment, understanding flooded her.

"Will's current position is more vital than any he's held. As I said, it pleases me. And so does *your* sacrifice to mankind and Halflings. It will be rewarded."

Rewarded? She didn't know what that could mean. And all she really wanted to know right now was w*here would she spend eternity?*

"And now you wonder what will become of you." He held a hand up. "Do you hear that?"

She listened until the faintest of sounds touched her ears. "It sounds like ... Mace."

"Yes. He's praying for you. I must admit, his persistence is commendable."

Mace was praying for her. Which meant he still thought she was alive. Her heart broke for him.

Mace would have to continue his immortal life without her.

281

Through the blinding tears and pain in his chest, Mace ran the halls of the Omega lab. At the far end of the longest tunnel, he spotted Raven. He skidded to a stop just as he turned. Their eyes met across the distance, and he realized Raven knew. The bag Raven carried dropped to the floor, and he ran to Mace, who now sagged against the wall. Strength came in spurts, as one second he was determined to find her and get her out, the next overwhelmed by the fact he'd never again hear her laugh, see her smile.

"What is it?" A midnight-blue gaze searched his face.

Mace stared back, but could only shake his head. Seeing Raven brought the last year flowing back. Moments with Nikki streamed through his mind.

"Is it Nikki?"

Mace's chest became tight. "She's gone. She's dead."

Raven collapsed into him. In the deadening silence, they gripped each other's arms. Raven's voice wavered as he half whispered, "I thought something had happened, but ... No."

"She's gone, Raven." Mace needed to say it. Hear it. Even though he couldn't believe it.

Raven clung to him, hands squeezing his forearms as his head shook violently. And Mace held him, knowing this is the closest they would come to an embrace, but yet it was enough. They strengthened one another. Somehow, Mace had to make it through this for Raven, and he'd need Raven now more than ever.

A prayer started, without solicitation, in the depth of Mace's mind. He heard himself crying out to God. "Please don't take her. She belongs here. With me." Over and over, his mind begged for Nikki to live. Though she was gone, he had no way of stopping the voice that pleaded for her life.

"Raven." Mace shook him. "I need your help. You know the lab. I can't leave her with these butchers. I need to find her ... body."

Raven swallowed and nodded. One hand released Mace's arm to swipe away the tears. "I know where she might be. You go to the front of the building and work your way back, I'll start here."

"If you know where she might be, let's go there."

"It's just a guess, and we need to hurry."

"Why? Most of the Omega employees fled after that explosion." As he spoke, he noticed a shift in Raven's posture.

"The explosion was no accident — the whole building is wired to blow. Mace, we have about two minutes to find her and get her out."

"Raven, what did you do? The authorities are on the way. They're going to search the building for evidence to put Vessler away."

"You can yell at me about this later. Right now, we have to find Nikki." He looked at his watch. "We've only got a minute and forty-five seconds. Go!" He shoved Mace and ran toward the back of the lab.

Mace stumbled toward the front, scanning rooms as he went. Time was running low, and he began to wonder if they'd find her. But then he heard Raven yelling for him. Mace bolted to the main aisle. His legs gave way beneath him when he arrived, forcing him to cling to a door frame.

Nikki's lifeless body was draped in Raven's arms.

No, no, no. God, please. Her hair swayed with each pounding step, the only sign of life left in her body. She was pale, and when Raven stopped at Mace's feet, he held her out to him. "Take her. You should carry her out."

He thought she'd be heavier, but compared to the sorrow he bore, she felt like nothing in his grasp. For a moment, he cradled her. "I'm so sorry I failed you, Nikki." Mace brushed strands away from her face. He sucked in a breath when he saw her brutally damaged skin. His grip tightened, a poor attempt to protect her from what she'd already suffered.

"Mace, go. I'm right behind you."

He tried to turn, but his legs were concrete.

"Mace, go!" This time, Raven turned him toward the front door. Just thirty feet away. Raven shoved him. "Go. We're almost out of time."

Somehow Mace's legs began to move, and soon he was racing to the door. Once they made it through, Mace turned to point Raven to the tree-lined parking lot ... but he didn't see Raven. He spun completely around, his eyes skimming past Winter, Glimmer, and Vine, who had rushed toward him. "Where'd he go?"

Glimmer was shaking her head, mouth covering her face as she stared at Nikki. Mace shifted his focus to Winter. "Where's Raven?"

It took her a moment to answer. "He hasn't come out."

"Vine!" Mace dropped Nikki in the younger boy's arms. "Don't let anyone back in. The place is loaded with explosives." He turned and bolted for the lab door; his foot cleared the threshold just as a blast hit him like a cannonball to the chest and threw him backward to the ground. A giant fireball erupted from the door and spewed over his head. For a moment, he thought the incinerating heat might melt his skin. Around him, screams rent the air and pandemonium broke out, people running in all directions. Before him, the lab was a hallowed cave of smoke, flames, and debris.

Mace crawled over the shards of glass that littered the area, his eyes fixed on the burning doorway. Raven was still inside. He'd lost his soul mate and his brother in the same day.

Smoke billowed over Mace's face, enveloping him in its darkness. His only thought a futile prayer running through his head. "No. *Please*. I can't lose them."

There was noise behind him. An irritating one calling his name, pulling him from the blackness. Mace fought it. This new darkness was beautifully simple. But the sound kept tugging him. First a request, then an order. He wished whomever it was would stop and let him enjoy the dark, inky sea he was sinking into, but then he recognized the voice.

The next voice was Winter's. "Mace, it's Nikki. She needs you."

Sheer will caused him to drag his eyes open and reject the dark he had wanted to succumb to. Vine and the others were there, and through the noise and the haze they helped him stand and stumble to the spot where Nikki's body lay. People parted as he neared her. Her pale form looked asleep there on the green grass, almost like she was waiting on a kiss to awaken her. But Nikki was gone. And even though he knew — had begun to accept — still, his mind continued to pray.

Many were standing around him as he knelt to her, and he could barely stand entering an atmosphere so heavy with sadness. Someone had arranged her hair so it framed her face perfectly. A tremor, small but noticeable, made its way through the crowd that had all but closed the two of them in. Mace took Nikki's hand in his. He bent forward and put his head on her stomach. And one more time, he prayed.

He couldn't stop himself; his spirit was determined. He'd

pray every minute of every hour of every day of every year if that's what he had to do to survive in a world without Nikki.

Someone gave his hand the lightest of squeezes. A collective gasp exhaled from the crowd. Someone whispered "Stop," and his head moved against Nikki's stomach again. But he didn't remember moving an inch. Mace shot to his knees and stared down at her open eyes.

"Stop praying, Mace. I'm here," Nikki whispered.

Everything went black around him. Someone — Vine? — caught him by the shoulders and held him fast while he tried to breathe.

He blinked away the haze, looked down at his hand locked in hers. She squeezed, little more than a tremor, but she did indeed move. Mace stared at her hard. *Am I hallucinating? Am I just seeing what I want to be true?* Then came her voice, a little stronger in tone.

"I was with him. It was beautiful. We walked by the River of Life and I drank. He took my hand. You know what he said?"

Mace couldn't speak. Alive ... she was really alive. Vine bumped his shoulder. And he remembered she'd asked him a question. He shook his head, the only response he could manage.

Nikki moved, which caused her to wince. "He said, 'You can't stay here.' And I was frightened, because I knew Halflings weren't promised heaven. But he told me that wasn't why. I couldn't stay because you, Mace, wouldn't let me."

And then Nikki passed out.

Nikki awakened to unfamiliar smells and the sound of someone shuffling across the room. She tried to focus.

"*Mace!*" someone hollered. A familiar voice. Lilting and beautiful. *Vegan.*

Mace appeared at Nikki's bedside and snapped his wings closed. He dropped to his knees and kissed her hands, her hair, her face. For a moment, she thought she was dreaming. But his feathery touch seemed so *real.*

"Where am I?" she whispered. The words were a gruff croak through a sand-dry throat. A horrid contrast to the perfect angel kneeling beside her.

"In my arms," he said, scooping her off the bed and onto his lap. "That's all that matters."

She tucked her head against his chest in the safe circle of his arms. He surrounded her so completely, so fully, it left no room for fear. He dipped a finger beneath her chin, and she realized his breaths were as ragged as her own.

Still weak, she glanced around the room, struggling for equilibrium. Giant rock walls, tall windows, and a wide wooden door. Viennesse.

"We're in Europe. You've been unconscious for three days."

"I was in … I saw …" The lab, Vessler, the cage rushed to her mind. "Zero?"

"Shh." Mace nuzzled her closer. "He's fine. Cranky as ever though. Right now he's downstairs with Dr. Spong fighting about where to set up the new computers."

"New computers?" she echoed.

"Didn't you hear? *Zero runs the network.*" Mace smiled, bright cerulean eyes sparkling and filled to their depths with love. "He said you called him a girl." But even as he spoke, he pulled her closer, as if to integrate their bodies so there'd be no distinction where one ended and the other began.

She supposed three days was a long time to watch your

perfect match fight to survive. When she smiled, her lips cracked, and she winced. "Think I may need some lip balm."

"No," Mace corrected. "I've been waiting for days to kiss away your boo-boos."

She tilted her head back, letting it fall against his shoulder. "Did you hear me tell Krissy you'd done that? That was forever ago, Mace." Not long after the beginning of this journey, shortly after her hands had been burned in the laboratory fire the night they'd confiscated a computer. A computer containing a file with Nikki's name on it, with the words *Genesis Project*. If only they'd know then it was a clue she was Vessler's prized creation.

"Yes, I heard you talking to Krissy that day. And I couldn't think of anything else afterward."

"That's a terrible waste of your time," she teased. His chest pressed against her, his scent wafting over her. Hints of soap from a recent shower, the cotton of his shirt, that faint tinge of spearmint all invaded her senses as he dipped closer to her mouth.

"And why was it a waste of my time?" His hand roamed over her shoulder, down her spine, and flattened against her back.

"Because you don't need an excuse." Her hands circled his neck, fingers sifting through his dark-blond hair. Nikki's lips met his. They were warm, moist, filled with anticipation and want, and a hint of sugar cookies. But mostly the promise of peace.

They were interrupted by a flock of Halflings, some materializing in the room with loud snapping wings, some opting for the more conventional method of running through the large door. "Wow," she said to the huge group. "You guys move fast."

Zero grinned. "All our ancestral homes were built with rooms large enough to leap in and out. It's good practice while we're training."

"Whoa, whoa," an unfamiliar voice hollered. She heard a crash at the window. Half in, half out, giant wings and one arm clung to the sill.

Mace shot a disgruntled look toward the window and shook his head. "That's Crash."

Two Halflings grabbed the arm and tugged him inside.

"Hoo-wee!" Crash said in a thick southern accent. "Y'all see that?" He leaned out the window and almost fell, clambering for the sill again. Somehow, his wings got tangled in the drape. He smacked at the thick cloth until he noticed every set of eyes in the room watched him. He flashed them a crooked smile. "I was follerin' Vine, then he cut left, but I was headed right. He was gonna show me this perty place. Then he shoved me into the wall."

Vine face turned pink. "I didn't shove you into the wall," he said through clenched teeth. "And don't tell people I was taking you to a 'pretty place.' It makes me sound like a little girl. I was going to help you work on your landings somewhere safe."

Vine moved next to Glimmer. Beside her, Winter sat down on the edge of the bed, and in one corner, Vegan was arranging the various plants and flowers that seemed to cover the room. Their scent saturated the space, offering life in great bundles of green and splashes of red. Nikki took in the other faces, several she didn't recognize.

Then, her heart thudded and a sick sensation rolled through her empty stomach. "Where's Raven?"

Gold and blue gazes ricocheted around the room. Glimmer dropped her head in her hands and let the tears fall.

Mace pulled Nikki closer, but she felt his chest constrict. "He ..." His stomach convulsed, and when she searched his eyes, she found only pain. "He didn't make it out."

She shook her head to clear it. "What?"

Silence answered her.

She pushed away from him. "No, no. That's not possible. You … you saved us. Zero and me. If we got out, he could."

Mace swallowed and looked away. "No, Nikki. There was an explosion."

"Couldn't he have leapt?"

"The hallways were too confined. He brought you to me and went back to stop more explosions from happening. The FBI was coming to investigate Vessler. Raven knew they'd need something concrete, so I think he went to stop the charges."

Nausea rolled through her system. She grabbed Mace's shirt and buried her head. "I'm so sorry," she finally uttered, mouth quivering. "He's gone?" But the very idea seemed inconceivable to her. Life without Raven.

"He made a choice to sacrifice his life for our protection." Around her, the Halflings all nodded. Glimmer hadn't raised her head from her hands, but tears fell in streams from her fingers. Several tried to sniff back their own tears, but the pain filtered through the room, unmanageable in its scope. "We have to honor that sacrifice. Even if this journey is over, there's still much work to be done. We must be ready to fight, Nikki."

She sucked in a firm breath and tipped her head back. "Then we'll fight." She raised a weak fist into the air. "For Raven."

A room full of Halflings answered. "For Raven."

Will materialized at her bedside. Bright blue eyes smiled at her. "You're looking fit, Miss Nikki."

"I just heard about Raven, Will. I know you loved him like a son." The words poured out of her before she could stop them, or even think about them. Will had sacrificed much. All for his Lost Boys.

His face collapsed, but his words were even and sure. "As a heavenly angel, I am not engineered to feel love as the humans do." He squared his shoulders. "Raven will be missed. His sacrifice was great." Will nodded, lips thinning. "A good fighter. A good soldier."

"A good son," Nikki insisted.

The giant of a man's shoulders began to quake. Not even a breath moved the air in the room. For a moment, life seemed to stop.

Dropping his head into his hands, Will wept.

Later that night, sitting in the gathering room of the mansion, Will hushed the Halflings with the only phrase able to stifle thirty teenage voices. "Heaven whispers."

Twenty male and ten female Halflings had been ordered to reside at Viennesse until further instruction. And while Will was somewhat used to the level of madness, the other caretakers were going crazy.

Normally, males and females crossed paths sporadically, but they were never meant to reside in large groups in a single dwelling for extended periods of time. Will worried what the implication might be.

In addition to the new Halfling relationships, something was changing. The earth groaned for the return of its creator. He had to wonder if the end of days was upon them.

Like volts of electricity, the room lit with power. Tongues of fire licked at the air. The ground shook as if the building quaked in fear. Dust rose from every corner, seeping from every crack. Brilliant light appeared, so radiant that even the ancient rocks comprising the walls glowed.

An angel emerged from the glow, carrying the essence of heaven upon him and its glory with him. Another angel appeared beside him, gleaming in the dingy room. They bowed as another became visible between them, appearing like fire wrapped in flesh.

"You are the product of the sons of God and the daughters of man," his voice boomed.

Will knew well the one standing in the center. He cast a glance to Nikki and saw the recognition in her face. She knew the lover of mankind as well.

"Halflings." The authority in his voice shook the room.

Thirty sets of eyes rounded as if the nitrogen had been sucked away, leaving the air pure and cold.

"You've chosen to pay a staggering debt. Not of yourselves, but of your fathers. Some have paid with their very lives. I am honored to have you in my service. A new dispensation is upon us. Male and female Halflings will work together until the end of days. Time is short. Know clearly which side you dwell on." When he said this, his burning eyes fell upon Viper.

Viper's gaze dropped to the floor.

"I will hold you accountable for your actions on the Great and Terrible Day."

No one moved, but apprehension had clearly developed in the onlookers.

Then the son of the Throne smiled, and like a warming sun rushes away the darkest winter night come spring, fear melted. He then looked to each Halfling gathered around. "But you have also captured my heart. I will petition the Father on your behalf."

Questioning looks flittered from one face to the other as he pointed to Nikki and motioned her to step forward.

Slowly, she rose and came to him.

"When I give a gift, I do not take it back. Open your wings."

Nikki closed her eyes and stretched. Almost instantly she felt the familiar weight of her wings on her back. The Throne's son reached out and touched the bend in each wing, and as she opened her eyes he said, "You were crimson, but I washed you white as snow." The blood-red color then drained away, leaving each feather as pure and white as porcelain.

He bowed to the Halflings, and they bowed their heads in return.

In a flash of light and fire, his feet lifted off the ground. Hovering above them, he spoke once more. "Oh, yes." A soft smile. "Raven says hello."

Chapter 29

THREE DAYS PRIOR.
OMEGA LABORATORY

When he realized there'd be no way to stop the explosives, Raven ran to the small air duct leading to the stables. Once inside, he'd hopefully be shielded from the bulk of the blast. That or he'd be like a baked potato wrapped in tinfoil once he entered the metal vent. Either way, it would be over quickly.

As soon as he shimmied out of the vent and stood up, the scent of hay and horses assaulted his nose. It was weirdly calming. He glanced to the right. At the end of the corridor, the equine leader, Debra, and the other horses roamed. To the left, the stable doors were wide open. Moments later he felt more than heard the blast coming from the lab. It shook the ground, causing dirt to flutter over him from the slatted roof above. The horses whinnied frantically, but within moments they began to calm.

Raven turned to leave. He needed to join the other Halflings, if only to let them know he was okay. Then he'd disappear and mourn Nikki's death alone.

From a vantage point at the open stall door, he could see the parking lot filled with his friends. They gathered around two beings. One was Nikki. The other was closer to the lab door. When someone moved, he caught a glimpse of his face. Mace.

Raven grabbed the door for support. "*No!*" The fool must have tried to come back in after him. But then the clump of flesh moved. Vine was there, supporting Mace, who soon looked up. Raven released a long breath. Mace was okay. But Raven's heart shuddered when he saw Mace standing and slowly going toward Nikki. The crowd made room for him. Mace knelt by her body and cried.

Bodies closed in around them, but from the distance Raven thought he saw her … move. No, it must be a mistake. He rushed to the other side of the door just as he heard a gun cock behind him. *Yes.* He was certain this time. Nikki was moving on her own. Alive.

"Turn around. Slowly."

Raven ignored the command. He wanted one more glimpse of her, but the Halflings closed in and he couldn't see her any longer.

"I said turn around, Raven."

Raven glanced over his shoulder.

"*Now.*" Adam Cordelle's voice shook along with the .45 caliber pistol in his grip.

Raven turned slowly, raising his hands in a show of surrender. "I'm not armed, Cordelle. Put down that gun before you hurt yourself." The man was the worst guard Raven had ever encountered. The two had actually become friends at one point while Raven was spying on the lab. Cordelle had thought him a vagrant and treated him like a wayward son.

Adam gripped the gun tighter. "You're with *them*, aren't you? You lied to me all that time."

Raven drew a long breath and let his weight rest on the edge of the doorjamb. "Nothing personal, Cordelle."

His mouth dropped open. "Nothing personal? I helped you. I trusted you."

"Yeah, uh, sorry about that. It was all for a good cause."

Adam's face reddened with indignation. "I'm glad you can be so flippant about it." His eyes narrowed and he leaned forward. "I know what you are. Mr. Vessler warned us about you ... you evil monsters."

"Whatever." If Raven could keep him talking for a few more minutes, Cordelle would eventually put the gun down or drop it from those chubby hands and scrawny arms. "You want to know who the monster is? Take a look at your boss. Vessler is the worst kind of evil, and you're working for him. You need to take your family and go away. Take that job you offered me at the chicken plant."

The barrel of the gun dropped marginally. Raven had him. But then the man's face hardened. "No. You lied to me. All along." The gun trembled in his hand as he raised it higher.

"You're not going to shoot me, Cordelle. You know you can't."

Something off to the right, beyond the door, caught Adam's attention. Raven then heard what Adam saw: men coming at them quickly. From where he stood, Raven wasn't sure if the men approaching could see him or not. Cordelle looked at Raven, then the group coming closer, then Raven. Then he fired the first shot.

Raven was so shocked he didn't have time to move. He felt

the bullet plunge deep into his side, tearing flesh and muscle. He dropped to the ground just as another shot rang out and caused fresh pain to sear through his arm.

Cordelle stood over him, yelling, "I got this one. He's dead. Go after the others."

Raven tried not to draw attention, but the pain in his flesh made his stomach muscles twist. He bit down hard to keep from groaning. When he heard Vessler's voice, he understood. Cordelle had decided to do his old stable buddy a favor.

"Stay with the body," Vessler yelled. "It'll be useful. I'll send a team back to pick it up."

As soon as the footsteps faded completely, Cordelle dropped to Raven's side. "I ... I shot you."

"Yeah, way to go." Raven's stomach convulsed, but he grabbed Cordelle by the collar. "Get out of here. Take your family and go. It's not worth it, Cordelle. Vessler will destroy you for helping me."

Adam swiped his hand across his face, where fresh tears mingled with sweat. "I gotta get you out of here. We can go. I'll bring my car around ..."

Raven clamped a hand over Cordelle's mouth. "No. You can't help me anymore. I'll go on my own."

"Go where? You can barely move."

"Help me to my feet. I heal fast."

"You're fooling yourself. You're bleeding out, Raven."

He tugged at the front of the man's shirt. "Just help me to my feet. I have to rest."

"Where can I take you?"

"Nowhere. Don't you get it? Vessler will kill you. Then, for good measure, he'll go kill your wife and kids. Take your family and get away from him."

The outburst caused Raven to black out for a moment. He awoke with Adam Cordelle trying to carry him. He'd managed two steps. Adam was mumbling. "I won't leave you. I won't leave you."

Raven reached up and turned Cordelle's face so their eyes met. "Okay. Listen, if I can get back into the vent that leads into the lab, I can rest there. It'll be safe."

Cordelle nodded. Once he was in place, Raven paused at the vent's trap door to regain a little strength, then he shimmied inside. Outside, Cordelle bunched leaves and pine needles to cover the blood trail they'd left.

"Now go," Raven said. "Before Vessler comes back."

Cordelle bent and peered into the vent. "Is it true you have wings?" he whispered, almost reverently.

Raven couldn't help but smile. "It's true."

"Sorry about shooting you. I was trying to help. The second shot was an accident. Didn't realize I was squeezing the trigger."

"I guess I should take that as a compliment. Good aim on the first shot, by the way. It's in my stomach, but I think you missed all my vital organs. If the bullet is where I think it is, the wound will heal in no time."

Cordelle's eyes widened. "I was aiming for your shoulder."

"Well, you got it with the second shot. You're not cut out for this kind of work, Adam."

He nodded eyes serious. "Everything happens for a reason. Maybe I was here to help you."

"Maybe. You saved my life."

Cordelle started to say something, but Raven shushed him. "They're coming back. You need to go."

Cordelle walked away from the vent as Raven scooted deeper inside. From deep within, words filtered to him.

"I was going to the barn to get a blanket to cover him — couldn't stand those dead eyes staring at me — and halfway there, I heard something. He rose, Mr. Vessler ... rose from the ground like a ghost with wings and he ... he flew. Blood and grass and dirt on him. He was dead. Not breathing. I know what I saw."

After a short inspection of the area, Vessler and his men lost interest in checking Adam Cordelle's story.

If the authorities came, Raven knew he would get some help, as the plan to hide in the vent wasn't working out that well. But it didn't sound like any of the good guys would be coming.

Just below him, Vessler was speaking to one of his lackeys. "Luckily, I was able to reroute that ridiculous FBI enquiry."

Tears of anguish stung Raven's eyes. He touched the wound on his shoulder. The shot had passed clean through. No bones hit, no arteries nicked, and already it was healing. But his side still oozed fresh blood, even if it seemed as though it was slowing. He told himself he just needed to rest. Give his body time to heal. There was no reason to hurry anyway. Nikki was gone. She may not be dead, but she wasn't his.

Trembling fingers reached into his back pocket and found the photo of Jessica Richmond. Through his blurred vision, the beautiful girl at the ocean's edge smiled at him as if her grin carried the secrets to life and the universe. Raven realized he was smiling back. He brushed hot angry tears from his eyes. But Jessica continued to smile. To coax.

Sleep well, my hero, she seemed to whisper, *for tomorrow another adventure awaits.*

Raven closed his eyes and slept. When he did, he dreamed. No, his journey wasn't over. In fact, *his* journey was just beginning.

Acknowledgments

My wonderful critique partner, Lynn Gutierrez. I couldn't do this without you.

My beta readers, Diane, Pops, and Mel.

John, Isaac, and Jake — for bringing me food, listening to me yammer about the story, and for having great plot ideas when I get stuck.

Thanks Dr. Alejandro P. Rooney, Research Geneticist with the U.S. Department of Agricultural Research Service, who spent time explaining genetics in laymen's terms and who knew about cold process experiments. Your insights made for a stronger story.

A special thanks to my church family, who prays for me continually, 'cause, well, I need it.

Talk It Up!

Want free books?
First looks at the best new fiction?
Awesome exclusive merchandise?

We want to hear from you!

Give us your opinions on titles, covers, and stories.
Join the Z Street Team.

Email us at zstreetteam@zondervan.com
to sign up today!

Also—Friend us on Facebook!

www.facebook.com/goodteenreads

- Video Trailers
- Connect with your favorite authors
- Sneak peeks at new releases
- Giveaways
- Fun discussions
- And much more!